# The Rise & Fall of Ryan

*by*

**William Holms**

# OTHER BOOKS BY WILLIAM HOLMS

***The Killing of Faith (2020)*** *Faith looks back on her life and describes a mysterious - but seemingly hopeless – situation. This mystery will draw you in, as you are given clues to solving the puzzle of Faith's whereabouts, the events leading up to her current nightmare, and how a woman's simple lies plunge her into a living nightmare beyond anything you can imagine.*

***The Beginning of Hope (2021)*** *Faith is forgotten by everyone until Hope, her youngest daughter, sets out to find her mother. She will uncover the dark truths of love, family, betrayal, and the haunting question - Who can someone really trust? Her search for the truth will put her life in danger and may destroy the Brunick family forever.*

***The Fall of Grace (2022)*** *takes you on another twisting, turning, suspense-filled journey as it continues the unforgettable story of Ryan and Faith Brunick. With both their mother and their father gone, Hope and Grace must learn to live without them as Grace's life unravels. These beloved characters make decisions that will surprise and shock you as they navigate the challenges of life, love, and loss.*

***The Rise & Fall of Ryan (2022)*** *takes you back to the beginning of Ryan Brunick's life and that fateful day when he met his future wife, Faith. Ryan must come face-to-face with his past as he works to get Hannah out of prison for murder. Will Ryan be able to pull out another miracle or will he lose his first case. The series concludes with even more twists and turns and another unforgettable conclusion.*

***The Intruder You Know (2023)*** *Paige Childers, a young college student left for college ready to start all over. But leaving your past behind is seldom clean and never easy. An intruder outside her home will change her life forever, the lives of everyone around her, and leave Paige in a fight for her life.*

# PART ONE

---

# RYAN BRUNICK

*Some people want it to happen, some people wish it to happen, other people make it happen.*

—Michael Jordan

*I had to wonder if men were so blinded by beauty that they would feel privileged to live their lives with an actual demon, so long as it was a beautiful demon.*

—Arthur Golden, Memoirs of a Geisha

# – CHAPTER 1 –

Ryan Brunick was born to Betty and Henry Brunick. His father was a truck driver who spent most of his time on the road, while his mother stayed home and raised the kids. They had four children in ten years. Ryan was the second child.

Ryan's father raised his family the only way he knew how—by the old school way of doing things. They lived on a farm, which meant early to bed, early to rise. All the time in between was filled with hard work.

When Dad came home from a long trip, it was work day. If you wanted to watch Saturday cartoons, you better wake up early. The girls worked inside cleaning the kitchen, mopping and vacuuming floors, folding clothes, and cooking lunch and dinner. The boys worked outside cleaning the yard, mowing the grass, and edging along the trees and fence line. His dad had an incredible ability to find some new job around the house that took days, weeks, or sometimes months to complete.

No kids were ever bored, for any such complaints would be met with their dad finding something around the house that needed cleaning, washing, painting, or moving. There were rocks and bricks that were moved just to be moved back the following day and holes that were dug just to be filled in again. If nothing else, you might be sent to clean your room.

Ryan's dad could recite a couple of scriptures by heart—like, *Spare the rod and spoil the child.* Listening to him, you'd never know the Bible said a word about love, kindness, and taking care of the poor. Punishments were harsh and swift and were usually found at the end of his leather belt. He never used words like, "Good job" or "I love you." It was Mom's job to tell the kids their father loved them.

Wives were to obey their husbands—another scripture he knew well. He became a regular ole' preacher when it suited his purpose. He was on the road for days, and when he came home from work after a long trip, he expected dinner on the table and a cold beer in his hand. Eating out was something other families did, but never the Brunicks. He often stopped by some bar on his way home, with dinner waiting on the table, to get a jump start on the rest of his evening.

When everyone left the table after dinner, the women cleaned the kitchen. Ryan's dad retired for the evening in front of the television with a cold beer in his hand. *Kids were to be seen and not heard.* Kids laughing and playing in the house might be sweet music in some homes, but it usually meant, *Shut those kids up!* in the Brunick home. No, kids were to be seen and not heard.

Boys were raised tough and girls were raised to be wives and mommies. The thought that one of these kids might actually work behind a desk never crossed his mind. To his dad, that wasn't really work. The Brunick kids learned at a young age to stay out of Dad's way. It was Mom's job to do all the mushy stuff like tending to a cut or giving goodnight kisses before bedtime.

Dad never had time to attend the kids' ball games, dance recitals, awards ceremonies, or other extracurricular activities. If the kids wanted to do those things, they had to finish their work first and ride their bike back and forth. Mom was always there for the children and told Dad about the award or the great catch at the dinner table, when he came home in one of his better moods.

Ryan's dad never cared much about school or grades. His motto was: *Less the learning and more the earning.* There was only one award he cared about. Every year, all the kids got the school's perfect attendance award; even if they had spent all night before school throwing up in bed. He never looked at report cards and couldn't have cared less if the kids made an A or a D. An F was a different story, although no one ever made an F. Surely, that wouldn't have been good.

Ryan didn't need encouragement from his dad, or anyone else, to make good grades. Some might say it came easy for him, but that would be an insult to the amount of work he put into his grades. He stayed up late studying for tests. He never cut corners on homework or term papers. While his brothers and sister made good grades, Ryan's grades were great.

The one time he showed his dad his report card, his dad looked at it for a second without saying a word. Then he sat it down on the table in a puddle of spilled gravy and asked Ryan's mom to pass the green beans.

After dinner, Ryan got up from the table, went to his room, and cried. You only cried in the privacy of your room because crying was for girls and sissies, and the Brunick boys would never be sissies.

"I hate you," he screamed just loud enough not to be heard outside his bedroom.

That was the day Ryan swore to himself that he'd be different from his dad. Ryan knew what a good parent looked like. He'd love his children like his mom loved him. No matter how hard it would be, he'd go to all school events, cheer at every ball game, never miss a doctor's appointment, and kiss his kids goodnight before they went to bed. Birthdays and Christmases would be grand celebration. Ryan's children would never have to wonder if their dad loved them.

The Brunick's home, with two parents, four children, a German shepherd, a beautiful yard, and a spotless kitchen, continued until Ryan was twelve years old. He was just about to leave for the bus stop when someone knocked at the front door. He opened the door on his way out and found a Texas DPS trooper standing outside the screen door. He had a bright star on his chest and a gun on his hip.

"Is your mother home?" he asked.

"Mom," Ryan yelled, turning to the kitchen.

Ryan's mom hurried to the front door but stopped when she saw the officer standing with his cowboy hat in his hand, and his eyes looking down just a bit. She slowly stepped forward, already suspecting why he was there. "Can I help you?" she asked.

"Mrs. Brunick?"

"Yes, I'm Mrs. Brunick."

"I have some bad news. I'm sorry to inform you that your husband was involved in an automobile accident last night."

"Is he okay?" she asked.

"No, ma'am," he said, looking down at his hat. "I'm afraid it was fatal."

Ryan's mom stood there without saying a word. Ryan looked up at her face. She looked so strong, like she had just been told the dog got out of the fence. She didn't cry or anything.

"Can I do anything for you?" the trooper asked.

"No, sir," Mom said, as somber as ever. "I'm just sorry you had to come here. Thank you for telling me."

"Yes, ma'am," the officer said, returning his cowboy hat to his head. He got back in his police car and sat for a few minutes. Ryan wondered if he was coming back to tell them more. Finally, the trooper backed out of the driveway and drove down the road.

Ryan's mom woke up his brothers and sister, knelt on the floor, and held everyone in her arms. Without shedding a tear, she told the kids their dad had been killed last night in a car wreck. Ryan didn't cry either—none of the kids cried. This was the only day any of the kids ever missed school.

Ryan's mom never worked a day outside the home before her husband died. Now, with no education and her only work experience being that of a housewife, she was forced to work odd jobs for little pay. She never made more than minimum wage and did the best she could with the little money had.

Ryan saw firsthand how difficult it is to raise a big family. Money was always tight. Ryan watched his mom work long hours and come home tired. When their lights were shut off, they lived by candlelight for weeks. The home phone was turned off, and was never turned back on again. Ryan ate free lunches at school that resulted in plenty of teasing from other kids who enjoyed the pain their words caused. *Not me,* he'd vow to himself. *One day, my life will be different.*

Although Ryan's mom was strikingly beautiful, she never remarried— or even dated. To her, this only took away the time she could spend with her children. Ryan had a friend whose mother and father divorced. His friend lived with his mom and often talked to Ryan about the things going on in their home. His friend's mom dated one guy after another, leaving the kids alone or with a babysitter they barely knew. One weekend, his friend stayed at Ryan's house when his mother left with some guy for the weekend but didn't come back for six days. It made Ryan sick. *How can a mother put some guy before her own kids?* Then, at the end of their junior year of high school, Ryan's friend died from an accidental drug overdose. Ryan, however, never believed it was an accident. He always blamed his friend's mother for his death.

Even though they struggled financially, Ryan was just glad his father was gone, and the home was peaceful. It was like he'd been carrying around a load of bricks in a sack slung across his back, and then someone just took that sack away.

Ryan might not have cared about lights or a telephone; but it all took a toll on his mother. She got a second job, but was still always two steps behind. She'd come home from work, cook a nice meal, fold laundry, and straighten up the house. But as hard as she tried, she still missed most of the kids' activities. This was especially hard for her since these were the things she once lived for.

Despite it all, Ryan's good grades never stopped. He won one award after another, graduated at the top of his class, and was awarded a full scholarship to the University of Texas at Austin. Thank God for the scholarship. Without it, he'd be taking classes at the junior college and working full time to pay for his tuition and books. After graduating from college, he applied to numerous law schools and was accepted at them all.

Then, in the middle of his final year of college, Ryan learned his mom was very sick. For the previous three years she suffered from terrible pain in her abdomen, which she did her best to ignore. She hadn't been to a doctor in years because she didn't have the time, or the money, or the health insurance for doctors and hospitals. When the pain got too severe to ignore, she went to the emergency room. She was diagnosed with cervical cancer, which she contracted from a sexually transmitted disease given to her by her husband before he died. It could have been treated if it had been caught early, but now her diagnosis was terminal.

Ryan dropped his classes and came home to be with his mom. By this time, she was looking tired, weak, and in a lot of pain. Ryan was devastated. He watched his mom moan in pain as her condition worsened. Ryan turned to God for the first time in his life and prayed that He would save his mother. God must not have heard his prayers. Five months later, his mom was gone, and Ryan was left without a mother or a father.

The night his mother died, Ryan and his sister held her hands and cried when she closed her eyes, took her last breath, and never woke up again. His oldest brother hadn't arrived yet from Pittsburgh. His younger brother was sound asleep in a chair by the bed.

Sitting on the front at his mother's funeral, Ryan didn't think about the lights being turned off, the phone that couldn't ring, or the Christmas presents he never received. All he could think about was how his mother loved her children more than she loved herself. She spent a lot of time at work, but every free moment she had, she spent with her kids. Every penny she earned, she spent on them. Every meal she cooked was for them. She often stayed up late at night to wash his uniform before his games. When she had no money, she somehow found a way to buy him a baseball glove. Maybe they didn't go on fancy vacations, but she always found time to take them to the park, the community pool, or to a free concert or festival in town. She was a great mom. Everything she did, she did for her children. She was the kind of mom his friend wished he had.

# – CHAPTER 2 –

Most kids who want to be a lawyer get a degree in political science. It gives them an idea how the government works, and it's the easiest way to get good grades. Good grades mean acceptance into an excellent law school.

Ryan had no one to help him through college, so he relied on scholarships, student loans, and working as a waiter. Becoming an actual lawyer seemed like a faraway dream at the time. *Always have a backup plan.* Whether it was school, living his life, raising a family, or trying a case in court, he lived by that motto. Ryan had a backup plan if this whole being an attorney thing fell through. He first got a degree in civil engineering—one of the hardest routes to law school. This was not the smartest move for someone hoping to get into law school, but he graduated with almost all A's and made one of the best scores on his Law School Admittance Test.

On the first day of law school orientation, the professor stood at the front and said, "Look to your left and your right. One of you won't be here after the first year." It scared most of the students in the room, but law school came easy for Ryan. His mind was made for this stuff. He had this ability to look at things from a different angle and see what everyone else missed. Where other students would ramble on and on about obvious facts or recite the law like memorizing it was some brilliant feat, Ryan applied the law in some clever, ingenious ways. He was often able to apply the law in a way that even the professor hadn't thought of. He always simplified things so a child could understand them. He was always the first to finish his three-hour exams and his answers were to the long test questions were much shorter than other students. It baffled his classmates when the A's kept coming in. Another student, who was struggling though law school, begged Ryan for help.

"Don't repeat the obvious," Ryan advised. "It's a waste of time."

It all seemed so plain and simple when Rya explained it, but when his friend tried this same tactic for himself, he failed all his classes that semester and dropped out of law school.

Ryan was the editor-in-chief of his law school's law review, the lead advocate in moot court, and won the state's moot court competition over all the other law students across the state. He did all of this while working part-time as a waiter at one of the local Mexican food restaurants.

He was young, handsome, smart, and was recruited by all the big law firms. There was no doubt Ryan had the grades, but the recruiters had their reservations about offering him one of their a high-paying jobs. Most law students have a mother or father who's an attorney or some other professional. They'd arrive at the interviews looking sharp—wearing a new suit, polished shoes, carrying a stylish briefcase, and sporting a fresh fifty-dollar haircut. Prouder than a mother hen, they'd recite their pedigree. Ryan, on the other hand, had no idea what a new lawyer was expected to look. He walked into his first interview wearing black slacks, a blue dress shirt, a cheap tie, Penny loafers, and a blue wool sports coat. It was obvious he was out of place in this new, high-dollar profession.

When Ryan walked into his first interview room, the high-priced attorneys gave him an uncomfortable stare as he took his seat. But as soon as Ryan started talking the mood changed and he gained the attention of every attorney in the room. Halfway through the interview, they knew Ryan had what his classmates couldn't buy with any amount of wealth and privilege. He was dynamic, personable, and spoke with the confidence rarely seen in a law student. These high-priced lawyers unbuttoned their expensive suit jackets or took them off altogether. As he drew them in, the room looked more like an after-work happy hour than some uptight interview room. Ryan talked like an equal and soon commanded the entire room. He talked about the law, discussed several of their pending cases, and offered strategies they might employ going forward. After the interview, the partners looked at each other like they had just witnessed the second coming of Christ. One of the senior partners joked, "Did this kid write the book, *How to Win Friends and Influence People?*"

But there was one other concern. Ryan was clear about what he wanted. Right off the bat, he claimed to be a trial attorney even though he'd never set foot into the courtroom, except to fight a speeding ticket during his first year of law school. "I want to try cases," he said with all the confidence of a seasoned trial attorney.

"That's wonderful, son," one partner said with a nod. "We have a large litigation section. Work hard and we'll see what we can—"

"No," Ryan interrupted, shaking his head with closed eyes. Then he looked right at them and said, "I don't want to spend all my time in some law library or behind a desk doing all the boring work for someone else to get all the credit. I belong in the courtroom. I want to try cases right away."

"Boy, you *are* ambitious!" the lawyer to Ryan's right laughed. He almost called Ryan arrogant, but for some reason, he knew it wasn't arrogance that was behind the young bravado.

"I like that," the senior partner chimed in. "I like someone who thinks big. But listen, son, you have a lot to learn and that takes some time."

"Oh sure," Ryan answered with the same self-confident smile. "I understand all that. I expect to spend a year or two learning the ropes before I try my first case."

*A year or two,* the head partner thought to himself. *If Ryan wanted to be in a courtroom in a year or two, he should hang a shingle and take criminal appointments. He could try a case where some poor guy's life is on the line.*

Big law firms work for big businesses and insurance companies who pay big bills. Their clients don't pay top dollar to have some kid right out of law school try their cases. An attorney doesn't even *second* chair an actual trial until they're a fifth—or sixth—year associate. After a couple of years, a new lawyer *might* be allowed to take a deposition or argue a meaningless hearing. *But try a case?* That takes a seasoned lawyer with at least ten or fifteen years of experience under their belt.

Still, Ryan's lure was very compelling. It would look great to have the top ranked law student at The University of Texas law school, a member of the law review, and the winner of the Lone Star State's Moot Court competition on the firm's bio.

In the end, Ryan received offers from ten different law firms. His starting salary would be more money in one month than his mother made in a year. Several firms gave him the best offer they'd ever presented to a new lawyer. What about all that talk about trying cases? They figured all that money, combined with his mounting student loans, would keep him pacified for years.

Ryan chose the most prestigious firm in town because they handled both plaintiff and defense cases. His first month on the job felt like paradise. Ryan was given an office in the middle of the hall with a small window that overlooked the building across the street. He arrived the first day to find a brand-new computer and laptop on his small desk. His phone had more buttons and gadgets than he knew what to do with. He was handed a catalog and told to pick any desk, chair, and credenza he pleased. Over the next few days, he filled his walls with his diplomas and an original oil painting he chose from some high-priced gallery.

Ryan was assigned a senior partner, Nathan Bannister, and worked alongside nine other lawyers. This would be his team. He shared a secretary who answered most of his questions, typed his letters, and helped him with anything he needed.

Every day for three weeks, Ryan was taken to lunch at a fancy downtown restaurant so he could meet the other lawyers in the firm. After work, the firm sponsored happy hours and other social events around the city.

Everyone knows that working at a big firm means being a slave to your job. Lawyers are judged by the number of hours they bill each month, and most lawyers find a way to bill more weekly hours than there are hours in the week. Lawyers live by deadlines, and the only way to keep up with their calendars is to work long, late hours during the week, and catch up on assignments on the weekends. But none of the partners ever mentioned billable hours. The first month, it looked like the law firm's only mission was to make Ryan happy. It was suggested a few times that he should take a few golf lessons and spent his free time out on the golf course. Three months later, he was offered full membership at the best country club, which boasted the nicest golf courses in Texas. Ryan would later learn this wasn't offered to most of his peers.

Well, it didn't take long before the honeymoon was over. No one told Ryan he needed to bill a lot of hours—they didn't have to. A lawyer who came into the office after seven-thirty in the morning would get "the look" as they walked to their office. The files, and then the boxes of files, soon filled Ryan's office. If he found a way to get ahead, more boxes would magically appear, often while he was out.

Ryan wasn't afraid of hard work or long hours—especially since he was about to be trying cases. But, a year into the job, Ryan was right where he said he wouldn't be. He spent more time in the library than in his own office. It was one memorandum after another. The closest he got to a courtroom was a brief or pleading he'd write for another lawyer to sign. But, just like they planned, the money was compelling. He was paying down his student loans, bought a nice car, and got a bigger, nicer apartment.

Ryan developed a rapport with all the other lawyers at the firm. Mr. Bannister, the partner he worked for the most, took a keen interest in him. He loved the way Ryan's mind worked. He gave Ryan more files than he gave the other attorneys—especially the cases that were important to him. He'd often call Ryan into his office to discuss some angle in a case. Ryan had this way of finding something everyone else overlooked, or never even thought about. Bannister relied on him more and more.

Ryan never stopped asking about going to court. He sounded like a broken record—which became a little irritating. Each time he asked, he was assured it was coming. "Be patient," Bannister smiled. "You're doing great. These things take time."

This went on for three and a half years. Ryan felt like his office was closing in on him—especially when they brought in a new file cabinet to get all the files off the floor. Well, it didn't work. Soon, the files were stacked on the floor again. Unlike the other attorneys who started with him, he was moved into a bigger office and now had his own secretary.

Right about the time Ryan was thinking of quitting, he had a meeting with Mr. Bannister to go over the cases he was working on. Bannister had just lost the first silicone breast implant case the firm had tried, which really hurt. They had almost three hundred thousand dollars wrapped up in that case. After a three-month trial, Bannister was tired and frustrated. Breast implant litigation was new and had just started popping up around the country. The manufacturers fought the cases hard and refused to settle; afraid a settlement would encourage more lawsuits. They aggressively defended every case and won one victory after another all across the country.

For the first time in front of Ryan, Mr. Bannister poured his favorite $350.00 bottle of McCallan scotch, and drank the entire glass without pausing. He didn't even offer Ryan a drink. "I never should have taken these goddamn cases," he said, still reeling from the loss. "I should have known better."

"What do you mean?" Ryan asked.

"The medical testimony is too damn complicated and confusing. People don't get it. The manufacturer blames the defective breast implants on everything and everyone. The plaintiff was negligent; the doctor put it in wrong; the drinking water was bad. Hell, they'd blame their own mothers if it'd work. They hire these…these doctors, who are just a bunch of prostitutes, to say the plaintiff isn't even injured. They practically called my lady a liar and a cheat. These cases are impossible to win."

Ryan had prepared most of the pleadings for the recent trial and had researched a lot of the issues in the case. He had summarized all the doctor's depositions in preparation for trial. In his mind, the case was pretty simple.

"So, the jury didn't believe the doctors who testified about her injuries?"

"Hell no. For every doctor we put on, they put on two. By the end of the trial, the jury didn't know who the hell to believe. Hell, I'm not sure if I even believed our own doctor anymore."

Ryan nodded and said, "I guess our client was pretty upset, right?"

"Hell, our client died two months ago. Her husband wasn't real happy, but he'll get over it."

Finishing his second drink, Ryan could tell the scotch was causing Bannister to be a lot more candid than usual. He didn't seem to care about the client at all.

"Don't we have another case coming up?" Ryan asked.

"Shit," Mr. Bannister said with a laugh. "Our clients pay us to win, not to get laughed out of the courtroom. They're our bread and butter. This loss will be all over the papers tomorrow and in the Austin Business Journal. They'll go somewhere else if we lose another big case."

"What are you saying?" Ryan asked.

"I'm out. I'm releasing the files."

The wheels in Ryan's head started turning. Then they started spinning. He had no reputation to protect or anyone except himself who cared if he won or lost. He just wanted to be in the courtroom. "Why don't you let me try it?" Ryan asked.

"Very funny," Mr. Bannister answered, almost laughing.

"I'm serious," Ryan said, leaning back in his chair. "I already know the medical and most of the legal issues in the case. We don't have to start from scratch…and we've already paid for the experts."

Bannister crossed his arms, sat back in his chair, and looked like he was actually considering the idea. The room went silent as a church on Friday night, while both men looked at each other.

"I don't know," Bannister finally said.

"How much do we have invested in these cases?"

"Over a quarter million dollars!"

"Don't you want to get that money back?"

Bannister drank down his third glass, poured another, leaned back in his chair, and whispered, "Oh God."

"What do you have to lose?" Ryan pressed.

Ryan didn't know if Mr. Bannister was just tired of looking at all the breast-implant files in his office, or if he was exhausted from the three months he had spent in trial. Maybe the scotch clouded his better judgment. Whatever the reason, Bannister stood up, grabbed a box off the floor, and dropped it with a *plunk* on the corner of his desk. "Here," he said with a wave of his arms. "Take this one. It's all yours."

The truth was, Mr. Bannister knew the case couldn't be won, but he figured, worst-case scenario, Ryan would lose the case, stop all this foolishness about being a trial lawyer, and get back to work in the library…or the dungeon as the young associates liked to call it.

Ryan grabbed the box and got out of his office before Mr. Bannister could change his mind. This was his birthday and Christmas all wrapped up into one. He went straight to his office and opened the box to find out what Santa Claus had just put under the Christmas tree.

Her name was Jodi Palmer. She was thirty-three years old and a single mother with two kids. When Ryan first met his client three months before trial, she wasn't impressed at all.

"Where's Mr. Ballister?" she asked.

"Mr. Bannister?" Ryan asked. "Well, you're still represented by this firm, but I'll be trying your case."

"You're an attorney?" she asked.

"I am. I graduated top of my class at U.T."

"How long have you been an attorney?" she asked.

"Almost four years now."

"I don't know," she said with a frown. "Mr. Bannister said he'd be the one handling my case."

Ryan walked around and sat on the edge of his desk. "I want to be honest with you," he explained. "Mr. Bannister was going to release your case. No one is taking these cases right now because juries haven't been very receptive to these claims. But I believe in you. I believe in your case. I'm willing to try your case. I think we can win."

"Do you?" she asked. "Do you think we can win?"

"I do," Ryan said.

Jodi took a cigarette out of her purse and started to light it up. "Can I smoke in here?" she asked.

"I don't think so," Ryan said.

She put the cigarette pack back in her purse and said, "How many cases have you tried?"

"None," Ryan answered coolly, like he had nothing to be embarrassed about. Always looking at things from the other side, he said, "But I haven't lost a single case either."

Jodi laughed.

"In law school, I won the state's moot court competition."

"What's that?" Jodi asked.

"It's kinda' like being in court. Law students from all over the state come to compete."

"And you won it?" Jodi asked.

"I did," Ryan replied, as if winning a law school competition gave him the credibility to try any case in the world.

"And Mr. Ballister won't try it?"

"Mr. Bannister? No…he's out."

"And you'll win?"

Ryan raised his hand and said, "Jodi, I didn't say I'd win." For the first time, Ryan called his client by her first name. It would be a practice he'd continue for the rest of his life. It established a connection between him and his clients. He had a way of lifting up, empowering others around him, and making them feel important. "I said I *think we* can win. I can't do anything by myself. It's your case and we have to this together. I think if you and I work together, we can win this case."

Jodi, who had been looking down, suddenly looked straight into Ryan's eyes and said, "Then let's go. Let's beat these assholes."

Unable to hide his joy, Ryan extended his hand to her with a big smile. The lawyer and client shook hands in agreement. It was a moment that changed Ryan's life forever.

# – CHAPTER 3 –

Ryan was determined to understand every medical record, study every deposition, and know every fact in the case. He took the file to his office, to lunch, to the bathroom, and to his home when he finally left each day. Night after night, he'd stay up until three, four, five in the morning; going over every little detail. He even dreamt about breast implants.

After forgetting to eat the day before—and maybe even the day before that—Ryan stopped off at a little diner on his way to the office for a quick breakfast. Sitting at a booth with his head buried in one of the defense expert's deposition, he looked up just long enough for the waitress to take his order.

"Good morning," she said with a friendly smile. "You look like you need a cup of coffee."

Ryan was staring at the most stunning girl he'd ever laid eyes on. This may sound like a cliché, but she was. She had beautiful ivory skin, shiny blond hair, and the most sparkly blue eyes God ever created. Her beautiful smile left him breathless—and speechless—which didn't happen often. Her name tag, pinned across her lovely chest, introduced her as "FAITH."

"Yes…coffee…please," Ryan said, doing his best not to stare too long. When she smiled, he could see that her teeth were perfect and beautifully white. Ryan was happy to see her ring finger had no wedding ring.

She was young and didn't seem like much of a waitress, but when you look like her, you don't have to be much of a waitress. She spoke with the giddy slang you'd expect from a teenager, so Ryan estimated this girl was seventeen years old—or maybe even younger.

When she left with his order, Ryan realized he'd just discovered the only thing that could distract him from his files. He did his best to concentrate on the deposition, but he couldn't help but look up each time she walked by or stopped to help another customer. Ryan kept thinking, *Jesus Christ, you're beautiful.*

After delivering three pancakes, two eggs, and two bacon strips, Faith looked at the stack of papers sitting on the table and asked, "What you reading there?"

"This," Ryan said, laying his hand on the tall stack. "It's a deposition."

"A deposition?" she asked.

"Yeah….you know, testimony a doctor gave in a case I'm handling. I'm an attorney."

She raised her eyebrows and with another beautiful smile, said, "That's incredible. I bet it's interesting."

"I don't know about *that*," Ryan laughed.

They exchanged smiles a couple more times while Ryan finished his breakfast. She refilled his coffee, spilling a little on the table.

"I'm so sorry," she said, and reached across the table for a napkin to mop it up. Her hair was shiny, and she smelled like she just stepped out of the shower. She was petite and had a beautifully trim figure.

Still chewing on his last bite of bacon, Ryan asked for his check. She dropped it off with another smile that lit up the room. Ryan wondered if she was just friendly to him or to everyone. He left enough cash on the table for the check and a whole lot more.

"You have a beautiful smile," he said as he stood up. "If I had a smile like yours, I'd smile all the time."

Blushing for the first time, Faith saw all the money sitting on the table and said, "Thank you so much. Good luck with your disposition thing."

Ryan returned the next morning and sat in the same booth. When Faith walked up, she was just as beautiful as she had been the day before. But she was not as cheerful. Ryan figured she was either having boy troubles or was on the outs with her parents. Her southern accent gave him an opening to find out which it was.

"Faith?" he asked.

"Yes….Faith."

"Hi Faith, I'm Ryan."

"Hi Ryan," she said with the first hint of the smile he fell in love with yesterday.

"Where you from?"

"I'm from Georgia. I just moved here three months ago."

Wanting to find out her circumstances, Ryan asked, "With your parents?"

She looked up, took a deep breath, and said, "No…actually with my boyfriend."

*BINGO!*

Surprised that a girl her age would move across the country with some boy, Ryan asked, "If you don't mind me asking…how old are you?"

"How old am I?" Faith repeated, like she was stalling for time.

"Sure, how long have you been living?"

"I'm twenty," she lied. This would be the first of many, many lies Ryan would hear.

"Wow, I thought you were much younger."

"Nope…twenty," she repeated, pretending to draw a large cross over her heart in a move Ryan would get used to seeing in the years to come.

"So, you live with your boyfriend?"

"Yep," Faith said, rolling her eyes and popping the "p":

"Everything okay?" Ryan asked.

With her eyes tearing up just a little, she answered, "It's nothing, really."

"Things not so good with your boyfriend?"

"Not so good? Not so good would be *great* right now."

The restaurant was busy, and Faith had already pressed her luck by staying at his table for a little too long. Plus, somehow this guy was able to get her to say more about her relationship than she'd told anyone. "Gotta go," she said, topping off his coffee, and walking away.

When he finished his meal, Faith dropped off the check, except this time she left a little heart at the top corner. Under it she wrote, "Nice to meet you Ryan…Faith."

Ryan would return for breakfast again and again. When she started working the evening shifts, he'd show up for dinner. There was something about this beautiful girl that drew him to her. Her eyes sparkled like diamonds, and she always smiled when she talked. He was smitten.

One evening, Ryan was the only customer in the restaurant. Some days Faith was upbeat and giddy, but other days she seemed down and sad—or maybe depressed. This seemed like a down day. "Why don't you have a seat…maybe keep me company," he said, pointing at the bench on the other side of the table.

Faith looked into the kitchen opening that had no door and said, "Maybe for a second." She sat down, rested her arms on the table, and said, "Well, hello there, Ryan."

She had the soft, tiny hands of a young girl. Her fingernails were short, with cracked fingernail polish that needed to be removed and repainted. She wasn't wearing a bracelet or even a watch to tell the time. Her breasts were smooth and ivory white, with no necklace and just the hint of her blue veins underneath. The only jewelry she had on was the kind of earrings you get when you first get your ears pierced. It was obvious she didn't come from money and no one was spending any money on her.

"Everything okay," Ryan asked.

Rolling her yes, she answered, "It's nothing, really."

"So, tell me a little about yourself," Ryan said, switching things up. "You came to Texas all the way from Georgia with your boyfriend?"

"Yeah," she said, like she understood how foolish that sounded.

"And how's that working out for you?"

"Oh, about like you'd expect."

"Young love is hard," Ryan said, hoping she'd tell him how she once loved her boyfriend, but she didn't any longer.

"Young *stupid* love," she nodded.

"What's got you down?"

"I don't know," Faith started, and then paused.

When it looked like she was finished, he asked, "What is it?"

"You're a lawyer, right? I guess you're used to hearing people's problems?"

"Sure," Ryan agreed.

"I don't know. I think he might be cheating on me."

How do you get a beautiful girl to fall in love with you, follow you across the country, and then cheat on her? Ryan thought this guy must be something really special. Feeling this out, he asked, "What's he do for a living?"

"Construction…when he works," she answered. "Mostly, he gets high and plays video games."

Ryan looked at this beautiful woman—or girl—and thought this had to be the craziest thing he'd ever heard. *She's the one working? He's the one cheating?* With a puzzled look, Ryan asked, "He doesn't work?"

"Off and on."

"And *he's* cheating on *you?*"

"I don't know. Maybe I'm just being paranoid."

"Usually, where there's smoke, there's fire," Ryan said.

"Well, there's lots of smoke," she replied, with another roll of her eyes.

"Follow your gut," Ryan said. "Your gut instinct is usually right."

Faith stared forward, but it was clear her mind was far away. It was like something he said had stung. Her eyes filled with tears, and she quickly wiped them away. "I gotta get back to work," she said before standing up and walking straight to the ladies' restroom.

The next time Ryan came in, Faith was back to the smiling, cheerful girl. Ryan figured things were straightened out at home. But a couple weeks later, Faith arrived at his table looking tired and upset. Her eyes looked like she'd been crying all night. It took almost no effort on his part to find out what was going on—mostly just a little heartfelt concern.

Soon, Faith would volunteer information about her relationship with her boyfriend without Ryan having to do a lot of prying. Anyone could see it was a toxic, unhealthy relationship. All Ryan could think was, *What an idiot. He has a beautiful girl who seems perfect.* Ryan had been dating someone new for the past five months. She was beautiful; but as much as he tried, he never felt for her what already he felt for Faith.

It was late, the restaurant was closing soon, and Faith was filling the sugar packets. They sat at the little bar and talked.

"I don't know," she started, resting her elbows on the table and dropping the sugar packets. "I found this phone bill under the seat of his car." Shaking her head in disgust, she said, "There were calls for hundreds and hundreds of dollars to Houston that lasted for hours and hours."

Offering his support, Ryan slid his arm halfway across the table, hoping she would take it, but she didn't.

"Well, I called the number, and some girl answered. She said she didn't want to talk and hung up on me."

"*Jesus,*" Ryan said, "I'm sorry."

"I asked Jake about it, but he denied everything."

"Of course he did," Ryan interjected.

"Then he said they were just friends."

"Right!" Ryan laughed.

"You don't think so?" Faith asked, like she was actually looking for the answer.

"You can't be serious," Ryan said with a scowl.

"I don't know. He says I'm crazy and they're only friends. I don't know what to think. Do you think I'm crazy?"

Ryan wanted to say, *yes, you're crazy...you're crazy for staying with this loser.* Instead, he placed his hand on hers and said, "No, I don't think you're crazy at all."

"So, I'm not being paranoid?"

Ryan sat there with his hand on hers—happy she didn't pull away, and wishing she'd turn her hand over and lace her fingers into his. He wanted to say, "If you were with me, I'd treat you so much better." Instead, he simply shook his head.

Like she'd just realized Ryan had been holding her hand for the past five minutes, Faith pulled back and said, "Well, maybe things are getting better."

"How so?" Ryan asked.

"Well, I was leaving and—"

"*Was* leaving?"

"I was leaving, and he stopped me. He told me that he loved me and wanted to get married."

*This is absurd—totally absurd.* Ryan took hold of both her shoulders and said, "Faith, why are you talking about marriage?"

"I don't know. I love him."

Ryan let go of her shoulders and said, "Fine, but you don't have to marry him. Slow down. Take your time."

"But this is what I've wanted…what I've always wanted. I want a family. Maybe seeing me walk out really changed him. I don't know…I have to see where this goes."

After talking for a few more minutes, the manager walked up to the front door and said, "Come on, guys. It's time to lock up."

Ryan walked with Faith out of the door. "Where's your car?" he asked.

Showing a little embarrassment, she answered, "I don't have a car."

"Of course you don't," Ryan said, shaking his head.

"I walk to work."

Trying not to laugh, he said, "Of course you do. How far do you live from here?"

"Hmm, I don't know…twenty minutes."

"You walk twenty minutes home at night?"

"Maybe fifteen minutes."

"Here," Ryan said, pointing to his car. "Let me take you home."

"I can't," Faith said firmly. "Jake is really jealous. My boss took me home once, and Jake blew a gasket. He wanted to know everything about him. I heard about it for months. I still hear about it. He acts like I cheated on him for letting my boss drive me home. God help me if I get out of your car. He'd kill me."

*This story just keeps getting worse.* Ryan felt so sorry for this girl. She has to wake up and see that she deserves better. Ryan took a step forward, so he was standing right in front of her. When he tried to look into her eyes, she looked down. He reached out, raised her chin until she was looking right at him, and said, "You know I care about you, right?"

For a brief second, they shared an intimate smile. Then she looked down, refusing to meet his gaze again.

At this point, Ryan was determined to kiss her like Sleeping Beauty and break the spell that's been cast over her. She has to know she doesn't have to be stuck in a terrible, toxic relationship. She can choose him—a lawyer who cares about her and can give her love, stability, a family—everything!

Ryan reached down, took her face in his hands, and brought her beautiful, soft lips to his. He'd dreamed of this moment so many times. As he closed his eyes, Faith pressed her body against his. A wave of pleasure spread over him. Caught up in the moment, Ryan slid his hand through her soft hair. Just as he turned his head to offer her his tongue, Faith pulled away and said, "I can't do this. I have to go."

With that one short, wonderful kiss, Ryan felt what it was like to have her, and he didn't want to let her go. "Faith, listen—" he said, hoping to put an end to all her fears.

Pulling out of his grasp, in a firm, sober voice, she said, "I'm sorry, I can't see you anymore."

With a look of weary desperation, Ryan shook his head and said, "I'm sorry. I shouldn't have done that."

"It's not that," Faith said, lowering her gaze. "It's just. . .it's just that I can't see you again."

Now full of regret, Ryan begged, "Please don't pull away from me. I really—"

Cutting him off, Faith gave Ryan one last hug and walked away.

Three days later, when Ryan returned to the restaurant and sat in her section, another girl took his table. The message was loud and clear.

# CHAPTER 4

Without the distraction of a gorgeous girl on his mind, Ryan could get back to obsessing about Jodi's breast implants. Plus, he'd been dating a pretty wonderful girl who left no question about her feelings for him. He might not be *in love*—whatever that means—but he did have feelings for her.

For weeks, Ryan had been straddling the fence with one foot on one side and one foot on the other. Again and again, his girlfriend would ask if everything was okay. He'd tell her he was thinking about his first big case coming up—which was partially true. It was also partly true that he had been hoping this beautiful girl named Faith would wake up one day and realize she wanted to be with him.

Well, Mr. Bannister had already tried the best case with the best chance of bringing home a win for the firm. His client had been a woman who was happily married with three kids. She had no previous medical history, went to church every Sunday, and eventually died after a battle with cancer that they blamed on the silicone breast implants.

Ryan wouldn't be so lucky. He didn't get the second-best or the third-best client. No, Jodi was a stripper who was a little rough around the edges. The way she described it, "I tell it like it is. If you don't like it, you can kiss my ass."

She had smoked all her life and not just cigarettes. She worked late hours at a gentlemen's club, often drinking more than she should. One unlucky night she was arrested for driving while intoxicated. She'd been married and divorced twice and had two kids—one from her first husband and the other from a boyfriend. She had an abortion that the defense attorney found out about after sending subpoenas all over the city. Ryan thought the abortion was irrelevant, but the attorney blamed all of her medical problems on that one decision. Ryan could never figure that one out. It seemed like a low blow. He was sure they were mostly hoping to inflame the jury against Jodi. Bringing up an abortion has ruined many good cases.

Jodi was still alive and made a number of serious mistakes in her deposition. It sounded like all the questions took her by surprise. Three hours into her testimony, she turned to Mr. Bannister and said, "What the fuck? Who is this son of a bitch?"

Bannister looked over at the other lawyer in embarrassment and said, "Maybe we should take a little break."

"I don't need no fuckin' break," Jodi yelled. "You're my lawyer. I need you to get off your fat ass and do something."

"Calm down," Bannister said, trying to explain. "He's entitled to ask these questions."

"Calm down! Well, you can kiss my ass, too!" Jodi snapped.

They left the deposition for a quick break. It took some coaxing to get Jodi back to the table.

It was obvious to everyone in the room that Jodi made a horrible witness. It was the worst breast implant case the firm had taken in. They only took her case in the hope that it would settle after Bannister won the first trial. Ryan couldn't help but wonder if he was given the worst case on purpose.

Jodi's case might have problems, but Ryan had one advantage. He had all the testimony from the first trial. All day and night he studied that testimony like his life—or his client's life—depended on it. He studied the cross-examination of Bannister's client. She was a sweet wife and mother, and they were still pretty rough on her. God only knows what they'd do to Jodi. No doubt, it'd be a regular street brawl. But Ryan wasn't deterred.

Ryan's biggest fear was the defendant's experts. Since it had worked once, he knew they'd follow the same game plan. He knew what they would say, so he worked tirelessly to poke holes in their testimony. He saw many instances where they gave conflicting—or at least he could make it *sound* conflicting—testimony. Digging deeper, he discovered their fancy studies were actually funded by the breast implant manufacturer. It took quite a bit of work to discover that, since the money was funneled through a parent corporation.

Then came Ryan's experts and all the medical testimony. Ryan figured out what worked and what didn't work. Most people don't know a red blood cell from a white blood cell. It's easier to explain how much rocket fuel is needed to land on the moon than to explain all this medical stuff.

So, he simplified the case. He told the doctors, "This time, don't get bogged down on things the jury won't understand, anyway. We don't want to bore them to death. Oh, and try not to use big medical terms. The case is simple and easy to understand. She was fine before the defendant's breast implants ruptured inside her, sending poison through her body, and now she's not fine anymore and she'll never be fine again. It's just that simple."

You can't storm out. Keep your cool. Don't say 'fuck off' or call him a 'son of a bitch.'"

By the time the trial came around, Jodi looked like a different person. She was ready to go to court and handle whatever they threw at her. Ryan gave her fifty dollars to get a pretty little dress and some flats like you'd wear to church—that same church she'll tell the jury she's been going to for the past year or so.

On Monday morning, Ryan walked into the courthouse in the new suit he had bought over the weekend. He rolled in four legal boxes, returned to his car, and came back with three more boxes. His client arrived in a beautiful blue dress, her hair straightened, and looking ten years younger than she did when this all started.

"Wow," Ryan said, stunned at the sight.

"Is it okay?" she asked, looking down.

"You look terrific. Are you ready?"

Jodi took a deep breath and said, "I don't know. I'm nervous."

Ryan took his own deep breath and said, "Don't worry. I'm a little nervous too."

The team of defense attorneys poured in, with their legal assistants following behind. Bringing up the rear were the men with dollies stacked high with boxes. There were so many boxes they had to leave some out in the hallway.

The team of defense attorneys poured in, with their legal assistants following behind. Bringing up the rear were the men with dollies stacked high with boxes. There were so many boxes they had to leave some out in the hallway.

Sounding really concerned, Jodi leaned over and whispered, "They have nine lawyers?"

"Nay," Ryan answered. "They only have five. The other four are legal assistants. Good thing this isn't an election."

The lead attorney looked around and asked, "Where's Mr. Bannister? Are you helping him try the case?"

Ryan, who looked way too young to be going up against this team of lawyers, said, "Looks like I'll be trying the case today. Please go easy on me."

The judge came in and took his place on his bench. After calling the case number, the judge asked both attorneys if they were ready for trial. Ryan stood first and said, "The Plaintiff is ready, Your Honor."

"Where's Mr. Bannister?" the judge asked.

"He's a little under the weather, Your Honor. He asked me to fill in for him."

With a slight grin, the judge said, "I'm not sure I've seen you before. What's your name, Counselor?"

"Brunick….Ryan Brunick."

"Very well, Mr. Brunick. Welcome to my court."

"Thank you, Judge."

The judge recognized each defense attorney by name, like they just spent the Christmas holidays together. He then looked at both tables and asked. "I understand mediation wasn't successful in this case. Have the parties made every effort to settle the case before coming to my court today?"

"We have," the lead defense attorney answered.

Ryan looked over at his adversary, back at the judge, and said, "If offering nothing is making every effort to resolve the case, the defense has made every effort."

The judge responded with another subtle smile and said, "Very well, I believe the jury has been empaneled. Let's bring them on in and pick a jury."

Each potential juror walked in one by one and took a seat in the visitor's gallery. Most looked like they'd rather be anywhere but here. As they closed the door behind the last woman, the place was packed.

The judge introduced Ryan and Jodi as "The Plaintiff and her attorney." Ryan stood and gave a nod. Jodi stood and gave the smile they had practiced yesterday. He then introduced the defendant and their lead attorney. It felt like the whole left side of the room stood up.

With a friendly smile, the judge said, "Mr. Brunick, since you're the Plaintiff you go first."

Over a hundred people came in so they could get a jury of twelve. This was his jury panel, and this was his first chance to address them.

Ryan started sounding young and nervous. He stood up, walked over to the podium in front of the crowd, and took a deep breath. When he reached down for his pen, a stack of papers fell to the floor. Jodi looked at the jury wondering where the Ryan she knew went. He gathered the papers up, gave a warm smile, and said, "Good morning, ladies and gentlemen. Thank you for coming here today."

The rest is history.

As Ryan continued, he soon looked at ease. He explained how Jodi was a single mother with two beautiful children. She works every day to provide for her family. Not wanting the defense to be the first to bring out the negatives about his client, he told them how she had left two abusive marriages, took the only job that paid enough for her to stay off welfare, and decided on breast implants for cosmetic reasons. It's true she started smoking when she was young, but she had quit a few months back. She never had any health issues from smoking. Ryan never brought up the abortion. By the time he was finished, he got every juror to agree these things had nothing to do with her case.

A surprising number of women on the panel also had breast augmentation. They listened carefully when Ryan, in plain non-medical terms, explained how breast implants can rupture, and the silicone can enter your bloodstream. The women looked concerned. The more Ryan talked, the more the panel smiled, laughed, and agreed with everything he said.

Ryan looked across the room and got real. Pointing at the Defendant, he said, "Jodi's life has been destroyed by the Defendant's defective product. We'll be asking you to right a great wrong here and award ten million dollars. Does anyone here have a problem giving a full verdict if the evidence supports it?" The jurors looked at each other and then shook their heads. Ryan thanked them all before sitting back down, happy with his first morning at the courthouse.

The defense attorney got up next and talked a lot about the experts and the reports they would be providing to help the jury understand the case. It was clear they were about to use the same strategy that had worked so well in the previous trial.

When they finally sat down, it was time to start the case. Ryan thought Mr. Bannister had made one big mistake during his trial. He tried to get his client off the stand as quickly as possible and focused most of his attention on the doctors, who looked surprisingly unprepared. He haggled endlessly with the experts and battled minor points to death. Ryan thought this was a mistake. The case almost became a theoretical back and forth debate about breast implants in general. The client was left out of the whole equation. No, Ryan wanted the jury to know his client. Sink or swim, she would talk…and talk a lot. Everything would focus on her. The case was simple, and all that confusing medical mumbo jumbo would take back stage.

After lunch, Ryan called Jodi to the stand. *Here we go,* he thought as he said, "The Plaintiff calls Jodi Lewis.

Jodi sat down in the chair looking like a mommy. The change was so drastic that the defense attorneys had to look back at her deposition to make sure they had the right Plaintiff.

"Good morning, Jodi. How are you doing today?"

She pulled the microphone a little too close, causing a boom around the courtroom. Pushing it back a bit, she said, "I'm pretty nervous."

Very different from her deposition, she was full of "yes sir" and "no sir." With the help of the throat lozenges she'd been taking for the last two months, she talked clearly with a warm Texas charm.

She talked about her life growing up in Austin and her two precious children. She went over all the wonderful things they do together and how they're the best thing that ever happened to her. She explained how she was in perfect health until she had the defendant's silicone breast implants inserted nine years before. They were removed three years later after one ruptured, and she developed severe chest pain, muscle pain, fatigue, and problems breathing. After her breast implants were removed, some symptoms went away, but other symptoms worsened. She developed what the doctors call autoimmune disease. She doesn't understand it all, but she knows it's serious. Now she's losing her hair. She understands her condition will continue to worsen. With tears falling down her cheeks, she testified how she feels depressed and suicidal. Only the love of her children keeps her hanging on. She prays she will live to see her youngest graduate from high school.

True to his word, Ryan asked for a fifteen-minute break. This testimony really shook the jury. They gave Jodi sympathetic smiles when they walked out of the room.

Jodi held her own on cross-examination. She decided on breast implants after breastfeeding her two children. She then corrected a few of the things from her deposition, just like they'd practiced. It softened the blows. The defense attorney made some points; but nothing was fatal. There was a point in the trial where they went back and forth so many times it looked like Jodi was about to explode. Ryan was certain the defense attorney thought, *there she is,* so he gave her the signal they rehearsed, and she calmed down and went back to answering with a smile. Unable to rattle her, or to get her to admit things that would end her case, the defense attorney stood up and said, "No more questions." The abortion was never mentioned.

*Well done.* Ryan thought. *We just dodged a bullet.*

Next came the medical doctors. Ryan spent plenty of time before the trial with each doctor, going over everything they testified to in the first trial and how to respond to the defense questions. He had new studies that bolstered their testimonies. He also cut their time on the stand in half. All the work paid off. In the first trial, the doctors just about admitted the case away. This time, they left the stand looking credible and trustworthy.

Two years after receiving her implants, Jodi was hospitalized for sepsis. It sounded confusing, but it was actually pretty simple. The body is overreacting to an infection. Jodi now suffers from connective-tissue and autoimmune disease caused by the breast implants, and there is no cure. She has a staph infection that threatens her life. Her condition will continue to worsen and, in all medical probability, it will be fatal. Jodi and three of the jurors cried, listening to this testimony.

After Ryan rested his case, the defense attorneys called their own experts. One after the other jumped on the stand, looking sharp and rolling out their impressive credentials. They had graduated from colleges like Harvard, Yale, Stanford, MIT; and, of course, The University of Texas. Each one testified that their breast implants were designed and manufactured just fine. They only ruptured because of the negligence of the Plaintiff, the Plaintiff's doctor, or a multitude of other strange reasons, including the water the Plaintiff was drinking and bathing in. Everyone was at fault except them. Several jurors seemed confused. Others followed closely and took notes.

Their doctors testified that silicone was harmless—it was simply absorbed by the body and flushed out by human waste. The Plaintiff had no real injuries, or her injuries were all psychological. They introduced thick studies in beautiful binders. They passed out each study to the judge, the court reporter, every attorney, and every juror. Some jurors followed along word for word, while others put the binders aside and simply listened. The science was clear—there was simply no evidence the silicone breast implants caused any of the Plaintiff's symptoms, and Jodi's claims weren't credible. It was almost laughable to believe Jodi would die from anything other than old age.

On cross-examination Ryan picked each expert apart piece by piece with a keen intellect, sharp wit, sarcasm, and by connecting dots no one saw coming. He had a study their experts hadn't seen before and brought up the thousands of claims by other women.

*"All these women all over the country—white, brown, black, rich, poor, young, old—were all mentally and physically healthy until their breast implants ruptured. Did they all magically develop the same psychological delusions? The women who passed away—I guess that was all in their heads too?"*

Unlike Jodi's doctor, they hadn't treated Jodi or even examined her. They'd never even talked to her. If the jury here, who just listened to the evidence,  believes her testimony—are all the jurors also suffering from the same psychological disorder? After a flurry of objections, Ryan withdrew the question.

Before it was over, Ryan was using their own experts against each other. After a tough cross-examination, two of their experts still appeared impressive. Three jurors appeared to be swayed by their testimony, binders, charts, and graphs. It was expert against expert, and their experts' studies seemed to carry the day.

Then Ryan finished his cross-examination with a stunning revelation. He had found a memo buried deep in the boxes and boxes of discovery that Mr. Bannister missed. The defendant had known for years that silicone gel would seep out of the implants. The jury looked outraged and the tide seemed to turn. The one woman on the jury who had silicone breast implants looked at the defendant with such anger the judge had to take a recess.

To get the case back on track, the defense attorney brought up the abortion. The doctor saw the medical records and explained how it was the abortion that caused all her injuries. Once afraid of this whole abortion thing, Ryan was now glad they went there. He thought it was a bridge too far, and he was waiting for it. When the defendants passed the witness, it was Ryan's turn. After spending four long, boring hours testifying for the defense, Ryan waisted no time.

"That must be it! An abortion that Jodi had when she was only seventeen years old caused all her injuries…right?"

"Oh, yes, sir," the doctor answered. "This procedure is not only immoral but also destructive. It can have serious effects on a woman's body many years later."

Ryan looked really confused and said, "Wait a minute…I thought you testified that she didn't have any injuries. Two hours ago, you swore under oath to this jury that all her injuries were in her head. Now you finally admit she *is* suffering from all these injuries?"

The expert was caught off guard.

"Let me ask you. In all your years and reading all your studies, have you ever treated, or even heard of, a woman with no breast implants having an abortion and fifteen years later suffering from sepsis, connective-tissue an autoimmune disease, and a staph infection? Does an abortion cause you to lose your hair?"

Each juror's head bounced from the expert to Ryan, and back to the expert, like they were watching a tennis match.

When the expert didn't respond, Ryan stood up and smiled. "I didn't think so. Thank you for your honesty." Then he excused the witness.

With a couple of questions, the Defendant just watched seven days of expert testimony how breast implants don't rupture and don't cause injuries fly right out the window They were ready to get him off the stand. The attorney stood up, buttoned his jacket, and said, "Uhm….no more questions, Your Honor."

Instead of lasting three months, this case was over in three weeks. As the case went on, the news spread around the courthouse and attorneys came in to see what all the talk was about. By the start of the second week of trial, Ryan stopped going into the office; but the news got back. Mr. Bannister and three other partners came down and sat in the front row to watch the show.

Ryan proved his true abilities in his closing arguments. The Defendant was cold and hard, focusing all his time on doctors, studies, and experts. He showed no sympathy for Jodi—mostly blaming her or her doctors for everything. Mr. Bannister listened with surprise as the defense attorney paid Ryan a pretty high compliment.

"Mr. Brunick is good. I'll give him that. He knows how to cross-examine a witness. But don't be fooled by his slick talk that tugs on your heartstrings. Remember the studies. You can't argue with studies."

Ryan, on the other hand, focused most of his closing argument talking about Jodi, barely mentioning all the experts. In a packed courtroom, with his boss sitting on the front row, Ryan finished his closing argument:

"This case is simple. Jodi was in perfect health before the implants. The Defendant's breast implants ruptured, and she's never been the same. If her injuries were not from the breast implants, then it's an unbelievable coincidence. Yes, it might get confusing listening to all these experts. The truth is, if you pay an expert enough money, he'll testify that an elephant can hang from a cliff with his tail tied to a dandelion. You're smart people. Use your common sense. That's all we ask. It doesn't take a bunch of overpriced experts to know the truth in this case."

Ryan looked at the defendants and said, "After this trial is over, these guys will return to their families and forget all about Jodi and her children. But Jodi didn't come all the way down from New York City to turn around and fly back. No, she lives in Travis County, just like each of you. You drive on the same streets, your kids go to the same schools, you shop in the same grocery stores. This is why we have you—real people who can think, and hurt, and feel—instead of some computer program who can't even see Jodi. Well, she needs your help. She has poison spreading through her body. She doesn't need your sympathy—she gets that from her family and her church. She needs justice. And what is justice? It's easy to get confused about justice with all these lawyers, the judge sitting up there, the bailiff over there, teams of doctors and experts, a bunch of law books, and confusing studies. It can be intimidating. To me, justice is simple. It's doing what's right. That's all Jodi asks…do what's right. This is her only chance to get justice for her and her children, and it's your only chance to give justice. It may be the most important thing you do the rest of your life. No one else can do it for you. If not, you…then who? If not now…then when? Thank you."

Ryan sat down, and in front of the jury, reached over and gave Jodi a hug.

When the jury filed out of the courtroom, Jodi turned to Ryan with tears in her eyes. She hugged him tight and thanked him for everything. The partners gave him impressive looks and nods.

Unlike the first case, the jury stayed out for the rest of the day and two more days. After the lunch break, the lead defense attorney tapped Ryan on the shoulder and asked if they could speak privately outside. Ryan knew this was great news.

"My client knows they did nothing wrong," he began. "Still, they want to help your client."

Throughout his career, Ryan always demanded his clients be addressed by their names. "Help Jodi? Her name is Jodi."

"Yes, they want to help Jodi.

"How much help?" Ryan asked.

"Actually, quite a lot of help. They're willing to pay fifty thousand to your client and—"

"Jodi"

"Yes, Jodi…and ten thousand to each of Jodi's children. I'm sorry, what're their names?"

"Lonnie and Karen."

This was Ryan's first chance to see just how compassionate defense attorneys really are.

"I thought you said a *lot* of help. That won't even cover our expenses."

"Come on, Ryan," the lawyer said with a scowl, now calling Ryan by his first name. "We both know those expenses were rung up in the last case your firm just lost. Give this money to your client."

"To Jodi?"

"To Jodi, it's a lot of help."

Ryan stood up and with a smile, said, "I'll take it to her. It's her decision."

"Oh, one more thing. No admission of liability. My client did nothing wrong…period! As far as the record will show, both parties walked away from the case. You know what I'm saying."

Ryan laughed just a little and said, "I understand exactly what you're saying."

As Ryan sat at the table explaining the offer to Jodi, the jury announced they had a verdict. Acting quick, Ryan asked, "Yes or no."

"Fuck…I mean forget them," Jodi answered.

Ryan turned to the defense attorney and shook his head. "I think she's going to pass."

No one said a word as the jury marched into the courtroom single file like soldiers coming home from battle. The first juror sat down and gave Jodi a smile. There was no time to negotiate. The defense attorney turned to Ryan and said, "Five hundred thousand."

Ryan saw the same thing—from three jurors. He closed his eyes and shook his head no.

The jury foreman held Jodi's fate in his right hand. As the foreman read the verdict, Ryan reached over and held Jodi's trembling hand. Jodi couldn't understand a word of the legal words until the courtroom exploded with gasps, cheers, and applause. *Who are all these people?* Jodi thought. *I arrived here with no one.*

They found the defendant one hundred percent responsible for the defective breast implants and awarded $10.6 million to Jodi for her injuries and $2.5 million in punitive damages.

Jodi cried. She had no one in the courtroom to congratulate her, so Ryan hugged her. She turned to Ryan and said, "We did it. We beat them"

"No, *you* did it," Ryan said. "*You* beat them."

David finally beat Goliath. One lawyer after another waited in line to shake Ryan's hand. The verdict was barely announced before the news spread like wildfire up and down the courthouse halls. Soon it was the legal gossip around the state and made headlines in one paper after another.

Ryan made his first appearance in front of the cameras, as local reporters were full of questions. Jodi was standing up front with four of the law partners, who caught the last week of the trial, standing on each side of her and Ryan at the end. Mr. Bannister did most of the talking, mentioning the law firm by name again and again. You wouldn't have known Ryan even tried the case, except when Jodi turned around, found Ryan at the very end, and said, "I couldn't have won this case without my lawyer, Mr. Brunick." Looking right at him, she wiped a tear away, and said, "He worked so hard on my case. He's the best lawyer there is." She walked to the end with tears streaming down her face and gave him a big hug.

This exact same scene would play out again and again in Ryan's career. No one worked harder to understand a case inside and out. He knew what his opponent would do and would beat him to the punch. He was a master of deception. When you think he's going right, he'd go left. He'd find some way to turn your own witnesses against you; and next thing, they're his witnesses. When his opponent had evidence that would doom most cases, he'd find some way to neutralize it or at least make his own points with it. Nothing seemed to concern him.

The cases kept getting bigger, along with Ryan's reputation. If you underestimated Ryan Brunick, you did so at your own peril. He was always two steps ahead. Lawyers who thought they had the case won would look at each other and say, "What are we missing?" By the time they found out, it was always too late.

He was raised by his mother, came from simple means, and had this ability to connect with a jury. He spoke in a way most jurors could understand. He combined a charm, quick wit, and sense of humor to get the jury on his side before he ever put on his first witness. More than anything else, he had passion and truly cared about everyone. Jurors could see how much he believed in his clients, and this caused them to believe in his clients, too.

The partners returned to their office, trying to figure out what to do with their rising star. Everyone agreed Ryan should be promoted to their litigation team, but it was way too early to jump to conclusions. They started going on and on about Ryan's sharp cross-examinations and incredible closing argument; but next thing they were talking about the rules of evidence and the objections Ryan missed. Mr. Bannister made sure everyone knew it was he who actually paved the way for the verdict. "Anyone can win a case if they're given all the testimony. It's always easier the second time around."

A single, uneducated mother might accept a lawyer right out of law school, but their sophisticated clients would never let some third-year lawyer handle their cases. They agreed to throw Ryan a bonus and keep him pacified for a few more years.


Ten days after the verdict, they called Ryan into the large conference room. Expensive Champagne sat on the table along with the most beautiful fruit and vegetable display, and an assortment of desserts. All the partners sat around the table and stood when he walked in. They congratulated him on his incredible performance with an applause, firm handshakes, and slaps on the back. Ryan was the man of the hour.

Once the hoopla died down, everyone took their seats. The senior partner handed Ryan a Champagne glass and said, "Good job on that trial, son."

Mr. Bannister raised his glass and said, "Good for you. You had a great client. She really—"

"Jodi," Ryan interrupted.

"Yes, Jodi did well."

Ryan raised his glass in agreement.

Ryan thought he should be the one to negotiate the final settlement numbers, but the file mysteriously left his office and landed back on Mr. Bannister's desk. Bannister fielded all the calls from the press and other attorneys. Most assumed he was the one who actually tried the case, and he didn't think it was important to correct them.

"And I've been in talks with the defense attorney," Bannister continued. "They're eager to get this case resolved. I got them up to three and a half million dollars if they won't appeal."

The partners clapped and whistled. Then they patted each other on the back.

Jodi was Mr. Bannister's client again. Each time she called in for Ryan, she was transferred to Bannister. Ryan won't even get the pleasure of handing her the settlement check when it comes in. But, that wasn't important to Ryan now.

"We have great news for you," Bannister said. "We're moving you to the litigation section of our firm."

*More applause and more pats on the back.* Now that's what Ryan had been waiting for. "Wonderful!" he said, lifting his glass to theirs. Thank you!"

"And we have a bonus for you."

They slid a $50,000 check across the table that Ryan opened with disappointment. The defendant was already offering $3.5 million to settle the case. Ryan thought it was ridiculous and they'd probably go higher. This case would pay the firm one and a half million dollars and reimburse them for the $285,000 they spent on experts and other costs in the first case they tried. Ryan wasn't altogether sure if swapping expenses back and forth was the way things were supposed to be done; and he was expecting more. *Bannister was about to throw this whole case away.* The good news? At least the bonus would cover most of his student loans and he'd be out of debt soon.

For him, it wasn't about the money, anyway. What he really wanted was the recognition so he could try more cases. Ryan put the check in his pocket and asked, "So, now I'll handle my own cases?"

The partners gave each other a few uncomfortable glances before looking at Ryan and saying, "Sure…with a little time."

Ryan closed his eyes and slowly shook his head. "A little more time? How much time?"

Mr. Bannister raised his glass. "Ryan, you did good…no doubt. Let's celebrate."

Cutting off the cheers, Ryan said, "I thought I'd be trying my own cases now."

The head partner, who Ryan rarely talked to, said, "Be patient. Your time will come."

Ryan took a deep breath and said, "I told you before I ever accepted this job, that I'm a trial lawyer—"

"We're not saying you aren't," Bannister interrupted.

Ryan set down his full Champagne glass, stood up from the table, raised the envelope in front of everyone, and said, "Thank you all for your generous bonus."

He tapped the side of the envelope on the conference table, then turned around and walked out of the room, leaving all the food and liquor on the table, and a bunch of partners looking at each other in disbelief. He stopped by his secretary's desk and said, "I'm leaving for the day."

"You're leaving?" she said, quite confused.

"Yep."

"You want me to forward your calls?"

"Nope."

## – CHAPTER 5 –

Ryan drove home in the Nissan Maxima he bought when he started his new job. It was the car he once dreamed of. He really thought he had proved himself. The partners' words kept bouncing around in his head.

*"Ryan, you did good last month…no doubt…but be patient.*

*"Your time will come."*

Driving down the road, he thought, *I won. I won the case Bannister was afraid to even try. Now I'm supposed to return to the library like it never happened?*

Thinking more about his life than the road ahead, Ryan suddenly realized he had just passed the restaurant where he always ate before he got wrapped up in this trial. He was stupid to kiss his beautiful waitress. She was so angry the last time he was there. She wouldn't even take his table. Apologies were in order.

Ryan made a quick U-turn and pulled into the restaurant. He walked in and sat down in his usual booth, hoping she wouldn't pass him off to a different waitress.

Faith walked up to his table, and he was surprised to see that her hair was uncombed, there were light circles under her eyes, and the smile he always looked forward to was replaced by the saddest look he'd ever seen. Still, she was the most beautiful woman in Austin.

Hoping she had put that kiss behind her by now, he gave a smile and said, "Hey, gorgeous, long time no see."

"Too long," she said, with the same smile he remembered.

Not sure if she actually married that loser, Ryan looked at her finger and said, "Well, I don't see a ring on your pretty little finger."

"Nope, you were right."

Feeling the pain he knew was deep inside her, Ryan said, "Well, I get no pleasure in being right."

For an hour, he watched as she walked around the restaurant—returning from time to time with fresh coffee, but without her lovely smile. There was something about this woman—something he'd never seen in any other woman. When he finished his meal, she dropped off a check with the most beautiful heart he'd ever seen. Even more nervous than that day he faced his first jury, Ryan took a deep breath and asked, "Would you like to get together sometime?"

They met at the park and Faith explained how she caught her boyfriend in bed with the same girl from before. As they stood beside his car, they shared their first kiss—their first real kiss. It was so wonderful. He would never get that kiss out of his mind. Her lips were soft as she pressed her beautiful body against his. She had this sexual dynamic that swept him away. Each time they'd talk, she seemed a little shy and nervous, but he'd never seen a woman, especially a woman this young, with so much sexual confidence. It would be the first kiss of many.

That evening, he drove her back to his house, and they made love. The look on her face as they slowly rocked back and forth was the most attractive sight he'd ever seen. The sounds she made beneath him were so beautiful and arousing that he never wanted the night to end. She was drop dead gorgeous and had a charm that was irresistible.

She also had a hurt deep inside her that was so strong he could feel it; and her hurt also hurt him. As they lay together in bed, she talked about her time growing up in Georgia. Her dad was nice, but her mother was impossible. She was always yelling about one thing or another. Faith was a good daughter; but as hard as she tried, she could never please her mom. Her mom didn't like the way she dressed, the makeup she wore, the guys she dated, the grades on her report cards…nothing. There was a point in her life when she actually felt like she hated her mom. Then she met Jake, the first guy she loved, who physically and mentally abused her and cheated on her.

Ryan was cursed with an abundance of empathy for other people. As Faith poured herself out in front of him, all he wanted to do was fill her with his love. It was impossible not to feel sorry for this girl. She had suffered a tough life and never got a break. He held her close, believing she only needed a chance…someone to love her. Once she realized his love was unconditional, she would blossom.

From that day forward, Ryan was hooked. Something about her touched his soul. Night after night, he felt a love and peace just lying there watching her sleep. All he could think was how lucky he was to have her…all of her. He was sure he'd never get a second chance to feel this kind of love again. He was determined he'd never let her get away.

Three days later, Ryan walked into Mr. Bannister's office and sat down in front of his desk. "I need to talk to you," he began.

Wanting to size him up, Bannister said, "Sure, what's on your mind?"

"I've given my situation here a lot of thought," Ryan said.

Not surprised how the conversation started, Bannister leaned back in his chair. He figured Ryan was there for a raise and he figured the partners would agree as long as it was reasonable. He crossed his arms and waited.

"I appreciate the opportunity you gave me, but I think it's time I move on. I'm giving you my two weeks' notice."

Bannister scrambled to fix the situation. "Ryan, wait a minute. I know you didn't hear what you wanted to hear the other day; but you have a great future here. Don't do anything—"

Ryan took the resignation letter he was holding and put it on Mr. Bannister's desk. "Really, it's all my fault. I knew I shouldn't have taken this job. I wanted to be a trial attorney, and I didn't want to wait ten years to do it. I thank you for everything you did for me, but I've decided to open my own firm."

Mr. Bannister picked up the letter and read it to himself. "Start your own firm?" he asked. "Do you know how hard that is? There's no need for this. I think the partners will agree to a nice raise. I'll talk to them. Maybe we can put you on the fast track."

Ryan stopped for a second and said, "You know, your work really helped on Jodi's case. I couldn't have done it without you."

"Sure," Mr. Bannister said. "We all did our part. That's what we're here for."

"I probably got lucky. I just don't think I'm cut out for a big firm."

"Hold on!" Bannister said, raising his hands in protest. "You just need more time to get used to it. You want a bigger office? I was just about to tell you that I'm moving you up to an office with a great view of the city."

Ryan shook his head and said, "That's very kind of you, but it's not about my office. I'm just not—"

"What if we doubled your bonus…tripled it?"

If anything, this made Ryan angry. If he was so valuable, why didn't they offer this three weeks ago? He shook his head, so Bannister continued.

"It's about Julie, isn't it? You want to wrap that case up? Hell, I don't care about that stuff. Call her in…you can give her the money."

"Jodi," Ryan corrected him. "It's not that. I'm just ready for a change."

Once Bannister accepted the inevitable, he extended his hand and said, "We're going to miss you around here."

Ryan shook his hand and turned for the door. Just before he could walk out, Mr. Bannister said, "Ryan, I'm only one vote. I wish I could have done more."

"I understand," Ryan said.

Bannister walked around his desk and placed his hands on Ryan's shoulders like you'd address a brother. "Ryan, you're a hell of a lawyer. I'm sure I'll see you down at the courthouse soon. I just hope we're not on opposite sides."

Ryan gave him a smile, then a wink, and said, "Oh, I'm sure you'll do just fine."


They actually tried eight cases against each other over the next twenty-two years when Bannister finally retired. Bannister never once did just fine.

# – CHAPTER 6 –

Ready to start the rest of his life, Ryan went home and asked the love of his life to move in with him. His whole world changed that day when she said yes.

When Faith went back to her tiny apartment to get her things, Ryan was left on cloud nine. He started clearing drawers, pushing his clothes to the right of the closet, and making room in the bathroom for two. Then the doorbell rang, which caught him by surprise. He just knew it was Faith coming back to tell him she had changed her mind.

Ryan opened the door and thought, *Oh shit!*

Jennifer, his now ex-girlfriend, looked at him with a smile, and said, "Hey, Ryan." Ryan knew she was wanting to come in.

Unsure what to do, Ryan said, "Jennifer. . .how you been?"

"I've been good. I've been trying to call you…and text you."

Ryan put his hand on his forehead, closed his eyes, and stammered, "Yes, I'm sorry. I've been so busy with my…with my trial and everything."

"Yeah, I saw it in the paper and on the news."

"I'm sorry. Everything's been so—"

"So, you did it?" Jennifer asked with a giant smile.

With a nod, Ryan said, "Yeah...I did it."

"You won your first trial!"

"My first trial," Ryan repeated.

Looking for some sign as to what was going on, Jennifer tried to look past him and said, "I just thought we would celebrate or something."

"Oh...yeah...it's just that—"

Afraid to let him finish, her lips began to tremble, as she said, "Well, we can celebrate now." When Ryan looked down without responding, a tear fell down her cheek. "Ryan, are we okay?"

Ryan looked up and said, "I'm sorry...I'm so—"

Wiping away her tear, she knew she had to do something. Her words came rushing out. "Ryan, what did I do? I'm so sorry. Just tell me what I did, and I'll make it right."

"You didn't do anything. It's me. I just—"

She put her hand over his mouth, like stopping him from talking might stop him from leaving. Holding him in place, she said, "Is it because I never said I love you? I'm sorry. I was scared. I didn't know if you felt the same way. I do love you. I love you so much."

The truth is, Jennifer had everything. She was beautiful, kind, smart, and honest. She had a master's degree, a high-paying job, and she was an intellect. They would talk for hours about Ryan's cases, politics, or the latest news of the day. Their arguments were always more like discussions. She was perfect for Ryan.

Faith, on the other hand, dropped out of high school, often talked without thinking, and played fast and loose with the truth. She always kept him off balance, and still talked about her old boyfriend, which often made Ryan wonder if she even loved him at all.

But Ryan was a savior; and Jennifer didn't need saving. Faith did. Even more, Faith was a romantic and had this sexual energy about her that Ryan could feel in their first kiss, when she pressed her body against his, and when they made love. The way she moaned, moved her body, and trembled in his arms—it was like she was a conductor and he was the orchestra. She was always on his mind and in his heart. They had this fire between them so big it would burn a perfectly good relationship down to the ground.

It was clear this wouldn't be easy. Ryan lowered her hand off his mouth and said, "It's not you…you're great. I don't want to hurt you."

"Then don't," she said, pleading for him to stay. "Let's go. Let's go celebrate together." When she felt Ryan resist, she said, "Ryan, I love you. I don't want to lose you. Just give me one more chance. All I want is one more chance."

She pressed her head against Ryan's chest and held him like she'd never let go. Not sure what to do, Ryan gently rubbed her back. For a second, she thought everything was going to be fine. Then Faith came driving up the road, turned into the driveway, and stopped Ryan's car in front of the garage. She popped the trunk and pulled out a stack of clothes.

This was really confusing. Jennifer couldn't understand why this girl, who looked like she was in high school, would be driving Ryan's car. She pulled away from Ryan, stood up straight, and watched as Faith came forward with an armful of clothes. She walked right by them, giving Ryan her pretty little smile and patting him on the stomach as she went through the open door.

Jennifer looked into Ryan's eyes and said, "Ryan?"

Faith put the clothes down on the couch and returned to the front door. In a voice that would make you think they'd been together for years, she moved in between them, extended her hand for a shake, and said, "Hi, I'm Faith. I'm Ryan's girlfriend."

Instead of shaking her hand, Jennifer gave Ryan a bewildering look and asked, "Your girlfriend?"

Ryan closed his eyes and Faith, sounding almost giddy, said, "Would you like to come inside?"

"You live here?" Jennifer asked.

Faith looked at Ryan and with another smile said, "Yeah, I do now!"

Tears filled Jennifer's eyes. She turned around and got back into her car, wiping her eyes on the way out. After she drove off, Faith asked, "Who was that?"

"It was my ex."

"Your ex? What's she doing here?"

Ryan looked down and said, "I don't know. She came to talk."

"She didn't know about us?"

"This all just happened over the last couple of days. I didn't even know there was an us."

Faith slowly shook her head. Sounding almost sincere, she said, "Well bless her heart, I hope she's alright."

That night, after making love, Ryan thought about his new life. Tomorrow he'd get some business cards and go looking for a little office and all the desks and furniture to go in it. He'd start by taking some criminal appointments and pass out business cards everywhere. He was already getting phone calls from other lawyers wanting to know how he had pulled off a miracle. One lawyer offered to refer his breast implant cases for a small referral fee. Surely after this big win, the defendants will want to settle with Ryan.

Jodi was also a great referral source. She'd already referred two auto accidents, a DWI, two possession of marijuana cases, and a couple of divorces to Ryan. Who knew that strip clubs were such a great referral source for attorneys?

What a change his life had taken. He just won his first case, would soon have his own law office, and was holding in his arms the sweetest, most beautiful woman he could ever want. Sure, she could be a little feisty and sometimes hard to reason with, but Faith knew how to make Ryan feel like the luckiest man on Earth. When he stood in the church and said "I do," he knew his life was complete. The skies had opened, the stars had aligned, and God had answered all his prayers. On that day, staring into the eyes of his beautiful bride, he swore to himself that he'd give her the world.

After they were married, Ryan believed Faith would finally meet him halfway—but that was something she could not, or would not, do. Little did Ryan know at the time that he had just stepped onto a roller coaster ride that he could never get off of again. The highs would take him to heaven and the lows to hell. He was hooked, but she'd leave at the drop of a hat. No, God had nothing to do with this. Faith Brunick would be the death of him.

# PART TWO

---

# FAITH BRUNICK

*The two most important days in life are the day you were born and the day you find out why.*

— Mark Twain

*Darkness cannot drive out darkness, only light can do that. Hate cannot drive out hate, only love can do that.*

—Martin Luther King, Jr.

# – CHAPTER 7 –

Standing at the back of this Thai courtroom in front of Ryan Brunick, the most evil man to walk the face of the Earth, a wonderful plan crosses my mind. It's the only plan I have left. The photograph of Ryan with Christian is sitting right here on the railing in front of me. It's my only hope for freedom. If the judge sees these two evil men together, smiling like two swindlers after a bank robbery, surely, he'll do something—if not today, then on my appeal. I'll send the photo to the media and cause an international firestorm.

I grab the photo and pull it to me. For a brief second, I have it in my hand, but with the speed of a rattlesnake, Ryan snatches it back and pulls it out of my grasp. "You can have all these other photos," Ryan says, putting the photo I want back in his briefcase and locking it closed, "but I think I'll be keeping this one for myself."

"Ryan, no!" I yell with all the strength left in my body. My scream echoes across the courtroom where order has just been restored. It startles everyone. I lunge for him. I want to kill him. I want to tear the flesh from his face, but the court officers who were once holding Ryan now tackle me, throw me to the floor, and handcuff me. When they lift me back to my feet, I finally see the first sign of emotion on Ryan's face. He has a smile that he cannot hide.

For almost a year, Ryan's been putting money into Faith's account so she has whatever she needs. Hearing Faith bring up Paul infuriates him. *Nothing's changed—Faith hasn't changed. Even after everything she's been through, it's still all about Paul.* Ryan takes a step back to make sure he's free of Faith's attack and says, "Faith, I hope you won't mind, but I can no longer deposit money into your account. You see, things are really tight for me trying to raise four kids. I'm sure you'll have no trouble finding someone else to take my place. Maybe Paul will send you money."

I hang my head in defeat. Looking up, and speaking barely louder than a whisper, I say, "You're a monster." I'm still in the grasp of both officers. I have the full attention of everyone in the courtroom when I scream, "YOU'RE A MONSTER!" again and again, as loud as my defeated body will allow until I'm forced out of the courtroom.

The door is slammed shut behind me. The last thing I remember is Ryan waving goodbye.

# – CHAPTER 8 –

With one guard on my right and another on my left, I'm dragged out of the courtroom with *fifty-five years* still ringing in my ears. The stack of photos I'm holding in my hand is my only chance to get out of here. I have to do something, and I must do it now. The prison has no phones, no internet, and all my mail is censured. The visitation times are so short that no one can afford to come. Prisoners in Thailand are simply forgotten. I cannot go back there. Once I'm taken out of this courthouse, no one will ever hear from me again.

Somehow, I have to get back in front of that judge. I have to show him the photos and tell him how I was set up—not by a faraway drug smuggler, but by the devil who's standing right there in his courtroom.

As soon as the guards close the courtroom door behind me, I lunge for the door and yank it open. I catch a quick glimpse of everyone inside, including Ryan, who's walking towards the door. The entire courtroom goes silent. Ryan and everyone else turn my way when I scream at the top of my voice, *"STOP! STOP HIM! HE DID IT! HE DID IT ALL!"*

A third officer runs up from inside the courtroom, breaks my grip on the door, tackles me from behind, and pulls me down to the ground. He first tries to get chains on my ankles, but I twist and kick him away. I'm doing everything I can to break free and run back in front of that judge.

"It was Ryan," I scream. "It was Ryan who did this to me."

The second I hear the first handcuff click on my right ankle, I twist to the left and try to kick it away with my other foot. It's too late. The handcuff is on tight. "Let me talk to the judge," I yell. "I need to tell him what happened!"

"Mi! Mi!" the guards yell while doing their best to take hold of my arms and legs and get me under control.

"Oh my God…no!" I scream, kicking one guard against the wall. "Take me to the judge…I've got to see the judge!"

Before they can handcuff my left ankle, I twist right, and then left, kicking anyone and anything in sight. A chair flies across the room, and a small table crashes on its side, throwing papers all over the floor.

"Hubpak!" the guards yell, which I know means *shut up.*

I don't care if they kill me. I have to get back to the judge. I kick a female guard; breaking her grip on my left leg. Suddenly, I see another guard running up from down the hallway. Before he can join in, I'm back on my feet and grabbing for the door. Right then, the new officer throws his arm around my neck and yanks me back down to the floor with a violent *crash.* He has his arm wrapped tight around my neck, and he's choking me in his firm grasp. Unable to breathe or even move, all I can do is shriek as loud as I can. Nothing comes out because I'm suffocating. The officer doesn't let up until I feel my face turn blood red. I feel dizzy, my brain goes fuzzy, and everything is going dark. My arms and legs go limp and I feel myself pass out.

I have no idea how long my lifeless body lay on the floor. Eventually, I feel the blood return to my head, and I start to breathe more easily again. I try to rise up and keep fighting, but my arms and legs are hogtied together behind my back.

"NO!" I cry, shaking my head, but my loud screams are now just sobs. I turn to the female officer for help. Crying, tired, and out of breath, I doubt she can hear me as I say, "Please help me. He did it….he did it all."

In my final act of desperation, I jerk left and then right, but it does me no good. All four guards lift me off my feet and drag me into the elevator, down the hall, and out the back door. They throw me back on the bus we came in on, causing my back to crash against one of the seats. They remove the hogties and chain my arms against a metal pole.

I lay my head on the seat in front of me, physically drained and mentally dead. Today was the first time I've seen life, real life, since the day I was arrested at the airport seven months ago. Just sitting in a chair—hearing people talking and laughing and feeling the cool air conditioning blowing against my skin—brought me back to another world. A world far, far away. Seeing lawyers in suits and people wearing normal clothes for a change is so different from the blue prison shirts, skirts, and flip-flops I've come to know. The only people I've seen for almost a year are all wearing blue prison clothes or brown guard uniforms.

I came to this courthouse so sure I was going home. I stayed up all last night praying and reading my Bible. I knew—I just knew—God was with me and would deliver me from this nightmare. Now here I sit chained to this bus heading back to that dirty, smelly, overcrowded, God-forsaken, hell.

I feel this emptiness deep inside me. It's the emptiness left behind from the flowers I'll never smell, the music I'll never hear, my children I'll never hold, the life I'll never live, and the love I'll never give or receive. All my life, all I ever wanted was to be a mommy…and I'll never be able to be a mom again.

The weight of it all is unbearable. Overcome by emotion, I bury my face in my hands, shake my head, and whisper, "Why?" I ask that same question again and again, but no one is here to answer. All my prayers have been for nothing. God has abandoned me. I ball over in my chair, doing my best to simply breathe.

I'm left all alone on the bus for hours, trying to understand how it all happened. How can the man who saved me as a young girl, and gave me life again, be the person who was behind everything? I thought he was here to rescue me, but the whole time he was actually planning the end of my life.

"Son of a bitch," I whisper with my head sunk low.

*He knew about everything—my affair with Paul, that night in the parking lot, the evening in the park on the blanket, the pictures I hid in my Bible, and our first time in San Antonio. He knew it all and never said a word. How? How can anyone be raging inside but still remain calm?*

"This can't be happening," I whisper as tears drop down my cheeks and onto my lap. My hands shake so hard they rattle the chains holding me in place.

*All the photos and cards from my children he brought to the prison.* I close my eyes and ask myself, "Who are you?"

Now I know exactly who he is. He's the devil, and the devil will be raising my children. I'm helpless to do anything about it. I lay my head down on the seat in front of me and cry.

*Why God? Why would you do this to me?*

Finally, the bus door opens and other prisoners step inside. Everyone's returning from their big day in court. Seeing people again causes me to come back to the land of the living—if you call this living.

As the bus slowly fills up again, there's not a cheerful face anywhere. Prisoners come in crying, yelling, or shaking their heads in disbelief. Most are guilty, but they had hoped for some sympathy, or leniency, or maybe a little understanding. It's clear from all the sad faces, and the tears they are trying to hide, that today the judge was full of justice and forgot all about the mercy. No one charged with drugs, theft, assault, or speaking out against the state, will be going home for a long, long time. Those charged with murder, rape, or dealing drugs are just like me. They will never return home again.

When the last person sits down, we drive back to the prison. I look up and feel the warm sun on my face. I take a deep breath in through my nose and out through my mouth. As we wait at a traffic light, I look through the wire screen on the window at the car beside us. There's a couple inside the car talking and laughing. A baby is sound asleep in a car seat in the back. *Never will I ride in a car with my husband again. I won't see my younger kids drive a car for the first time. I will never see my first grandbaby sleeping in a car seat.*

When the light changes, we drive through the city past beautiful trees, flowers and bushes along the road. A lovely river runs under us. We slow down long enough for me to catch a glimpse of a park full of children playing and laughing on the playground. It's been so long since I've seen what the real world looks like outside the prison walls. I don't know how, but now I must live the rest of my life without it. I have to get out of Thailand. Maybe that appeal Sassen once talked about is my answer. It's the only chance I have left.

Back at the prison, the gate opens and we drive through. *This is the life I know. The walls are still covered with razor wires, guards are still walking around with guns, the air is still hot and sticky, and prisoners are still crowded shoulder to shoulder.*

The line heading inside moves as slow as it always does. With every ounce of dignity and self-respect stolen from me long ago, I look up and whisper, "I don't give a shit." I walk up to the guards and, without blinking an eye, strip naked in front of everyone, throw my arms out on each side of me, and open my legs. Most of these guards know me by now. I turn around, bend over, touch the ground, and let them do their thing.

When the guard opens the door to our cage, Mali and Tian are waiting to hear what happened. In the seven months I've been here, we haven't seen a single prisoner leave for court and not come back. They actually thought I'd be the first, but the bad news is written all over my face.

Mali gets this sad look, and with a wince, she asks, "No guilty?"

I put my hands over my face, look down, and start bawling again. I can't even talk. I slowly shake my head no.

"Noooo," Mali says, like she might cry too. She steps forward and takes me in her arms. I hold her tight and cry. Between my tears and my gasps for air, I say, "It…it…it was him. He set me up."

"Christian?" Mali asks, looking confused.

I shake my head, try to catch my breath, and cry, "No…not…not… Christian. It was Ryan the whole time. He was behind everything."

"You guilty?" Tian asks.

I wipe my runny nose with the palm of my hand and nod my head. Trying to regain control of myself, I say, "Yes…guilty."

Tian drops her head and tears up. Looking back up at me, she asks, "Many years?"

I nod my head. "The Judge gave me fifty-five years."

This might sound shocking to anyone back home, but here it's no surprise. I had hoped my sentence would be less, but that wasn't realistic at all. Mali puts her hand on my leg and asks, "Judge no think you girl?"

"No *believe* her?" I clarify.

"Yes, judge no *believe* her?" she repeats, trying to understand what happened.

As another tear rolls down my cheek, I cry, "There was no girl, Mali. It was all a lie."

Tian is just learning English. "Lie?" she asks.

"Not true," I try to explain. "No girl was ever coming to help me."

"Why no girl?" Mali asks.

I knock my head against the back wall hard enough that it makes a *thud*. I breathe in deep and exhale, blowing the hair in my eyes out of the way. My lips and my jaw quiver as I try to find the words to explain it all. How do you explain something so cruel—so evil?

I look at Mali, then back at Tian, and say, "Ryan was not helping me. He never found a girl to go to court. He *wanted* me to be guilty."

I'm pretty sure Mali gets it. Tian is still trying to understand. "Ryan no love you?" she asks.

I close my eyes, shake my head, and whisper. "No, Tian, Ryan doesn't love me." I wipe the tears from my right cheek and say, "Ryan hates me."

"Why hate you?" Tian asks.

*What a good question. Why would Ryan hate me? Why would he hate me so much that he'd put me in this hellhole for the rest of my life?*

I shrug my shoulder and say, "I don't know."

This isn't the truth. The fact is, I do know. I've just tried to block it out. There's only one explanation. Somehow, Ryan found out. It wasn't Paul, or the divorce, or the custody thing. He would have dealt with these things—he probably would have taken me back to court. There's only one thing that would make Ryan so angry that he'd hate me this much. I knew it was wrong. I knew it would be bad if he ever found out. Well, he obviously found out, and now I'm paying for what I did.

# – CHAPTER 9 –

Over the next hour, all the women come back from work. Here I am back in the same cage, sitting on the same sticky floor, and feeling the same women crowd in on all sides. I've seen this same routine every day for the past seven months, but now it seems different. Somehow I'd gotten used to things, but this time it feels like I'm seeing it through fresh eyes. It takes me back to the first day I arrived here. *How is this possible? How can they fit so many women in this room?*

Before, I felt like a visitor here—it was all a big mistake and I would be returning home soon. But it wasn't a mistake, was it? It was a sadistic plot and I'm not ever going home again. *So, this is my life? I've been given one life to live, and now I'll spend the rest of my life in this hell.*

For the first time in my life, I finally wanted my life to mean something. I wanted to accomplish something good and real. I wanted to help others. There's nothing sadder than a life without meaning, but that's the only life I have left. It will never have purpose or meaning again. No, I'm no longer a stranger here. Now, this is my home, and I'd rather die than live here a day longer.

When the bell rings for dinner, we stand up and get in line like we always do. We walk single file out of our cage, down the hall, and into the cafeteria. Waiting for me on the front table is the dinner I ordered at the beginning of the week. While most people are eating rotten rice, I have a beautiful bowl of yellow curry with white rice, a bowl of fruit, and a slice of cake for dessert—all from a nearby restaurant. There's a can of cold green tea and a separate bottle of water. So many times, I've eaten at a steakhouse, an Indian or Thai restaurant, or a simple sandwich shop, and we bowed our heads and thanked the Lord for the food, but no one at the table knew how blessed they really were. Now, I sit down and divide the meal between Mali, Tian, and me. We enjoy the last good meal we'll ever eat.

Back in our cage, I take my spot against the back wall. With all the cigarettes I've been handing out over the past few months, other women have become much more agreeable. Instead of pushing me away, they move over and give me a little space.

I sit against the wall and think about everything. *How did he pull it off? Even now, when the bitter truth has been laid bare in front of me, I can't understand how he did this to me. I thought I was so smart…I'd show him. I took the house, the kids, and got a big check in the mail every month. He wanted Colt, but I refused to even talk to him.*

I may not know how he pulled it off, but now it all makes sense: Christian liked everything I liked—every meal, movie, music, faith in God—everything. Our last-minute trip to Thailand and he didn't want to have sex; the anonymous call to the airport; and Ryan popping up at the prison out of nowhere, wanting to help me. I feel so stupid. *How could I be such an idiot?*

Back at the courthouse, I had the stack of photos Ryan left me. They were all in my right hand when I started fighting to get away from the guards so I could talk to the judge. When I lunged for the door, the photos fell out of my hands and all over the floor. Then I blacked out. When I came to, my hands were handcuffed behind my back, and the pictures were gone. I could feel some of the photos underneath me, so I grabbed them as they pulled me up to my feet. I was once holding about twenty photos, but now I only have six, and they're all bent and crumpled.

There are two photos of Paul and me in San Antonio, a photo of Christian and me walking along the beach, two photos of me sitting on Christian's lap by the pool, and a photo of me painting on the balcony at the resort.

I look at each photo in disbelief. I hate Christian as much as I hate Ryan. They're both snakes. I clench my teeth and whisper, "You bastard!"

I take the two photos of me and Christian together in the pool, and rip them up again and again until there's nothing left but a bunch of small pieces. Then there's the photo of Christian and me walking hand in hand along the beach. I look so carefree and happy in the bright sunshine. I want to remember my last days of freedom. I carefully tear him out of the picture and keep the half that only shows me.

Suddenly, a guard opens the door to our cage and steps inside. This rarely happens after dinner, so everyone looks his way. He walks right up to me with an envelope in his hand. I missed all mail delivery because I was at my trial. I take the letter from his hands and see it's a letter from my mom.

It's a small, pink envelope with my name and the address for this prison written in my mom's handwriting. As usual, it's open on one end where the guards took it out and read it. I remove the letter inside and sit next to Mali as I read:

========================================

*My sweet girl ---*

*By now your trial is probably over. I've been praying for you every day. All the ladies in my Bible study are praying for you too. I just know the Lord will deliver you. I haven't heard from you, so I figure you're on your way home.*

*I'm writing to you to let you know your father passed away yesterday. It's been a long, tough struggle for him, but now he's finally at peace.*

========================================

I cannot believe this news. Can things get any worse? I'm so shaken I have to stop reading. I ball over and cry into the letter, *"Oh Daddy. I'm so sorry. I love you so much."* Mali sees me crying and puts her head on my shoulder as I finish the letter:

=================================================

*I called Ryan, but his wife said he's out of town. Your father's funeral is this coming Wednesday, March 23rd. By the time you get this letter, you may already be home. I know you want to see your kids, but everyone would love to see you at the funeral. Please try to make it.*

*Love you and miss you,*
*Mom*

=================================================

I drop the letter in my lap, turn to Mali, and cry in her arms. When I don't stop, she pats my back and asks, "What wrong?"

"It's my father. He's…he's…gone."

"Gone?"

It's hard to get any words out, so I cry, "He…he…he died."

She takes my head and pulls me to her.

"My father died and I'll…I'll never see him again."

Two days later, Mali, Tian, and I go to the cafeteria and approach the guard to buy our food for the next week.

"Mimi ngein," the guard says with a wave of his hand.

My Thai isn't great, but I think I know what he just said. "What?" I ask.

"Mimi ngein," he repeats.

I turn to Mali, who says, "No money."

"No money?" I repeat.

She closes her eyes and shakes her head. Tian says nothing. I look at them both and say, "I'm so sorry."

"It kay," Tian says with a sad smile. "We be kay."

## – CHAPTER 10 –

Nothing makes sense anymore. Over the next months, the dark hole inside me just keeps getting darker and darker. I haven't slept in days. Everything keeps going round and round in my head.

I spend every night going over the trial. I think about everything I said…everything I didn't say.

*What could I have said to change things?*

*Maybe if I had only said more.*

*Maybe if I had said nothing at all.*

*Why did I lie about Christian being my husband?*

*Why didn't I get the judge to believe me?*

Things are supposed to get easier with time. Time might heal all wounds, but in here, time just stands still. It's been three months since my trial, but I feel like I'm still at square one. In less than two days, I was convicted of trafficking heroin, I was sentenced to fifty-five years in prison, I found out my ex-husband set me up, and then I got a letter telling me my father had died. I feel so defeated. I can't function.

After months of having food delivered, I forgot just how awful the food here really is. Everything is undercooked and almost raw or overcooked and burnt. Most of the food is literally rotten. There are no fruits or vegetables. You're either eating rotten rice with something that looks a little like watery curry or soup with almost nothing in it except a lot of things you'd never eat—unless you're locked up in a Thai prison.

The only way I can earn money to buy decent food, drink clean water, or buy a few of the things I need to survive in here is to get a job that pays slave wages. Good luck there! Mali has been waiting for a job assignment for two years now. There aren't enough jobs to go around. One of the problems—some women who haven't been here as long as I have, suddenly leave for work with the other women.

"Wait," I say, looking at Mali. "She came after me!"

It didn't take long to figure out that a fistful of money or a carton of cigarettes in the right hands can land you a job. Well, I have no chance at that. It also helps if you know someone on the outside who can pull some strings for you, but, the only person I know is Mr. Taylor, and I don't think he operates like that. Then there's *Plan C*. Some women—I think lots of women—trade sexual favors for just about anything.

If you're reading this and think, *I'd never do that*, then you've never been locked up in a Thai prison. Things like pride, dignity, modesty, and morals were tossed aside the first time I stood naked in a room full of men, spread my arms and legs, and squatted three times to prove I had nothing hiding up there.

I see the way the guards look at me. Have I thought about giving myself away to get good food and clean water, or to be first in line at the water trough, or to receive the next available job? You bet I have! Right now, I'd sell my soul to the devil to be back in Austin with my children again.

After two more weeks, I start sharing glances with one of the guards. When I give him a little smile, he looks down, blushing. He's the most attractive of them all, but the thought of it still makes me sick. *Maybe one day, but I'm not quite that desperate or that hungry yet.* For now, I'll just wait my turn.

# – CHAPTER 11 –

Three months later, I'm choking down my last bite of rice when a guard comes up and tells me I have a visitor. I get up from the table and follow him to the visiting room. Halfway there, I realized no one is left to visit me other than Ryan. *Why? Why would he dare show his face here?*

I almost turn around and head back to my cell. Then it occurs to me he might be here to help me. Maybe he got back home and realized what he did to me. I pray he's here to get me out.

I'm escorted to the front of the line and walk right past the other prisoners. Sitting here with the dirty phone in my hand, I wonder who's here. I don't have to wait long before a man in a suit and jacket sits down in front of me.

"Faith…Faith Brunick?" he asks holding the phone away from his mouth.

"Yes, I'm Faith Brunick."

"I'm Justin Taylor. I'm with the United States Consulate office."

"Where's Mike Sassen?"

"Mike Sassen's no longer working as your prison liaison. I've taken his place."

"Where is he?" I ask. "I need to talk to him."

"I'm sorry, but that's not possible. He returned to the U.S. a few months back. He left to care for his mother." This man looks much younger than Sassen—and not as experienced. I developed a rapport with Sassen and now I feel like I'm starting all over from scratch. Not sounding real empathetic, he says, "I heard about your trial. I'm very sorry."

"Do you know anything about my case?" I ask.

He looks down at my file and fumbles through the pages like he's looking at it for the first time. "Your case? Let's see…well, it looks like you were arrested at the airport with a large amount of heroin. It appears the judge sentenced you to fifty-five years." When he looks up from his file, he asks, "If you don't mind me asking, why didn't you just plead guilty? The judge might have given you twenty years."

"Oh my God," I laugh, looking up at the ceiling. "You know nothing."

"Hold on, hold on," he says, holding up both hands. "I took over for Mike. I've got a lot of files to look over. I'm trying to play catch up here."

I just sit here as he reads over everything. Finally, he looks up and says, "I understand you're angry. It's natural to be upset right now. That's why I'm here. I'm here to help you…help you adjust to prison life. If you're going to survive in here, you've got to stay mentally and physically healthy. You know what I mean? You need to stay active…exercise regularly. Have you ever tried yoga? There's a book on yoga that many prisoners–"

I cover my mouth with my hand and burst out laughing. "Oh my God. This can't be happening!"

"Mrs. Brunick, many prisoners swear by it. They—"

"I'm innocent!" I yell, cutting him off. "I was set up!"

He puts down his pen and says, "Ms. Brunick, I don't mean to upset you. I'm only trying to help."

I bang the phone against the window and scream, "Are you listening to me? I need Sassen. I have to talk to him!"

"Mrs. Brunick, you can talk to me."

"What's your name again?"

"Taylor…Justin Taylor."

I lower my head and take a deep breath to calm down. I look back up at him and, sounding defeated, say, "Mr. Taylor, I was set up from the beginning. I came to Thailand with a man I thought was my boyfriend, but he set me up. He planted drugs in my suitcase."

He nods his head and says, "I see that in your file. You claim you knew nothing about the drugs in your bag, right?"

"That's right."

"But it *was* your suitcase?"

"Yes, it was my suitcase, but it was all a setup."

"I'm sure Mr. Sassen told you how difficult it is to win a case like yours. Just about everyone claims they were set up. It's hard to prove—"

"Mr. Taylor, I was set up by my ex-husband. He planned the whole thing from the beginning."

"How do you know it was your husband?" he asks.

"My ex-husband."

"How do you know it was your ex-husband?"

I close my eyes and clench my jaw. I look down and shout, "Because he told me all about it."

"Ms. Brunick, you must stay calm. If you keep shouting, they're going to end our visit."

I calm down and try to explain. "He was at the trial. He was supposed to be helping me get out, but the whole time he was setting me up. He came up to me after the trial and confessed everything. I have to get back in front of the judge. Can't I appeal or something?"

"The Thai system does provide for appeals, but I don't know much about it. I believe you have to hire your own attorney. Do you have an attorney?"

I lower my head for a second and say, "I have nothing. I just found out my father died. I don't even have money to buy toothpaste."

"I'm so sorry to hear that," he says.

"Then how can I appeal? How do I tell the judge what happened?"

He taps his pen against the palm of his hand and says, "I don't really know. Appeals in Thailand aren't like appeals in the U.S. The same judge who heard your case will probably hear your appeal."

"Then I'll tell him," I say. "I talked to him in my trial, so I'll talk to him again."

"Do you have proof?"

"What kind of proof?" I ask.

"I don't know. You said your husband confessed it all. Can you get him to fill out an affidavit or something?"

"My *ex*-husband," I say, looking astonished. Sounding as sarcastic as possible, I nod my head and say, "Yeah, why don't I just get him to sign an affidavit? Or maybe he'll talk into my private microphone. While we're at it, why don't I just make the doors to this prison magically open up and I'll just walk right out?"

With a little grin, he says, "I don't mean to be cruel, but you have to have evidence to have any chance at an appeal."

"I have no evidence other than a couple of crumpled photos that don't show anything that will help."

Mr. Taylor places both hands on the file sitting in front of him and says, "There is one other avenue. It's a realistic chance to get you out of here."

"How?"

"Well, you're an American, and you're a woman with children. It doesn't look good to have an American woman locked up overseas—especially here. There's a treaty that allows a prisoner to serve their remaining sentence in the States. With the amount of drugs you were convicted of, you don't qualify, but perhaps an exception can be made."

This is the best news ever. I can't believe my ears. "This is wonderful. Please…please try. I have to get out of here."

"I'll try. I'll file the paperwork and contact someone in the U.S. who can advocate on your behalf. But, it's not so simple. First, you must serve part of your sentence here."

"No problem," I say with a nod of my head. "I've already been here a year and a half. How long do I have to stay?"

"I'm not sure," he says. "With the sentence you got, I would think ten or twelve years."

"Ten years!" I shout. "I can't survive ten years."

He raises his hand and says, "Maybe less…maybe less. After five or six years, we'll start the process, but you have to stay out of trouble. You can't—"

I look down and cover my teary eyes. My hope of getting out of here is now shot down. Without looking up, I speak into the phone, and say, "I can't. I can't wait ten years. I'll go crazy in here. I really thought I was going home. It was the only thing keeping me hanging on this long."

"But you still have hope you can go home one day," he says, as if those kinds of words matter in here like they do on the outside. "You've got to hold on to that hope."

I pull up my sleeve showing the infection on my arm and say, "Look at my arm."

He looks through the glass with an awful grimace and says, "That looks like a staph infection, which is pretty common here because of the overcrowding and lack of hand washing. It's a bacteria. If you touch someone who has the bacteria, it can be passed on to you…usually through a scrape, a scratch, or a wound."

I put my arm back down and say, "This one is actually looking a little better. I have another one on my leg. It's getting bigger, and now it's oozing puss. It hurts to even touch it. It stings when I walk."

"A lot of prisoners have staph infections. The antibiotics to treat them are expensive and don't always work, so they hope it goes away on its own. They rarely send someone to the doctor until it's quite serious. Do your best to wash it out regularly."

"That's easier said than done. I no longer have money for food or clean water. My ex-husband was putting money into my account, but he stopped. I'm back to waiting in a long line, and it's usually empty by the time I get there."

"The ex who set you up put money in your account?"

"Yes, the ex who set me up."

"Why would he put money in your account if he planted the drugs on you?"

"I know it's twisted," I say. "He did everything to keep me pacified until the trial. Now I have nothing."

"What about a job?" he asks.

"I don't know. I've been waiting for a job, but I don't think I'll get one any time soon."

"Ms. Brunick, you've just got to keep moving forward. You need to make friends, start exercising, start doing a craft or hobby, get a job. You can't think about solving everything right now. That's just too overwhelming. Keep your eye on the next goal. Just one step at a time. How old is your oldest child?"

"She's fifteen now….why?"

"So, she's what…in ninth grade? Doesn't it feel like she just started kindergarten yesterday? How quick did nine years go by? The years go by faster than you think."

For a brief second, it actually sounds doable. He's right. It doesn't seem that long ago that Ryan and I found out I was pregnant after coming back from New York. For a few brief seconds, I feel good about things, but my will to continue doesn't last long. It's easy to talk about things going by quickly when you're looking back. It's a whole lot different looking forward. The thought of ten years in here comes crashing back like a car wreck. I look back at Mr. Taylor, shake my head, and say, "I don't know. I just don't know."

Not ready to give up on me, Mr. Taylor continues, "Now that your trial is over, there is something you can do. Write letters. Write to your family and friends. You need people back home who are helping you—fighting for you."

I nod my head in agreement and say, "You know, I haven't been writing much. I guess I was too ashamed. I didn't want people to know where I was."

"Do you know your governor? You can write him, or your senator, or your congressman. Write to anyone who can help."

I roll my eyes and say, "I don't know anyone like that. I don't even know the name of our mayor."

"Well, write people—but be careful. They monitor any letters you send or receive. Say the wrong thing, and the letter might disappear and you'll never know about it. It won't help your chance of getting a transfer if you're saying negative things about Thailand, the prisons, or the Thai legal system. They don't want to be embarrassed. They're more likely to let you go back if they're not afraid of what you might say. Until you get out of here, make it all sound positive."

A guard stands behind me with his arms crossed to let us know our time is up. They're a little more subtle when I'm talking to someone from the Embassy. Mr. Taylor gives him a quick nod, gathers his stuff, and says, "Be patient. I'll talk to my supervisor and see if there's anything I can do about the job thing. Like I said, I think the transfer is your best shot."

At this point, he's all I've got left. "Thank you," I say, standing up. Right before I put the phone back in the cradle, I try to catch his attention. "Oh, Mr. Taylor, just one more thing. Could you get me a book?"

"I'll try. What kind of book?

"I want an English book about Buddhism."

"No problem," he says with a nod. "I'll drop it off today or tomorrow."

# – CHAPTER 12 –

Three months after Mr. Taylor left, I'm still walking around like some kind of zombie—a sad, depressed zombie. I guess I just feel numb. I've been losing weight again from eating the crap they feed us. I practically choke on it just to get it down. I've also been so tired lately.

I'm always so exhausted and I have this chill I can't seem to shake. I just want to sleep, but when I finally fall asleep, I dream of my dad and the pain is unbearable. When I wake up, I think about my horrible life.

I know I'm supposed to write letters, but I don't really know where to start. After I was arrested, I was so ashamed and embarrassed to tell anyone what I had gotten myself into. I figured I'd be going home soon, and I'd come up with some story to explain everything away. Well, that's not happening anymore. So, if I do write, what do I say? This story is just too crazy. Little me from Austin, Texas, is set up for smuggling drugs on the other side of the world. Then to find out it was Mr. Perfect, Ryan Brunick, who did it all. I doubt anyone would believe me if I told them. It's kind of ironic when you think about it. When I finally decide to be an honest person, my story is so unbelievable no one will believe me.

Writing letters won't be so easy. I have a small box with everything I own inside it, and I don't have a lot of paper to spare. I only have half a notebook tablet left, a handful of envelopes, and a couple of stamps. I have to choose carefully who I write, so the first letter I write is to my mom. I'm not sure how to tell her everything that's happened and I can't bear to tell her I was actually convicted. I open my tablet and do my best.

===============================================

*Dear Mom,*
*Thank you so much for your letter. It's always a joy when I get a letter from you. Thank you for your prayers...tell everyone how much they mean to me.*
*I'm so sorry about dad. I think of him all the time. I wish I could have been at the funeral. You know, I was his little girl.*
*You might have guessed by now that my trial did not go my way, but I don't want you to worry. The judge listened carefully and was very fair. I'm told that I might be home in eight years.*
*Mom, I never told you and dad a lot about my case. I didn't want to worry you. I guess I was ashamed about everything I got myself into—ashamed about the person I became. Well, I met a man I thought I loved. We went on a trip to Thailand and he planted drugs in my suitcase. Yes, he set me up. After the trial, I finally learned the truth. This man I thought I loved, was working for Ryan. The whole time I thought Ryan was helping me out, but he wasn't. He was behind everything.*
*I know this has been hard on you and dad. I don't want you to worry about me. I'm treated really well here. I'm sorry I can't call but I will try to ~~right~~ write more. Mama, please know how much I love you. I wish I would have been a better daughter. Please don't blame yourself. I know you and dad did the best you could.*
*Love you , Faith*

===============================================

After I seal the envelope, I start my next letter to my brother. We were close when we were kids, but we stopped hanging out in high school. He was in Honor Society and played in the band. I was more interested in partying than studying, so we ran in different circles. He hated my first boyfriend, Jake, which led to some pretty ugly words between us. Like my dad, he wasn't happy when I divorced Ryan. I'll just start at the beginning.

===============================================================

*Hey Big Brother,*
*How you been? I'm sorry I haven't wrote you before now but I didn't really know what to say. You probably already know by now that I was arrested in Thailand with drugs in my bag. Well, I promise you it was all a lie. I was set up. I went to Thailand with a man I loved. He planted the drugs in my bag. I went to court and was found guilty and sentenced to fifty-five years in prison. I didn't stand a chance. PLEASE DON'T TELL MOM—I DON'T WANT TO WORRY HER. It's not as bad as it seems. With a little luck, I can come home in eight years. (This is all I want mom to know.)*

*Mom and dad might have ~~infor~~ told you Ryan was helping me. This was a lie too. After the trial, I found out he was behind everything. He hired this man to take me to Thailand and put the drugs in my suitcase. Please believe me. After years of giving him everything, this is what I get.*

*I'm so sorry about dad. I wish I could have been at his funeral. How is mom doing? I hear her health is not too good.*

*I know you're disappointed in me. I wish I listened to mom and dad (and you). I know I didn't always show it, but I always loved you. I know you were just looking out for me. Please forgive me.*

*I would love to hear from you. I can't receive calls but maybe you can write me sometime. Better yet, come and visit me (ha ha).*

*I love you brother,*
*Faith*

===============================================================

I don't know who else to write. *What about Sharon?* I received one letter from her a couple of months after I got here. I pull it out of my box and read it again.

====================================================

*Faith,*

*I'm really sorry to hear about you getting arrested. I can't believe it. I think you're right. Christian had something to do with it. Something about him never seemed right. I never liked him.*

*I wish I could come visit you, but I don't have the kind of money to fly all that way. It's such a long flight to only see you for twenty minutes. Plus, by the time I could get there, you'll probably be home. I hope you understand.*

*Hey, some good news! I met a great guy. We've been dating now for four months. We already used the "L" word. I think he's the one. Well, he just asked me to move in with him. I have to see where it goes. He lives in Oklahoma City. You gotta come visit us when you get out. I think you'll really like him.*

*Anyway, I just wanted you to know. I wish we could email (it would be so much easier.) Well, I gotta go. I'll send you my new address when I get there. Please stay strong. I'm sure everything will turn out okay. I'm praying for you.*

*Friends for Life,*
*Sharon*

====================================================

I received this letter a long time ago. She never sent her address, and I never heard from her again. She was once my best friend, but when I needed a friend the most, she couldn't send me a penny. I've let that go a long time ago. I have no way to write to her again even if I wanted to.

*Who else can I write? What happened to all my old friends—the housewives who lived in our neighborhood?* We seemed close at the time. We got together for lunch or wine, played bunco, got the kids together for playdates, and shared the most intimate details of our lives and our marriages. Then everything changed after the divorce. Sandy told one of our friends about my affair with Paul—it was one of those, *don't tell anyone about it* stories—and soon *everyone* knew. They made me feel like

I was less than them. They stopped hanging out with me—or maybe I stopped hanging out with them. After a couple of months, I pretty much spent all my time with Paul. Since Sharon and I were both divorced with the same visitation schedules, we spent the rest of my free time together.

I consider writing to my last boss, but I don't think it will do any good. I left for Thailand without calling or anything. I thought about emailing him from our resort, but I was too busy going here and there. As far as he knows, I just stopped coming in. Time and time again, he warned me about being late or missing work. He was always explaining how the office was small and, as the front receptionist, I was the first person the clients saw. It didn't look good when I was gone. I don't think he'd respond, even if I did write to him.

Suddenly, it dawns on me. There's one person I might be able to turn to. We once had something special. I helped him when he needed it the most. Maybe he'll help me. If nothing else, he can sell the watch I bought him for Christmas. I flip my tablet to the next page and write to Paul:

====================================================

*Dear Paul,*

*I know it's been a long time since we last spoke. I hope you and your wife and little girl are doing good. I really do.*

*The reason I'm righting is because I need your help. I went on a vacation to Thailand with a friend and someone planted drugs in my suitcase (yes it sounds crazy, but it's true). I was arrested and now I'm sitting in a Thai prison. The prison conditions aren't good. I have no money for food or water.*

*I know this is asking a lot but I really need your help. My dad died and now I have no one. I once ~~gave~~ loaned you a lot of money. I was hoping you could pay me back. You could also sell the watch*

*I gave you for Christmas. I really thought you would return it after we broke up, but you never did.*

*We were once in love. At least I loved you. I hope you loved me to. We had something special…I've never forgotten about you. I hope you still think about me. If I meant anything to you, I ask you—no, I <u>beg</u> you for help. It would also be nice to see you again if you could come to Thailand to visit me*

================================================

As I finish the letter, I realize how stupid this is. *What the hell am I doing?* Paul doesn't give a damn about me. I won't give him the satisfaction of hearing how bad things are. I tear the paper out of the notebook, crumple it up, and rip it into pieces.

# – CHAPTER 13 –

I put away my notebook and pen. *Sitting here is the Bible I've been reading since I got here.* I open my Bible and read the scriptures I had marked.

*"If you remain in me and my words remain in you, ask whatever you wish, and it will be done for you."*

*"This is the confidence we have in approaching God: that if we ask anything according to his will, he hears us."*

*"And if we know that he hears us—whatever we ask—we know that we have what we asked of him."*

*"And whatever you ask in prayer, you will receive, if you have faith."*

As difficult as these last months have been, I always held onto my faith and tried to be the best Christian I could be. I carried this Bible around like a life raft in a storm—reading every night and praying in faith. I prayed with other prisoners, even though they only knew Buddhism. Now I know that my mom and her entire Bible study were praying for me. What was it all for? In the end, I was all alone. It was only me standing in front of that judge, so afraid I might say the wrong thing. It was only me who got sentenced to fifty-five years. When I needed God the most, He was nowhere to be found.

I lay my head against the wall. Angry about everything, I whisper, "Where were you? What about all these scriptures? Where were you when I needed you?" I remember Jesus' words on the cross and wonder: *Why? Why have you forsaken me?*

With my Bible in my arms, I bow my head and try to pray but nothing comes out. I no longer know what to say. I feel like I've prayed myself out, and I have no prayers left. My soul feels dark and empty. I open my eyes again and sit here in silence.

Along with the rest of my stuff, I see the two books Mr. Taylor left me about Buddhism. I pick up the first book and stare at the cover, almost afraid to start reading. A part of me feels like I'm turning my back on God—or Jesus—if I even read it. Another part of me wonders if I've been reading the wrong Bible all these years. I close my eyes, shake my head, and start reading from the beginning.

This book is easy to read and easy to understand. It seems Buddhism is a religion that is deeply focused on personal spiritual development and the achievement of a deep insight into the true nature of life. Buddhism is also about equal treatment for everyone, helping others, and being respectful towards nature. *Nothing so crazy here.* It sounds like the same things I read in my Bible. So far, it makes a lot of sense.

Buddhism does not believe in an eternal or everlasting soul. Buddhists believe there is no permanent soul, because there is no unchanging, permanent essence or soul. Buddhists talk more about good and bad energy and rebirth, rather than souls. They believe in *sentience*—that all things are to be respected and you must love all things. This includes people, animals, insects, plants, trees—everything.

Buddhism believes in Karma, which is different from fate. It's about action and reaction, cause and effect. Any thought, word, or deed conditioned by desire, hate, passion, and illusion creates karma. Karma reaches across lifetimes and brings about rebirth. This process of being reborn is associated with suffering. It's called *samsara*. Someone who cultivates positive karma through right actions in life may reincarnate as someone who will enjoy a positive and pleasant life. This continues until you reach the highest level, called *Nirvana*. After you reach Nirvana, there is no more rebirth.

*"One road leads to wealth; another road leads to Nirvana. Let the mendicant, the disciple of Buddha, learn this and not strive for honor but seek wisdom."*

My reading is interrupted by our dinner bell. I sit down at the table with Mali and Tian and think about the words on karma and living a morally good life. I always thought of myself as a pretty good person. *I'm not that bad,* keeps running through my mind.

After dinner, I return to our cage feeling sick from the food I ate. I want to throw up. The infection on my thigh stings so bad when I walk or barely even touch it. Once the size of a pimple, it's now maybe two inches wide. It's bloody red, full of puss, with this nasty pimple in the middle. When I complain to a guard, I'm ignored. I'm not sure how bad things have to get before they'll finally help me. It's hard to read, or even concentrate, when I'm in so much pain.

A week later, I get back to reading again. I learn Buddhism knows five moral precepts, which are rules that help Buddhists learn what is right and what is wrong, and how they should behave in a moral and ethical way. These five precepts are: abstain from taking life; abstain from taking what is not given; abstain from sexual misconduct; abstain from false speech; abstain from intoxicants that cloud the mind. When these precepts are followed, Buddhists are assured they are living a morally good life. They will slowly be relieved of their suffering, and eventually they'll achieve enlightenment and assure a better future for themselves.

Buddhists hope to either gain enlightenment or to ensure a better future for themselves. These good actions are set out in the Eightfold Path, which includes right speech, right livelihood, and right concentration. Good actions will result in a better rebirth, while bad actions will have the opposite effect. I pause a minute to consider my past and my own karma.

Over the next weeks, I read more and thumb back over the things I've already read. The more I read, the more I reflect on my own life. *Living moral, right speech, and good thoughts.* This whole karma thing starts to scare me. I remember all the things I did in my previous life.

Further in the book, I learn Buddhism revolves around respecting our elders. You must hold your parents in very high regard and do nothing to hurt them or make them cry. If this happens, it is believed it will bring bad luck. If a Thai person commits a crime, he's not the only one who gets punished. Their parents also suffer from their image being stained.

*What the hell!* I remember my time with Jake so long ago—how stupid I was. My mother and father did everything to stop me, but I wouldn't listen. They talked; they yelled; they grounded me; they demanded I stop seeing him. Instead of listening, I talked and yelled back—telling them again and again how much I hated them. I lied to them to be with Jake, snuck out of my room while they were sleeping or at work, and spent half my time high.

I'll never forget the day I told my parents I was leaving to go to Texas to live with Jake. My mom and dad were devastated, but I didn't care a bit. When my dad dropped me off at the bus station, a tear fell down his cheek after he kissed me goodbye. I knew I was breaking his heart, but I didn't care. I couldn't get out of there fast enough. Is this my karma? Am I getting back the karma I sent out?

Years later, my mom and dad practically begged me not to divorce Ryan. They wanted me to go to counseling, but I wouldn't listen. I was already in love with Paul. I lied to my parents—I lied to everyone. I told them my divorce was all about Ryan…and nothing else.

Sure, the Bible warned against sexual impurity and adultery, but I told myself we were in love. Isn't love enough? Isn't God all about love? Now, for the first time, I realize it wasn't love at all. I never truly loved Paul, and he certainly didn't love me.

*What have I done?* I barely signed the divorce papers when my dad had a stroke. He had bleeding in his brain—and then over the next hours—his condition worsened significantly. My brother called me while I was in Mexico—although I never told him I was there with Paul. My brother said I should come to the hospital right away. Instead, I continued my vacation with Paul. I told myself I'd go to Georgia after we came back, but I didn't.

To our surprise, my dad was released from the hospital and held on longer than we thought he would. I called now and then but couldn't really understand him when he talked. He was never the same.

So many times I said I would go visit, but I never did. Now he's gone, and I never apologized or even said goodbye. I sit here crying as it all sinks in. For the first time, I realize just how bad I treated my parents. Now my dad is gone and I can't be there for my mother. *Is this because of me?* I treated my parents so terribly. Now I can't leave this place and tell my mom how much I love her.

I can't help but worry about what my next life will be like. I've really screwed this one up pretty bad. I'll probably come back as a roach or something. I don't know how long it takes to reach this Nirvana place, but I'm pretty sure for me it's still many lifetimes away.

# – CHAPTER 14 –

The burn on my thigh keeps getting worse and worse. The infection that was once two inches is now large and gross. It's still bright red, but now it's covered with these white spots and the center has turned bright green. It looks so nasty. I spend most of my nights wracked in pain. I can't sleep, and I'm afraid to pass it to Mali or Tian. Desperate to do something, I reach down and scrape my nails across the top, ripping the head off. I scream and cry in agony as the yellow, bloody puss pours down my leg. Most people can tell from the smell what just happened. I wrap it the best I can and spend the night crying in pain.

When a guard arrives the next morning, I remove the wrapping that's stuck to my skin and show him my wound. It looks worse today than it did yesterday when I scraped it. When he sees the bloody, smelly sore, he takes me to the medical facility for them to look at my wound.

I wait in a room full of people. Just looking around, I can see why I wasn't taken earlier. Some of the sores and injuries I see makes my leg sore look like nothing. Some look so horrible, I have to look away. Men and women, young and old, are racked with agonizing pain. Everyone looks like they should have received medical treatment long ago.

After spending all day waiting, I'm finally taken into the treatment room. A woman who looks like a nurse pours something over my wound that burns like gasoline. She shows little concern for my screams as she tries to scrape, cut, and clean my wound before she applies some type of topical medicine. The pain is so bad I'm unable to sit still.

"Stop," she yells, angrily.

"I can't," I cry. "Please give me some anesthesia!"

"Mi!" she screams.

When I won't stay still, she gets up and walks out the door. She comes back with a doctor and points at me in anger and disgust. He looks at my wound, pokes around, takes out a needle, and deadens the area.

I feel no pain for the first time in months. She's now able to cut away the dead skin and clean out the infection. It leaves a nasty hole in my leg that she wraps in bandages so it can heal. I sit here for another hour before the guards come to get me.

When the guard directs me out, I turn to the nurse and ask, "Is this it? Will I be alright?"

"Right?" the woman asks.

"Will I be okay?"

"Chi," she says, which means yes.

I tell her I'm sick, I have terrible stomach pains from food poisoning, and I'm burning up and feel weak and dizzy.

"You kay now," she says, and the guard sends me back to our cage.

# – CHAPTER 15 –

Three weeks later, my leg feels better, but I feel worse. Every time I get a little food down, I throw it all back up again. All I want to do is sleep. As I finish the first book on Buddhism, a guard tells me I have a visitor.

I sit in the chair, barely able to hold myself up. I pick up the phone and Mr. Taylor asks, "Ms. Brunick, are you okay?"

I can only imagine how bad I look. I haven't washed in weeks, I've thrown up everything I've eaten, and I can tell by the fit of my bra, and my boney arms and legs, that I've lost too much weight.

It's hard for me to speak, but I say, "Something isn't right. I'm sick. I can't eat, and I throw up whatever I do eat."

"I did what I could," he says, shaking his head. "I thought they sent you to the hospital?"

"I went to the hospital, and they cleaned my infected leg. I told them how sick I am, but they didn't really care."

"Jesus," he says.

"I hope you have some good news. I've got to get out of here."

"Ms. Brunick, I spoke with my boss. We can process your request right away, but he doesn't think they'll release you for at least five years."

"Five years?" I mumble, barely above a whisper.

"I don't know," he says. "You don't look good. Maybe they'll release you given your condition."

"Please try," I beg.

"Ms. Brunick, I'm concerned about you. I called Mr. Sassen. He remembers you. He remembers you very well."

All I can do is smile a little.

"I told him about your trial. It really affected him. I think he's coming back. They offered him my boss's job, and he acts like he's going to take it. I told him about your staph infection, but I didn't know when I talked to him that you were this sick. Maybe he can do something more."

I feel myself about to throw up again. I bow my head and whisper, "Please…please hurry."

I can tell from the look in his eyes that he feels my pain. He puts the phone closer to his lips and says, "I got a call yesterday. It was from Ryan Brunick."

I'm not even sure if I heard him right. "Ryan, my ex?"

"He called and was asking about your case. He asked about your appeal, and I let him know how difficult appeals are. Then, he said something incredible. He wanted to know if we could get you out, if we were able to prove that you were set up."

I cannot believe my ears. *He sets me up and now he wants to know about getting me out?* I look up and ask, "What did you tell him?"

"I didn't want to let him know I was aware he was the one who did it. I told him we'd have to get the person who set you up in front of the judge. He paused like he was thinking about it all. The truth is, I don't think he'll do it."

"No," I say, laying my head back down.

"Then I told him about getting you released after serving part of your sentence. He wanted to know all about it. He wanted to know if there was anything he could do to help."

"No!" I shout. "I don't trust him. He is a snake. Don't take any help from him. He wants to kill me."

"I understand," he says with a nod. "I won't talk to him again."

I look at Mr. Taylor through the wired glass and say, "Please…please help me. I'm not going to make it in here."

He looks back at me like he doesn't know what to say. I'm tired, weak, and barely able to hold myself up. Showing genuine compassion for the first time, he says, "Ms. Brunick, you've got to stay strong. I'll try to get you back to the hospital. We're going to get you out…you just have to hold on a little longer."


As the weeks go by, I only feel worse. I've eaten nothing over the last four days. Mali finally got a job, but she refused to go so she can stay with me. Sweating profusely, I lie with my head on her lap. She puts a wet towel on my head and tries to cool me down. The guard comes in and tells me I have another visitor.

I look at Mali, and say, "It's Mr. Taylor. He's here to get me out. I have to see him."

She helps me up, and I slowly stumble to the visiting area. The guard takes my arm for help. When I finally sit down, I'm overcome with emotion. It's my brother on the other side of the glass, holding the phone.

# – CHAPTER 16 –

The second he sits down, I can see the shock written all over his face. His eyes tear up, and he has to look away to keep himself from crying.

"Faith…oh my God…Faith," he says, shaking his head.

Just holding myself up in the chair isn't easy. Tears stream down my face, as I say, "Jonah…Jonah you came."

"What have they done to you?" he asks.

My lips are so dry I can barely talk. "I'm not good. I have this…this staph infection. I'm sick and I'm not getting better. I'm afraid I don't have much time."

He can't hold back his tears any longer. "Oh Sis, I'm sorry. I'm so sorry."

"It's terrible," I get out. "It's so terrible in here. They put so many people in a room. The food is—"

"I know," he says. "I looked it up online. That's why I came. I had to see you. I had to see what I could do."

I put my head down and whisper, "Thank you…thank you so much for coming."

"Faith, when are you getting out of here?"

I wipe the dry saliva that's built up in the corner of my mouth, look up with tears in my eyes, and say, "I'm not getting out. They say it will take a few more years, but I know I won't last that long. I'm going to die in here."

"Don't say that, Faith," he says, looking so sad and depressed. "You're going to get out if you just stay strong. I'll get you whatever you need."

I shake my head and whisper, "It's too late. I can't hold on any longer."

"You have to," he begs.

I do my best to look up and say, "Jonah…it was Ryan. Ryan did this to—"

His tears are about to pour out of his eyes again. "I know, Faith. I called him over and over. I just wanted to talk to the kids, but he wouldn't allow it. I went to his house. I told him I knew what he did. Of course, he denied it, but I could tell he was lying. He ordered me off his property. He actually threatened to call the police."

Barely able to speak, I look back down and whisper, "He's the devil. I did everything to be a good wife. I spent our whole marriage taking care of him. I gave him everything he wanted. No matter what I did it was never enough for him."

"I know, Faith. It wasn't you. He was lucky to have you for a wife."

I nod my head in agreement and say, "I wasn't perfect."

He shakes his head, and says, "It wasn't your fault. I saw the person he was when I went to his house. He never deserved you.

Crying again, I say, "Do you know how long it's been since I've seen my babies?'

"I know," he says.

"He didn't even want our kids, and now he has them. I'll…I'll never see them again."

He puts his hand on the glass and says, "Yes, you will. You're going to get out of here. I'm going to make sure of it."

I look up, shake my head, and say, "It's just too late."

He moves closer to the glass and asks, "What can I do? Just tell me what to do."

"Do one thing for me," I say, and then I start coughing again. "Promise me…whatever it takes, promise me you'll look after them—even if it's when they're older. Please don't let them forget me."

"I will," he says with a nod. "I'll make sure."

I wipe my eyes and lick my dry lips. Putting my right hand on the glass, I say, "Jonah, I love you. I'm so sorry I wasn't a better sister to you. I shouldn't have ever—"

"Don't say that," he interrupts. "You were a great sister."

Barely loud enough for him to hear me over the phone, I slowly say, "I have to say this. You were such a good big brother to me, and I was so mean to you. Please forgive me. You were so sweet and I was so stupid. I said things I can't take back. No matter what, you never stopped loving me." Struggling just to breathe, I say, "I never even saw Dad in the hospital. He died without me telling him goodbye." My eyes close as I start to fall asleep. With my head still down, I cough into the phone.

My brother closes his eyes and asks, "Are you okay?"

I shake my head and say, "I love you. Please know I love you."

"I know," he says. "And I love you too."

"Please tell Mom—"

"Faith…Mom passed away."

I look up and ask. "What happened?"

"She was never the same after Dad died. I was staying with her. I went into her room to wake her up and she was unconscious. An ambulance rushed her to the hospital, but she never recovered."

Somehow, I knew I would never see her again, but finding out this way is just too hard. I hide my face in my arms and cry.

"Faith, she loved you so much. That's all she talked about the last days. She gave me this letter and asked me to give it to you."

He slides the letter under the glass. I take it and look at the envelope that says, "My Little Girl" in the handwriting I've known all my life.

Sounding desperate, Jonah says, "Faith, I put money into your account. I don't know what else I can do."

With my head still down, I feel too tired and too weak to answer. The guard approaches for us to wrap things up.

"I'll be back tomorrow," he says. "I promise I'll get you out of here."

When the guard lifts me up, Jonah starts yelling, "She's sick! Can't you see she's sick? Get her some help!"

The guard carries me away. I will never see my brother again.

With the help of the guard, I go back to my cage. I'm so exhausted that I collapse into Mali's arms. "Mr. Taylor get you out?" Mali asks.

"No, Mali. It was my brother."

"You brother?"

Laying in her lap, I say, "Yes…my brother came to see me."

I rub my face with the wet towel and slowly—painfully—open my mother's letter.

*My Dearest Faith,*

*It's been so long since I last heard from you. I hope you are still okay. I'm sorry I wasn't able to come and visit you. Please forgive me.*

*Please know how much I've always loved you. You were my little girl. I remember when I brought you home from the hospital. I remember my sweet girl playing house in your pretty dress and ponytails. I remember times you helped me cook in the kitchen and the girl who worked so hard to be the best cheerleader. I loved holding you in my arms until you fell asleep. These are the happy times I remember.*

*I know when you got older I was too hard on you. It was how I was raised, and it's all I knew. I know I pushed you away and caused you to go to Texas. Please know I was doing what I thought was right. I'm sorry about that. Please forgive me.*

*Faith, you will always be my darling daughter. I should have told you more how much I love you. Please know that I love you with all my heart. I know one day we will see each other again.*

*Love you*
*Mom*

Her letter crushes me. As far back as I can remember, my mom and I were always fighting. I didn't think she ever loved me, so I never really loved her back. I realize for the first time, she always loved me but didn't know how to show it. Why did it take her dying for me to finally see it?

I lay there crying as Mali wipes my face, my arms, and my legs. My throat is so sore it hurts when I talk or cough—and I cough a lot. I fall asleep in her lap as she looks down and strokes my hair.

– CHAPTER 17 –

For the next four hours, Mali lays with me, fanning my body to keep me cool. I'm burning up, but I'm freezing to death. Other prisoners give their blanket to keep me covered and break my fever. Exhausted, Mali finally falls asleep with my head still in her lap.

The next morning, she shakes my head and says, "Faith…Faith, time to wake up." When I don't move, tears pour down her face, and she says, "Faith…please wake up. Wake up, Faith."

She moves my face in her hands, but I'm lying here lifeless. When I don't respond, or even budge, she screams, "Ch̀wy ͞chạn d̂wy!" which means, "HELP ME!"

Everyone gets up and yells, "Ch̀wy, Ch̀wy, Ch̀wy" until a guard comes to the cage.

I wake up two days later in a hospital bed with Mali at my side. "Hi, Mali," I whisper with a smile.

"Hi, Faith," she says, holding my hand.

Still barely able to talk, I whisper, "How did you get here?"

"I come wif you," she says with a smile. "They say no, swing they club, but I no leave. I come hospital wif you."

I squeeze her hand and say, "I love you, Mali."

She picks up a water glass with a straw and puts it to my lips. After I take a sip, she asks, "You be right?"

Unable to drink more than a sip, I pull my head away, knowing I'll never be alright again.

"You sit up?" she asks.

I shake my head no.

"Here," she says, reaching over to the table beside me and grabbing my Bible. "I bring you."

With another smile, I take my Bible and say, "Thank you, Mali."

Seeing I'm too weak to talk, Mali sits beside me and strokes my hair over and over again. I want to spend as much time with her as I can, but I'm just too tired and weak. My eyes get heavier and heavier until I fall back asleep.


As I lie there asleep, I feel a peace come over me like a breeze blowing through the leaves of a tree. My body that just felt like it was on fire now feels cool and light. The pain that was just burning my leg is gone. My body feels whole again. I feel the strength I haven't felt since the day I arrived here.

I move my foot until it touches the floor and sit up on the side of the bed. I lower my other foot to the floor and stand without the help of Mali or anyone around me. I turn to Mali, who's just watched me stand to my feet, and say, "I love you, Mali."

She holds my hand as I walk away until I'm out of her reach and we let go. "I love you," she says.

I look down and see my bare feet moving underneath me. The bandage on my leg is gone and the sore on my thigh is gone. I take one step after another, not knowing where I'm going. I move so effortlessly, with none of the pain I've come to know. Unsure if this is actually happening, or simply a dream, I raise my hands in front of my face and see the smooth, beautiful hands I haven't seen for so long.

As I continue forward, a soft breeze blows against my face and gently through my hair behind my back. My nose is filled with a wonderful, sweet perfume. It's sweeter than any fragrance I've ever smelled before. It brings a smile to my face as I breathe deeply until my lungs are so full, I can't take any more in.

As I continue forward, a light pours over me, like the rising sun spreading across the sky. It's so warm and bright, I have to look down. I'm afraid it will burn my eyes if I dare look directly at it. Standing in place, I feel this peace and inner serenity flow through me. I spread my arms wide and slowly look up at the light. With a smile on my face, I keep saying, "It's wonderful….it's so wonderful."

Then this feeling inside me pulls me forward.

As I walk closer and closer to the light, I realize it's not a light at all. It's pure love, and it shines right through me. In that moment, I feel the same wonderful love, joy, peace, and kindness that I felt when looking into the eyes of the angel in Central Park so many years ago.

I want to stay here soaking in that love forever, but the light seems to pull me towards it. Suddenly, the love takes the form of a man who comes towards me with such a beautiful and easy grace. I freeze in my tracks, afraid to move any closer, but He doesn't stop at all. He keeps walking to me until he's standing right in front of me. His eyes and His smile seem to look into my heart and illuminate my soul. Standing in front of me, He opens His arms, and invites me into his embrace. I want to come forward, but I'm overcome with shame. I fall to my knees, wrap my arms around His legs, and cry. I hold on so tight, afraid if I let go, I'll lose Him forever.

"Shhh," He says, putting His hands on each side of my face with a touch that's gentle and warm. The second He touches my face, a love flows from His fingertips and into my body. This love is so overwhelming, it feels like it might burst right out of me. I'm frozen on my knees in front of Him until He raises my face to His, and asks, "Faith….why are you crying?"

With trembling lips and tears streaming from down my cheeks, I cry, "Because …because I don't deserve to be here with you. I don't deserve to go to heaven."

With a beautiful smile, He slowly shakes His head and says, "Faith, no one deserves to go to heaven."

I look up, and for the first time it all becomes clear.

"Faith," he continues, "I love you. I loved you when you came into this world, and I've loved you ever since."

He raises me to my feet and wraps His arms around my shoulders; holding me close. I wrap my arms around His waist and cry against His chest. When we finally pull apart, he reaches out to hold my hands and smiles at me tenderly.

"I just love your name," He says. "Do you know where it came from?"

"My parents gave it to—"

He closes His eyes and gives me this look that stops me cold.

"Really?" I ask.

"Really," He answers, with the most beautiful smile.

I hold Him tight again. It's like I can't get close enough to Him.

Without me asking, He answers the question I've been asking since the day of my trial. "Faith, I know you felt alone, but I was there. I've been with you the whole time."

"Was that you in Central Park?" I ask.

"Yes, I was with you in the park. I've always been with you, but you couldn't see or hear me. Faith, my Father created humans to live a full and abundant life. Instead, most live consumed with regret about the past and anxiety about the future. They spend so much time worrying about things like money, a job, family, past relationships, or something as trivial as what someone else said or did to them. This robs their minds and hearts of the peace and serenity they were born with. Think about that day in Central Park. In that moment, was your mind free from all stress and worry?"

"I was happy," I say. "I felt so full of love."

"Exactly," He says. "I've always been there drawing you near, but only in that moment were you able to hear me. Your mind, body, and soul are the greatest gifts you have in this life. They must be cherished and guarded. Instead, most people let negative thoughts and actions destroy this precious gift. Think of all the things you allow to enter your mind and consume you."

With a sense of clarity, I realize this is so true. I've lived my whole life in fear. I gave no thought to the things I let into my mind or out of my mouth. I think about my daughter who spends every waking hour on her phone filling her head with clutter. "This sounds easy, but how? How do you do it?"

"It's not hard," He says with a smile, "Just love one another. Love everyone and everything, excluding no one and nothing. Love me, love yourself, and love others."

"Is it that easy?" I ask.

"It's that easy."

When it came to God and religion, all my life I've heard about all the things I shouldn't be doing, or all the things I'm doing wrong. God was always about fear. Now, for the first time, I see how great true love really is. Now that I've felt and touched it, it's all I want. I cannot imagine being without it. I lay my head back down on His shoulder with His arms holding me tight. My soul is full and I want to stay here forever, as He strokes my hair, sending this incredible serenity through me. Without looking up, I say, "I will never leave you again. I will stay here forever."

I barely get these words out when He rubs my back and says, "Faith, there's someone here who wants to see you."

I raise my head off His shoulder and look around. "Oh my God," I cry, as I see Colt walking towards us with his arms open wide. Jesus takes a step back and watches as I take my son into my arms, holding him as tightly as I can. The second I touch him, I feel the same overflowing love I just felt when I was in Jesus' arms.

"Oh, my beautiful boy," I say, looking at his precious face. "I've missed you…I've missed you so much."

With such a loving smile, he says, "I've missed you too, Mom."

I never knew about the accident, but I don't have to ask. It's like my eyes are open, and I have an understanding of all that has happened in my life. Staring into Colt's face, I realize all my tears are gone. For the first time, I feel like I've changed. I not only feel this love flowing into me, but now it's also flowing out of me. Sharing this love is even more beautiful and overwhelming.

"You're so beautiful," I say.

"So are you," he says, still smiling.

"I love you," I say with a heart filled with joy.

He looks at Jesus and says, "Isn't love great?"

There's no sense of time as we hold each other for all eternity. Colt looks into my eyes and says, "Mom….Grandma is here. Grandpa is here. Everyone is here."

I turn to Jesus and say, "Can I see them?"

Jesus gives a little laugh, and says, "They just got here. They're in the presence of my Father—soaking up His love. I think they'll be there for a while."

"How long?" I ask.

"Faith, on Earth you're born, you age, and you die. You deal in minutes, hours, days, weeks, and years to maintain a chronological order to things. It has to be that way. On Earth time limits you, but there aren't the same constraints here. A second is a thousand years and a thousand years is a second. Do you understand?"

I start to nod my head and then say, "I have no idea what you just said."

He laughs and says, "How long will they be there? Maybe two or three hundred of your years."

A smile spreads across my face. I return to Colt and kiss his left cheek, his forehead, and then his right cheek.

Jesus steps back in and says, "Guess what? The love you feel now doesn't even compare to the place I've prepared for you since the beginning of time."

"Praise God," I say. "I want that. I've got to have it. I want to spend two or three hundred years with God."

Colt kisses my lips and says, "I've got to go, Mom."

"No," I beg. "Please don't go."

"Colt's with me," Jesus says. "And you will be too."

"But I want to stay. I want to stay right here with you."

"And you will," Jesus says. He gives me another smile and asks, "But can you do something for me first?"

Unable to speak, I simply nod my head.

"Faith, I brought you here to fulfill *My* purpose and further *My* kingdom. I need you to go back."

"Go back?" I ask. "I thought I died?"

He closes His eyes and shakes His head. "I want you to go back and tell them I'm there. Tell them I'm there, and I love them."

"I can't," I say. "I'm stuck in a small room. I don't even have a job. I can't meet people without a job."

He looks at me like this doesn't concern him at all.

Trying to get him to understand, I say, "And I can barely speak Thai. I can't even communicate with anyone unless Mali—"

He gives me this look and I see it all. "Mali?" I ask.

He smiles, closes His eyes, and nods His head. "Teach her as I taught you. Tell Mali how much I love her so she can tell others. And tell her that her children are safe. I'm watching over them."

"How do we tell people how they should live?" I ask.

"Faith, remember this. You will be judged the same way you judge others. When you came here, did you want judgment and condemnation, or did you want forgiveness and love?"

My eyes open wide and I say, "Forgiveness and love! Definitely forgiveness and love!"

He smiles at my reaction. "Just tell them I love them. Tell them to love me, to love themselves, to love one another. Why don't we leave everything else to My Father?"

I've spent three years in a prison believing it was all for nothing. I was forgotten by everyone, and my life was a waste. But now I know. The whole time, I was sent here for a reason. I look at His bright face and say, "I'll go...I'll go back."

"That's my girl," he says, reaching down and kissing my cheek. A tear shoots down my face. Not a tear of sadness, but of overflowing love. He wipes it away and says, "Now those are the tears I like to see."

I give Jesus one last hug and pull away. I look into His eyes and say, "I'll be back. I'll go and come back."

"Yes, you will," He says.

"It won't be a thousand years, will it?" I ask.

He shakes his head, smiles, and says, "More like a second."

I kiss Colt goodbye and touch his face one last time. You'd think I'd be devoured by sadness, but overcome with this love, I say, "I love you, Colt. I can't wait to hold you in my arms forever."

With an easy smile, he says, "I'll be waiting for you."

I turn around and walk back down the same path from where I came. Now that beautiful fragrance fills my whole body. I look up, breathe deep, and smile up at the sky as I walk forward. When I look back over my shoulder, Jesus is gone. Colt is gone. But the love inside me grows stronger and stronger with every step I take.

# – CHAPTER 18 –

Back in my hospital bed, I open my eyes and see Tian and Mali beside my bed; with Mali's head lying on my chest. I look up and cannot believe my eyes. Mr. Sassen is sitting in a chair next to my bed. I can't believe he came back.

Mali looks up when she feels me reach out and stroke her face. "Faith," she says, with her eyes filled with tears.

"I'm here, Mali."

With a face also stained with tears, Tian takes a step forward. I reach out, take her hand, and pull her close.

"I love you, Tian," I say. "Do you know I love you?"

Unable to talk, she nods her head. Then she wipes her tears away and says, "Love you, Faith."

I turn to Sassen and say, "You came."

He nods his head and asks, "How you feeling?"

I let go of Tian and reach out for his hand. He takes my hand in his and moves to the side of my bed. I do my best to scoot myself up a little and say, "You're such a good man. God sees everything you do. He loves you so much. He's with you. Do you know he's with you? He's with you in everything you do."

A tear falls down his cheek.

I look down at my leg and see the bandage with blood soaking through the top. The anesthesia is gone, and my leg burns like a hot iron is sitting on it. My throat is so dry I can barely talk. "Can I get a little water?" I ask.

Mali grabs the cup of water next to my bed and directs the straw to my dry, chapped lips. "You seep for long, long time," she says.

I put my hand against her cheek, shake my head, and say, "I wasn't asleep. I went to Jesus. I saw my son, Colt."

Mali looks over at Tian and then back at me. "You see Jesus?"

Doing my best to smile, I nod my head and say, "I did."

Not sure how to take this, Sassen takes a step back and gives me a look of confusion. I look at Mali and say, "Jesus loves you, Mali." I turn to Tian and say, "Jesus loves you, too."

Looking at them both, I say, "Jesus is here. He's right here in this hospital room with us. He's in the cell when you return."

As I try to lift the water glass, I realize I'm back in the same body I was in before I left. My hands are weak, and I shake as I take another sip. This causes my stomach to cramp again, and I lean over feeling I'm about to throw up.

Mr. Sassen watches me gag and says, "Just rest."

I shake my head and ask Mali to put my pillow behind my back so I can sit up a little. I strain to lean forward as she moves my pillow. Once I lay back against its softness, I turn to Sassen.

"Mr. Sassen, what's happening to me?"

He looks at me and shakes his head as if he doesn't want to answer.

With a half-smile, I say, "It's okay. I need to know."

He looks into my eyes and says, "Faith, the staph infection has entered your bloodstream. Your kidneys are shutting down and it's going to spread to your other organs."

Showing no fear at all, I ask, "Am I going to be okay?"

His eyes tear up. He shakes his head no.

"Will I be going back to our cell?" I ask.

He wipes his eyes and shakes his head again.

"It's okay," I say. "I need you to do me a couple of favors."

"What do you need?" he asks.

"I need you to bring me a Bible, written in Thai."

"That's not a problem," he answers. "What else do you need?"

"Mike…can I call you Mike?"

"Please," he says.

"Mike…Mali and Tian cannot survive in here unless they get food and clean water. Please make sure they have money in their account."

"Don't worry," he says, squeezing my hand. "I'll take care of them myself. Anything else?

"I need Mali and Tian to stay here with me. I need to talk with them as much as I can in the time I have left."

"I don't think that's possible," he says. Before turning around and walking out the door, he says, "Let me see what I can do."

I lay against the pillow, saying nothing more, while I wait to hear back from him. Mali asks me again and again if I need anything, as she wipes my face and lips with a cold towel. My eyes grow tired as the hours pass. At some point, I fall back asleep.

I'm stirred awake by Mali shaking my arm. A nurse is standing in the room holding soup—real soup—and a bowl of chopped peaches in a small bowl. It's been so long since I've seen a bowl of peaches.

"You eat," Mali says.

"I can't," I say, feeling nauseous even thinking about eating.

"Eat, Faith," Mali says, putting the spoon closer to my mouth.

I shake my head and say, "I don't feel good."

"Please eat for me," she begs.

She moves the spoon to my lips, and I take a sip of the soup. I'm surprised I'm able to keep it down. I take another sip, and then another, and then another. Just when I think I might finish it, I feel my stomach cramp. I lean to the side of my bed and throw up all over myself, Mali, the bed, and the floor.

"I'm sorry," I say, laying back on the bed.

"No sorry," Mali says as she grabs a towel and wipes my face. Before cleaning herself, she gets down on her hands and knees and cleans up the bed and the floor. Once everything is cleaned up, she leans me forward and takes hold of my gown. She grabs the clean rag beside the sink, turns to me, and washes my body like I once washed my own children. The cool water feels so soothing against my skin.

Lying naked in front of her, I'm humbled to tears. Since the day I first arrived, she's done everything for me, and I've done nothing for her. I couldn't understand at the time why, after we first met, she lay over me and took the guard's blows that were meant for me. Now I know why Jesus chose her and is protecting her children. She's the embodiment of God's love.

I lean a little closer, and whisper, "Please tell the nurse, I have to go to the restroom."

Mali walks into the bathroom and comes back with a bedpan. She helps me and then cleans up after me.

I lie back in my bed, feeling a little better from the cool water against my skin. Just when I'm about to fall asleep again, Sassen comes back into the room. He walks up to my bed and says, "I don't believe this. They're going to let Mali and Tian stay here…at least for a while. They've never done this before."

I take his hand and move it to my cheek, doing my best to talk. Feeling so weak again, I whisper, "Mike, I'll never forget the love and kindness you have shown me. When I had nothing, you put money in my account. I was hungry, and you fed me. I was thirsty, and you gave me something to drink. I was in prison, and you visited me. God has seen everything you do. Your work here is so much greater than you'll ever know."

With heavy eyes full of tears, Sassen nods his head.

I look at both Mali and Tian and say, "God has a plan for each of you. Will you please stay with me?"

"I stay," Mali answers. Tian nods her head.

I turn to Mali and say, "He gave me a message for you."

Feeling too exhausted to talk any more, I turn to Mali and say, "I need to sleep now. Please move my pillow back under my head."

Sassen takes my hand for a brief moment and gives it a light squeeze before walking out of the room. Mali gently lifts my head and pulls away the extra pillow. So sweet and tender, she lays my head back down. I close my eyes and fall back asleep.

# – CHAPTER 19 –

I'm not sure how long I've been asleep. I'm always nauseous, even when I'm not eating, feeling like I might throw up at any time. I'm burning hot, and I ache so bad from the poison that's spreading through my body. Just trying to stay awake takes all my effort.

Sleep is my refuge. I'm also hoping God will bring me back to Him. I got just a taste of what's waiting for me, and I want to feel it again—even if it's only for a few minutes—but that doesn't happen. If it were up to me, I'd stay asleep forever, but I know I must come around. When I open my eyes, Mali and Tian are sitting by my bed.

"How long was I asleep?" I ask.

Tian lifts up two fingers and says, "Tree days."

"Two days?" I ask.

"Ah…yes," she says with a laugh. "Two days."

My mouth is so dry and my lips are crusted over. Before I even ask, Mali puts the straw in my mouth.

I sip the water that feels cool going down. I do my best to wet my lips but it doesn't help a lot. "That's good," I say.

"Hugry?" she asks

I'm sure I'll just throw it up again, so I shake my head no.

Once another pillow is behind my back and I'm sitting up, I turn to Mali and Tian and tell them about everything.

"I've been so sick lately," I start.

"Chi," Mali says. "Uh…yes."

"I was so tired and sick. I didn't think I would ever wake up again. After I fell asleep, I felt myself rise up from the bed. All my pain was gone. My bandage was gone and my leg no longer burned. My stomach was good and my fever was gone. I saw you standing beside me, holding my hand. I started walking, but I didn't know where I was going. When I walked forward, I could smell the most beautiful smell. It was like thousands of roses in a field all around me. When I walked some more, there was this beautiful light. It was like the warm sun on a beautifully cool day; but it wasn't the sun. It was Jesus. The light was the love coming from Him." I look at her with this magical smile, and say, "I could see it; I could feel it; I could touch it. His love was everywhere. It was the most wonderful feeling I've ever known."

Tian's eyes open wide as she listens while I talk.

"When I saw Jesus, I was so afraid. I stopped walking forward, but He walked up and stood in front of me. I fell down in front of Him and cried. He lifted my face to His and asked me, 'Why are you crying?' He told me He loved me and He's always loved me. Love was flowing out from Him like the sun shining from the skies. He raised me to my feet and wrapped His arms around my neck, holding me tight. I wrapped my arm around His waist and cried against His chest. He looked at me and said my son wanted to see me. Then my son, Colt, walked up to me with his arms spread wide." With a big smile, I spread my arms to show how he looked. "I didn't even know Colt was there. He was so beautiful. I held him and kissed him. I told him how much I loved him."

Mali's face lights up upon hearing this. I take both their hands, and say, "Jesus is real. He's real, and He loves me. He loves you, too."

Mali nods her head. I look at her and say, "He wants you to hold your children again. He's waiting for you in heaven."

Mali looks down and says, "But I kill. I try kill my husband. I don't deserve heaven."

This is the first time I've heard her say this. I did not know this was so heavy on her heart. Maybe the scriptures we read together convicted her about that terrible night.

I take her face, raise her head so she will hear me, look into her eyes, and say, "I did many bad things, too. I asked for forgiveness for those things. He forgives me and He forgives you, too."

"Forgive?" she asks.

"When you ask for forgiveness and turn your life to God, He doesn't care what you did. He loves you so much."

Mali is looking down when I say, "He asked me to give you a message."

She raises her eyes and gives me the strangest look, like she's afraid to hear the message. "Don't be afraid," I say. "He told me He's watching over your children. He said not to worry about them. He's keeping them safe for you."

Mali's eyes fill with tears. "Do I see them again?" she asks.

Still holding her face, I nod my head. "Yes, Mali. You will see them again. Just like I was with my little boy, you will be with your children again one day. Maybe you see them here. Maybe you don't. But you will be with them in heaven forever and ever."

Tears fall down her cheeks. I wipe them away and with my best smile I say, "Isn't God wonderful?"

She puts her hands over her face and nods her head.

With a smile, I say, "God is here even in this horrible place."

Mali nods her head.

Struggling to breathe, I say, "I won't be here much longer. I'm going back to be with Jesus, my son, and my mom and dad. God wants you and Tian to tell everyone here that He's with them, and He loves them."

Looking down, Mali shakes her head and says, "No. I no do that."

I take both Mali and Tian's hand in mine. Holding them tight, I say, "You can. Don't be afraid. God will be with you."

I feel like this is too much for them. I turn to Mali, and say, "Mali, don't be afraid. Just like God is taking care of your children, he will take care of you."

Shaking her head, she says, "I no how."

"Before I leave, I'll tell you what to do. I'll show you the words in the Bible to read. You speak Thai. Just tell everyone Jesus loves them. He loves them and is waiting for them. Start with Tian. Read your Bible to Tian so she can tell other people, too."

She smiles big and says, "I get job!"

"You got a job?" I ask.

"Yes, I get job."

"That's wonderful! Don't you see? Jesus is taking care of you already. Now you can talk to many, many people. Tell them, Mali. Tell them how much Jesus loves them."

She nods in agreement.

I reach out and pull her to me. "Mali, God sent you to me. I was so afraid, and you held me. I would have quit, but I had you for my friend. God knows what a good person you are. He will be with you when you tell people about Jesus. Don't be afraid. He will help you know what to say."

She gives me a hug and says, "I tell, Faith. I tell them Jesus love them."

I turn to Tian, who looks terrified. I squeeze her hand and say, "I need you to help Mali. Can you help her?"

She shakes her head and says, "I girl. I no old."

"Right now, all you have to do is help Mali. She will tell you about Jesus. I need you to listen to everything she teaches you. I need you to pray with her. Will you help her?"

Tian looks over at Mali and nods in agreement.

I reach out for her to come closer. I put my arm around her neck and pull her to me. I kiss her cheek and say, "You will be leaving to go home soon. When you get home, I need you to tell others about Jesus. Will you do this for me?"

"Chi," she says with a nod.

I pull back and say, "I want to pray for you. Is that okay?"

They both nod.

I take their hands in mine and pray. "Oh, heavenly Father, thank you for these beautiful women. They love you so much. Please fill them with the Holy Spirit. Show them how to talk to others. We pray you touch everyone in this prison. We pray your Word spreads across this country. Please give them the strength and courage to do Your will. In Jesus' beautiful name, we pray. Amen."

They're both still looking down, so I ask, "Can you say Amen?"

They both say, "Amen."


Over the next seven days, we spend all our time reading the Bible. We focus all our attention on the New Testament. My Bible is already underlined with notes in the margins. Every scripture I marked in my Bible, Mali marks in hers. We continue to underline and mark her Thai Bible as we move forward.

Mali gets a notebook and I make notes to help her know what scriptures to read, what they mean, and what to say to others. At first, I do all the reading.

The first day, we learn how Jesus was born in a manger and how He began his teachings with the Sermon on the Mount. Mali writes in her notebook in Thai. She tells me what she's writing in Thai: *Love everyone. Forgive people. Always help poor people.*

Then we come to the Lord's prayer—

> "Our Father in heaven, hallowed be your name,
> your kingdom come, your will be done,

on earth as it is in heaven.
 Give us today our daily bread.
 And forgive us our debts,
   as we also have forgiven our debtors.
 And lead us not into temptation,
   but deliver us from the evil one.


"I pray this?" Mali asks.

I've never actually prayed *with* Mali. I've always done all the praying while she listens. I shake my head and say, "Don't worry about the words you say. You don't always have to pray the Lord's prayer. Jesus already knows how you feel. Just talk to Jesus. Tell Him you love him. Thank Him for everything."

I take Mali's hands in mine and say, "Mali, you can help other people learn how to pray. This is how they talk to Jesus. Let us pray again, except this time, you pray."

She lowers her head and says, "Heaven Father, thank you. I love you much. Please make Faith better. Help Faith eat she food."

My eyes tear up and I squeeze her hands. I've heard the best preachers give prayers that go on and on. I've never been so overwhelmed by any other prayer in my life. It's her first prayer, and she nailed it!

"Say Amen," I whisper.

With a big smile, she says, "Amen."


As the days go by, she's able to read everything on her own. Actually, she insists on it. Tian mostly sits beside her, doing her best to follow along. Watching her read one scripture after another brings such happiness to my heart. We had already read most of these scriptures over the past year, but Mali seemed confused. She often nodded her head, even though I wondered if she understood. Now it's like her mind is open and she's soaking it all in.

When I fall back to sleep, she can't wait for me to wake up. She shakes me awake and says, "Here Faith. Here light!" I find where she is in my Bible and read:

> *"He came as a witness, to testify about the Light, so that all might believe through him."*

She looks right at me with this amazing look. "Faith, this light! This light you see!"

"Yes Mali, this is the light I saw. It was beautiful. It was everywhere, and it felt so good."

"I want light," she says.

Tian nods her head in agreement.

"You will," I say. "One day, Jesus will meet you just like He met me. You will feel His love all around you. You will feel His love inside you."

I put my head down and fall back asleep. When I wake back up, I can tell it's late at night. Mali's still busy reading her Bible and writing in her notebook with Tian right beside her. I sit up and ask them what they just read. Mali's amazed by the miracles Jesus performed.

"He make man no die. He feed many people with little bread and fishes. Some follow when He go."

"Those are His disciples," I say.

"Disciple?"

"Disciples are the people who love Jesus and follow Him. You are His disciple too!"

Mali raises her eyebrows and says, "I?"

"Yes, both of you. You are His disciple."


Four days after we started, we read about Jesus dying on the cross. I've heard this story so many times, going all the way back to vacation Bible school when I was a child. Every Easter, the preacher told the same story from another angle. But this is very different. Seeing how these scriptures affect Mali hits me really hard. For the first time, I truly appreciate Jesus' sacrifice so much more.

Not even trying to stop her tears from falling down her cheeks, she asks, "Why Faith? He love us. Why kill Jesus?"

I'm not sure where my words come from. I pull myself up and say, "Mali, they didn't kill Him. He died for you. He died for me. He died for everyone. He died so you can go to heaven."

"Why kill Jesus so we go heaven?"

"Remember when we talked about sin? Everyone has sin. Jesus took our sin away. By dying on the cross, He took our sin so we can go to heaven just like Him."

"Why no one help Jesus?" she asks.

"I don't know," I answer. "Some people don't understand. Other people are like your husband. They don't know Jesus."

"I hate him," Mali says.

"No, Mali," I say, shaking my head. "Jesus loves everyone. It's so much love. All you want to do is give this love to everyone else. When you have this much love inside you, there's no room left for hate—not even a little bit of hate. That little bit of hate will take away from all the love. You don't want that, do you?"

"I want love," she says.

"Then don't hate your husband. I no longer hate Ryan. Love everyone and let Jesus take care of everything else."

"I want heaven," she says.

"Then pray," I say. "Tell Jesus how you feel."

This time, Mali reaches out and takes *my* hands. She lowers her head and says, "Heaven father, thank you. You love me. You die for me. I love you. I want heaven. Amen."

I look up, feeling so emotional. "Mali, that was beautiful," I say. "You're very good at praying."

"I like pray," she smiles.

# – CHAPTER 20 –

Each day that goes by, I feel weaker and weaker. As hard as I try, it's difficult for me to keep any food down. Sassen comes by every day to check on me. Some days I'm alert, but other days I'm asleep, and the only way I know he came by is because Mali tells me about it.

After another week, I'm wracked with pain and feel my body fading away. Each time I wake up, Mali is busy with her Bible. I feel so weak all I can do is pray for her. Tian is sitting in a chair, barely awake. She looks right at me and starts to cry. I hold out my arm and whisper, "Tian…come here…I want to talk to you."

Still crying, she slowly walks to the bed. "You no kay?" she asks with a sad face.

I hold her in my arms and shake my head.

"Stay," she says wiping tears from her eyes. "Please don't go."

The next day, I raise my hand to my face and see that my skin is yellow. My fingers look like bones covered with skin. My lips are dry and chapped. I moan a little as I turn on my side. Mali puts the straw to my lips so I can take a drink, but I don't have any strength left to even take a sip.

"Please drink," Mali begs.

I try to shake my head, but can't move. I struggle just to take a breath. Wheezing, I say, "I can't."

Mali takes Tian's hands in hers, and prays, "Jesus, help Faith." They both start crying when Mali says, "Please make Faith sit up and drink she water. Make she eat she food."

Sassen walks in, and I motion for him to come closer. I struggle just to take a couple of breaths before I continue. I swallow hard and ask, "One last favor."

He leans in to hear me, as I whisper, "When you meet people, give everyone two Bibles even if they don't ask. Give them an English Bible and a Thai Bible. Tell them to give one Bible away. Tell them about Mali. She will help them survive in here."

"I will," he says. "I'll tell Mr. Taylor to do the same thing."

I nod a little and fall back asleep.

I spend the next day asleep. Late at night, I wake up with Mali and Tian lying over me praying. I'm not prepared for this. My eyes tear up when I hear their pain. When they see me awake, they stop praying. I look at them both and struggle just to smile.

Mali takes the bowl of soup and says, "Faith, please eat."

I close my eyes, letting my tears fall down my cheeks, and shake my head. She puts the water cup in front of me, but again I shake my head.

Mali takes my hand in hers and says, "I love you, Faith."

With eyes still full of tears, I cannot talk. I mouth, "I love you."

Seeing me slip away, Mali and Tian both cry uncontrollably.

Knowing my time has come, I open my eyes one last time. Even though it's late, Sassen is sitting in the corner of the room. He stands to his feet, walks to the side of my bed, and puts his hand on my leg.

Mali wipes my face with a cold towel and starts to cry again. She looks at my face and says, "Faith….Faith."

I take one last deep breath and say, "Don't cry, Mali. I'll be alright. I'm going to Jesus now." I close my eyes and whisper, "I'm free, Mali. Now I'm free."

# PART THREE

---

## HOPE BRUNICK

*It is amazing how complete is the delusion that beauty is goodness.*

—Leo Tolstoy

*Beware. Some men will sell you a dream and deliver a nightmare.*

—Author Unknown

# – CHAPTER 21 –

After three weeks of walking along the canals of Venice, touring the wineries outside of Florence, seeing all the sites of Rome, visiting Pompei, and traveling down the Amalfi Coast, Hope is ready to go home. She has a wedding to plan. Grace, on the other hand, isn't ready to go back to the chaos she left behind. Not to mention, she has to convince her dad to take Hannah's case, and Bonnie wants to stay here with her grandpa forever.

Back at his home, Ryan asks Hope if they can talk before she leaves. Gone are the old days when he'd discuss things behind his desk. They walk hand in hand out to the firepit overlooking the ocean.

"I never get tired of sitting out here," Hope says as they walk to the chairs.

Letting go of her hand so they can sit down, Ryan says, "You know this is your home, too."

Hope considers this for a second, and says, "For some reason, it doesn't feel like it,"

"That's because it's new. Remember when we moved out to the hill country? It was strange at first, but you grew to love it."

"That's probably it," she says.

"You keep asking for Tylenol. You feeling okay?"

"I've had this back pain for a couple weeks now. It won't seem to go away."

"Did you hurt your back?"

"I don't think so. It's probably the long flight and all the walking we've been doing. I haven't been sleeping too good lately."

"Well, get back and get some rest. Let me know if it doesn't get better."

After a few minutes, Ryan says, "Hope, you're such a beautiful woman. You got into one of the best schools in the country, you're making good grades, you're doing great. I can't tell you how proud I am of you."

Hope takes a deep breath and says, "It hasn't been easy."

Ryan looks out, brushes his hair back with his fingers, and says, "I know…and I'm sorry for that."

Hope rests her elbows on her knees, takes a deep breath, and lowers her face down to the palms of her hands.

"Hope, I've spent my whole life taking care of you. You kids are all that matter to me. Now I've caused you so much hurt. God, I wish I could go back and change everything."

This stirs the anger in Hope that she's been trying to avoid. She looks at her dad and says, "Yeah, now you wish you could change everything…now because you got caught."

Ryan reaches out and touches her forearm. "That's not true," he says. "From the day I got back from Thailand, I've been racked with guilt. I couldn't eat. I couldn't sleep. I went to therapy and dove deep into church. Nothing helped."

Hope looks over and says, "I wonder why?"

"I know," Ryan says.

Hope looks right into her dad's eyes and says, "How could you do something like this?"

Ryan sits back and closes his eyes. Then he looks up at the sky and says, "Hope, life is pretty simple for you, and it should be. Marriage can get pretty ugly sometimes. Something horrible happened in our marriage that you know nothing about—no one does. It wasn't Paul, and it wasn't Colt either. It's the worst thing you could ever imagine."

Hope looks over while Ryan is still looking up. Having no idea what he's talking about, she asks, "What is it, Dad? I want to know."

Ryan looks directly at Hope with tears in his eyes. She thinks he's about to let go, but he simply says, "I can't, Hope. It's something I'll take to my grave."

Hope looks at her dad like she really wants an answer to her question. "Then why didn't you get her out?"

"I tried. It just wasn't that easy. The Thai legal system doesn't work like it does in the United States. I hired a lawyer in Thailand. He told me that even if I came forward, it probably wouldn't get her out. At best, it'd reduce her sentence. I spoke to the guy at the embassy. He told me our best shot was to get her transferred to the U.S., and then she'd be sent here and released. Then….then she was gone."

Hope first hides her face as if to say, *I told you I didn't want to talk about this.* Then she shakes her hands in front of her face in anger, and says, "Then I don't know what to say, because it was *you* who did this!"

Ryan slowly nods his head as the shame pours over him.

Hope stands up and says, "You know, Dad, I don't like talking about this. All it does is bring back a lot of old feelings that make me so angry. I miss my mom. I think about her all the time, and how my life could have been different. You're my dad. You'll always be my dad. Yes, part of me loves you so much and will always love you. Another part hates you…or hates what you did. I don't think I can ever forgive you for that. I've had to learn how to live with it. Let's just leave it at that."

Before Hope can walk off, Ryan takes her arm and eases her back down into her chair. Looking down with trembling lips, and tears falling from his eyes, he cries, "Hope, you know what the worst part is? I once felt like I was a good man, and I derived so much strength from that. Ever since I did that horrible thing to your mom, I've never been able to believe in myself like that again. Even worse, I now question the purity of God's opinion of me. You have no idea how awful that feels—especially knowing that I did it all to myself. I deserve everything that's happened. You might think I walk around here like everything's fine, but every time I look at you kids, it reminds me of what I did and how much I hurt you…hurt all of us. You have no idea what that's done to me. I will never be the man I once was. I destroyed the best part of myself."

Seeing her dad so broken, Hope starts to tear up.

"I can never expect you kids to ever forgive me. I don't deserve forgiveness. I will never forgive myself."

Hope sits back down and puts her hand on her dad's knee.

"You have no idea how many times I've thought about taking my own life. Remember after Colt died? I was so low I almost killed myself. You thought it was about Colt, but it wasn't just Colt. It was this thing I had done. I couldn't live with myself anymore. You know that road my car went over? So many times, I've almost driven my car right off that road and ended it all. There's only one reason I didn't—you kids. I couldn't face the pain it would cause you and Grace to be left all alone. I didn't want you to live without a mom and a dad."

Hope looks down and says, "You know, her gravesite was beautiful. At least she got that. It was the most beautiful thing I've ever seen. I thank you for that."

Ryan puts his head down in his hands and cries. Hope leans over, puts her arm around his shoulders, and says, "I do love you, Dad. I'll always love you."

# – CHAPTER 22 –

After dropping Hope off at the airport and saying their goodbyes, Ryan, Grace, and Bonnie stop at a restaurant on their way home for dinner. When the waitress takes their order and walks away, Grace builds up the courage to talk about Hannah again.

"Dad, have you thought about Hannah?"

"Of course, I've thought about her."

"Well?"

"Grace, I feel sorry for Hannah. I really do. But you're my daughter. I have to put you first."

"But I did this. I have to do something about it."

"Grace, I don't think I could represent her…not really. I'd be too concerned about keeping everything off of you. I can't bear losing you. I don't know what I'd do if you were convicted and went to prison."

"But you're going to lose me, anyway. I'll turn myself in before I'll let her go to prison for murder. I did it, and I'll make it right."

"Even if it leaves Bonnie and Wesley without their mother?"

Grace looks over at Bonnie, who's busy coloring the paper they gave her when they walked in, and says, "I guess so."

"God no, Grace. Don't say that."

"That's why I need you. You're the only one who can save her."

"She doesn't need me. There are other good lawyers. I'll pay for her to have the best lawyer I can find."

Grace gives Ryan this sideways look and says, "Come on, Dad. No one's like you. We both know it. Everyone knows it. Plus, what if one of these hot-shot lawyers digs too far? What if he finds out about Sean? What if he finds out Sean wasn't just some random hiker who just happened to walk by and find Jackson? You know how you lawyers always try to point the finger at someone else. You know the internet. It won't take too much digging to find out we went to the same college at the same time. Maybe they'll find some old pictures. Then what? It all comes back to me."

Ryan hadn't considered this.

"You can do it, Dad. I was in Thailand. All you have to do is keep things away from Sean."

"Then how do I prove she's innocent?" Ryan asks.

"I don't know, I'm a doctor," Grace says, shuffling her hands across the top of the table. "Do your thing. Mess up their case. You'll think of something…you always do."

"It's not so easy. I never know how I'll handle the case until I see their case. I have to comb over the evidence and find a crack in the case."

"Yes!" she says. "Shuffle…find a crack in their case."

"Sometimes, I just catch a break."

"Then catch a break. She's innocent. You get guilty people off. Getting an innocent person off should be a piece of cake."

Ryan stops for a second to think things over. Then he says, "You know, people always ask me how I can represent guilty people. I always tell them it's not representing guilty people that bothers me. It's representing the innocent people that's hard. It's terrifying. I could never live with myself if I had an innocent client go to prison."

"Dad, I've seen you in court. You never lose. I've heard you talk. You always find a way."

Ryan nods a little before saying, "There's one other problem. I really shouldn't go back to the United States for a while."

"Shouldn't?" Grace asks. "Are the police after you?"

"It's not so much the police. That crazy Flint hired a guy to kill me. Flint was found with my fake—I mean my new—passport in his pocket and almost thirty-five thousand dollars. He always uses this guy Jesse to take someone out. Well, later that afternoon, Jesse arrived at the park. He said he was there to go fishing. I'm sure Flint hired him to kill me. That's a lot of money. He'd only pay him that much if he was paid to go all the way to Europe. Who knows what would happen if I go back to the United States."

"So, he knows your passport?"

"Well, sorta. I bought that passport from this guy I know in Houston. Flint knows the same guy. I figured he'd be looking for me and sooner or later he'd go to Houston. So, I had this guy give me a second passport and birth certificate. Anyway, I flew with the first passport to Italy to throw them off. From that day on, I've used my second passport they have no idea about."

"Jesus….Dad. How do you think of this stuff?"

Ryan raises his pointer finger and says, "Always have a backup plan. When they look for Scott Edwards Richards, it'll be a complete dead end."

"So, you're safe now?" Grace asks.

"As long as I stay here. But what if I go back and try Hannah's case? I can't just go back and practice law under the name of a guy who's not licensed with the state bar. I'll have to go back and use my real name."

"But this is in Aspen, Colorado. Where does this guy live?"

"Alice, Texas. A little city between Austin and Laredo."

"Do you really think he'll go all the way to Colorado?"

"He's the best. He'll go there if he finds out I'm there."

"But Flint is dead. He probably doesn't give a damn anymore."

"I don't know. If he got paid and he knows where I am….who knows what he's capable of. Killing is nothing to him—I think he enjoys it. Plus, if I get Hannah off, it will probably make the news in Austin."

"Then leave," Grace says. "The day after the trial, we get the hell out of there and come back home."

Ryan sits there in deep thought. Grace knows it's best give him time to think it over. Finally, Ryan says, "Let me think give it some thought."

With a nod, Grace says, "We don't have much time."

"I know," Ryan agrees. "I'll let you know soon."

# – CHAPTER 23 –

The next day, Ryan makes a few calls to Colorado. He found out Hannah was brought in front of a judge for arraignment and said she didn't want a court-appointed lawyer—at least for now. *This is perfect.* Ryan will find a competent criminal lawyer to act as co-counsel. He can handle all the pre-trial matters and Ryan will show up to try the case. He seems like the perfect lawyer for the job and calls his office.

"Hello. . .Mark Zimmerman."

"Hello, Mark. This is Ryan Brunick. I want to talk with you about a referral there in Aspen."

"Brunick. . .Brunick," he mumbles, like he's searching his memory. "How do I know that name?"

"I'm an attorney in Austin."

"Yes, Ryan Brunick! You represented that woman who was convicted of killing her own baby. You took over and got her off."

"That was a long time ago," Ryan says. "It was a little more complicated, but that was the gist of it."

"Oh yeah, it was all over the news. You must have been paid a mint on that one."

"Actually, I did the whole thing pro-bono."

"Really?"

"Yep," Ryan says.

"Wait a minute," the lawyer says, a little puzzled. "I thought you were killed in a car wreck a while back."

"Oh brother, not that rumor again," Ryan says, trying to remain vague about it.

"I'll be damned. Well, how can I help you, Ryan?"

"I'm about to represent a young girl there in Aspen. She's accused of killing her husband."

"Hannah Jackson?" he asks.

"That's her."

"Good for you, Ryan. I was in court during her first appearance. Case sounds pretty strong….but what the hell do I know?"

"Listen, I'm looking for local counsel. I hear you know your way around the courthouse."

"Well, thanks for that, Ryan. I scratch out a living, but I'm no Ryan Brunick."

"I need someone to handle all the pre-trial matters. You know, get the discovery and forward it to me. Just talk with the prosecutors and see what they have to say."

"I can do that," Mark says. "My expertise is pleading cases out. I'll get her the best deal I can."

"I'm pretty sure this case is going to trial."

"Really?" he says, like this is amazing.

"For now, I want you to keep my involvement pretty low key. Your name will be on all the pleadings. I'll prepare them and you file them. You know what I'm saying?"

"No problem....low key."

"Exactly. I'll do most of the work. You just show up for all her appearances and help gather whatever evidence we need for trial. Once we have a firm court date, I'll take over."

"Listen man, I just want to see you at work. Can I second chair the case if you go to trial?"

This isn't the first time Ryan's been asked this. "No problem. You can help with the trial, but I handle all the witnesses."

"Hell yes...hell yes! Thank you, Ryan. I've tried four or five cases and they didn't go too good. That's how I got so good at pleas. I want to try more cases—I really do. Maybe you can show me how."

"Actually, this is perfect," Ryan says. "The prosecutor will think we're heading for a plea. They won't be as prepared."

"I love it," Mark says.

"Okay. I'll send you a check for twenty thousand dollars. Does that sound okay?"

"Twenty thousand! I get $350.00 for a plea." He pauses for a minute and says, "I don't want your money. Don't worry about it. I'm just—"

Ryan stops him. "I'm not gonna have you work for free. I'll get the check in the mail right away."

Zimmerman gives a little whistle and says, "You're paying me twenty thousand? You musta' been paid a hell of a retainer."

"Nope," Ryan says. "Pro bono."

"How do you do all this pro bono stuff?"

"Let's just call it karma. I've made a good living. Treat people right and they'll come back and refer others."

"I really thank you for this. To be honest, I'm afraid to try a case. I convinced myself the first case wasn't my fault. After five losses in a row, I kinda' got the hint."

"You want to know the secret?"

"There's a secret?"

"Sure, have passion…care about your client."

"I'll try to work on that," Zimmerman says. "Anyway, thank you, Ryan. I know your reputation. You were once the key speaker at a criminal law trial conference. I tried to sign up, but it filled up too fast. I really appreciate this opportunity."

"For now, I want you to meet with Hannah. Explain the situation. Tell her I'll be representing her. Tell her Grace says hello. She'll know who you're talking about."

"No problem, Ryan. I'll go there this afternoon."

"Great, let me know how it goes."

"I will, Ryan. Thanks again."

"Oh, I'm seven hours earlier than you are, so we'll always talk in the mornings."

"No problem.'

"Talk with you soon."


Ryan hangs up the phone and calls Grace into his bedroom. Sitting beside her on the bed, he says, "I just got off the phone with a lawyer in Colorado."

She taps her fists against her forehead and says, "No, Dad! I told you I want you. I don't want some other—"

Ryan raises his hand and says, "He's going to handle the pretrial stuff. I'll be the one who's actually representing her. I'll be the one who tries her case."

Grace leans over and tackles her dad. Wrapping her arms around his neck, she says, "I love you, Dad. I love you…I love you…I love you. I want Hannah to come visit when she gets out. Her little girl will have so much fun here. I can't wait to—"

"Hold on," Ryan says. "We don't have her out yet."

Grace rolls her eyes, and with a smile, she says, "Yeah, right."


A couple of hours later, Mr. Zimmerman walks into the county jail and signs in as Hannah's lawyer. In jail, lawyers don't have to talk through a phone or glass window. Zimmerman's led to Meeting Room 2 where he walks in, opens his briefcase, and sits down at the table.

Twenty minutes later, Hannah comes in wearing an orange prison suit. She's prettier than most of the clients Zimmerman represents. Zimmerman stands up when she walks in and says, "Hello, Ms. Kennedy. I'm Mark Zimmerman."

Hannah pauses for a second and says, "I told the judge I didn't want a court-appointed lawyer."

"I'm not a court-appointed lawyer. I'm here for Ryan Brunick." He points across the table at the chair and says, "Please take a seat."

"Thank God," she says and sits down.

"Mr. Brunick is going to be your lawyer. I'm going to help him with all the local stuff like filing pleadings and getting the evidence from the prosecutor. If the case has to be tried, he'll be your man."

"Let me ask you. Is he good?"

"You don't know him?" Zimmerman asks.

"No, I'm friends with his daughter, Grace."

"Oh…Grace says hello by the way." Zimmerman leans back and says, "Is Ryan good? He's the best. As far as I know, he's never lost. He teaches other lawyers how to try cases, if you're lucky enough to get into one of his lectures. Trust me when I say you're in good hands."

Hannah puts her head down. With her hands laced in front of her head like she's praying, she says, "Thank God."

"Ms. Kennedy, I need to go over your case. Really, I don't want to know if you did it or not."

"I didn't," she says.

"It doesn't matter. I'd rather not know."

"Well, I didn't," she repeats.

"Then tell me what you know."

"I don't know a whole lot. My husband Jackson was coming home. We were supposed to meet at our vacation home in Aspen. I went there to meet him, but he never showed up. I turned around and went back home."

"That's it?" he asks.

"Pretty much."

Writing everything on his tablet, he asks, "And you know nothing about his death?"

"Everything I know, I got from the news…and when I sat down with the investigator."

"Oh, shit," he says, sounding alarmed. "You were interrogated by the police?"

"Yeah," Hannah says. "They asked me to come in. I wanted to cooperate."

"Shit, shit, shit."

"Is that bad?"

"That must be it. You must have said something. I know you thought you were doing right, but you never talk to the investigators."

"I didn't confess, that's for sure."

"Yeah, but they twist everything around. They make you sound guilty even if you're not."

"Honestly, I didn't think I was a suspect. Then they said they already knew what happened. They said they had evidence against me."

"Yeah, that's what they do. They lie. They'll tell you they have evidence they don't have."

"How can they do that?"

"Well, they can. Our Supreme Court is so conservative. They always rule against the accused. They've pretty much given police the green light to do or say whatever they want. They'll lie, they'll question you for days without sleep, they'll coerce a confession—"

"This is crazy. It sounds like Russia or something."

"It kinda is. One big difference—you don't have to talk. You just don't do it."

"That's why I stopped it. I told them I wanted an attorney."

"You asked for an attorney?"

"I did, and they let me go home."

"Great! How long were you there?"

"I don't know. Maybe an hour?"

"That's the best thing I've heard. We gotta find out what they got."

"How do we do that?"

"I'll get the discovery at your next appearance. By now, they'll have everything together. Let me ask you. How do you know this Grace woman?"

"We became friends after she came and visited me."

"Who is she?"

"You don't know?" Hannah asks.

"Know what?"

"She was married to Jackson."

"Married to Jackson? *Your* Jackson? So that's his ex-wife?"

"No….we were both married to him at the same time. He had two wives. He had two whole lives."

"Holy shit!" he says. "She's Ryan Brunick's daughter?"

"She is," Hannah says.

"Well, there's motive….for both of you. How do you know she didn't do it? She has as much reason to do it as you do."

"She couldn't have done it. She was in Thailand at the time."

"When was she in Thailand?"

"I'm not sure. She left a few days before he left and came back weeks later. Actually, she didn't even know about me."

"Did you know?"

"I found out when the police questioned me."

"Well, that's the end of motive—if they believe you."

"Why wouldn't they believe me?"

"Did they ask you about it?"

"Oh shit. They asked me if he was having an affair. I said he probably was."

"Damn," he says, writing this down. "Why would you say that if you didn't know about it?"

"I didn't really know. He was gone all the time. It just made sense."

He shakes his head and says, "Well, there's motive again."

"I was just talking. I didn't know one way or another."

"I know, but that's not how they'll take it."

Hannah lowers her head and says, "Oh, God."

"Listen, Ms. Kennedy, there's no reason to worry. I don't know anything right now. Let me get the discovery. Let me see your statement. We'll know a lot more after that."

He gathers up his things. Before leaving, Hannah says, "One more thing. An officer just served me with these papers." She hands over the papers she's been holding.

Zimmerman reads through the document, saying "hmm" here and there. Finally, he says, "It's a custody suit. It looks like the state is asking the court to take custody of your daughter."

"They want to put her in foster care?"

"Savannah?"

"Yes, her name is Savannah."

"Yeah, it looks like they do. Where is she now?"

For the first time, Hannah starts to tear up. "She's with my mom."

"Well, I'm not a family law lawyer, but they're asking the court to give the state temporary custody for now. This means they'll be asking for permanent custody later."

"How? How can they do this?"

"They're probably doing this to pressure you to plead guilty. They know you can't do anything since you're locked up in here charged with murder. They put your daughter with some strange family, and they get you to plead guilty just to protect your daughter."

Hannah starts crying. "I can't lose my baby. She's all I've got. I'll die if I lose her."

"There's an emergency hearing scheduled next week."

"I saw that."

"I don't know what to tell you. I'm here for the criminal case. You need a good family law attorney. Even if you hire an attorney, it's pretty hard to do anything if you're not at the hearing."

"Can't I bond out?"

"It's highly unlikely. I know this judge. He never grants bail in a murder case."

Wiping her tears and unable to stop crying, Hannah says, "This is a nightmare. I did nothing wrong. I didn't kill anyone. All I did was take care of Jackson and my baby. She's my life. She's my whole life. If I lose her, I'll just die."

Trying to change the subject, Zimmerman asks, "How are they treating you here?"

"Everyone's nice, as long as you do what they say. But I'm in prison. I sit around all day with nothing to do. I pretty much stay to myself. The food is terrible here. I have to shower in front of a bunch of women I don't even know. It's pretty humiliating. I feel like I'm losing my mind in here."

Zimmerman shakes his head and says, "Yeah, I understand."

"How soon can I get to trial?"

"These courts are pretty backed up. It's taking a year and a half, two years, to get to court."

Now Hannah really cries. "Two years? At least my mom brings Savannah to see me every week. I'll never see her if they put her in foster care. She won't even recognize me in two years."

With Hannah crying, Zimmerman simply looks at his watch and says, "Look, Ms. Kennedy, I've got to go. I'm scheduled to talk with Mr. Brunick in the morning." He hands the custody papers back and says, "Right now, we need to get you out of here."

Hannah takes the papers and stands up with teary eyes. "Thank you for representing me."

"You're welcome, but it's Mr. Brunick who'll represent you. Your next appearance is a week from Wednesday. We'll talk more then."

Zimmerman pushes a buzzer, and an officer comes in to take Hannah back to her cell.

# – CHAPTER 24 –

Zimmerman calls Ryan back two days later. Ryan spends every morning in prayer and meditation out by the firepit. When he hears the call, he runs to his phone.

"Hey, Mark," he says, breathing heavily.

"Hi, Ryan. Sorry I didn't call you yesterday. I met with the prosecutor. He gave me the discovery in the case. By the time I got out of there, it was too late to call."

"What'd you find?" Ryan asks.

"Well, it doesn't look good. They got plenty. They allege Hannah was the last person to see this guy. They have texts showing he was on his way to meet with her. They got Hannah's cell phone pinging off the cell phone tower where Jackson disappeared. They know he arrived because he was wearing her wedding ring when he died. Are you aware she talked to the police?"

"Yeah, I heard that."

"Well, evidently, she admitted that she knew he was having an affair. She said something very incriminating."

"What's that?"

"She said they'll never find him. This sounds pretty bad. How would she know where he is?"

"Hmm," Ryan says.

"She bought a gun five months before he was killed. She paid for the gun with her damn credit card. Oh…and her computer is full of searches about those hiking trails."

"Is that it?"

"Evidently things weren't as rosy as Hannah let on. They have an email and a few text messages a couple of days before he disappeared with some pretty testy exchanges. You know, the usual stuff. One last thing. A neighbor next door to the Aspen home says she saw Hannah and Jackson together the same day Hannah said he never showed up. It's all circumstantial, but pretty incriminating. Did you know Jackson had a million-dollar life insurance policy, and she was the beneficiary?"

"I had no idea."

"Well, she bought a policy six months before the murder. I think she was planning this for quite a while."

Ryan takes it all in without saying anything.

"What about this neighbor? Do you want me to go over there and talk to her?"

"Nah," Ryan answers. "I have an excellent investigator. I'll send him to Aspen to handle it. He'll talk to all the neighbors. He'll go out to those trails. If there's anything to find, he'll find it."

"Sounds good," Zimmerman says. "I'll email these papers to you. Take a look for yourself. If you ask me, they got a damn strong case. I'm not sure what there is to try. This is a case I'd definitely plead out. Do you want me to work on a plea?"

"Where are they at now?"

"You know, they're screaming capital murder. Maybe they'll go life in prison without the possibility of parole."

"Tell them she's wanting a plea. At every hearing, try your best to get them lower and lower. Tell them you don't want to try the case. Make them believe you're scared to death. I don't want them to think for a second we'd ever try this case."

"Will do," Zimmerman says.

"How's Hannah doing?"

"Not so good. She got served with custody papers. The state filed to take her kid and put her in foster care. Do you think they'd actually do that? Would they take a little baby away from her grandma and put her with strangers?"

With disgust, Ryan says, "They don't give a shit. It's all a game to them. They do this all the time. They want to put as much pressure on her as possible. You want your kid out of foster care? Plead out and we'll give her back to your mother."

"That's what I told her."

"Does she expect us to help her with her daughter?"

"I don't think so. I let her know she needs a family law attorney to take care of it."

"How long is it taking to get to trial there?"

"It's pretty backed up. Most people I represent don't want to go to court. They're happy to continue the case. I'd say at least two years. Since she's in custody, her case will take precedent. If you press it, maybe a year."

"I tell you what, we'll file a motion for our constitutional right to a speedy trial."

"But what about all this plea business? I thought we want them to think we're not going to court."

"You've never won a criminal trial…right?"

"Well, I did get a hung jury once. I got this bleeding heart juror to buck all the rest. After the trial, my guy took a plea. He swore he was innocent, but I got him to take involuntary manslaughter and fifteen years."

"We'll file the motion," Ryan says. "They'll think you're bluffing."

"You know what? I'll tell the prosecutor I only filed it because my client ordered me to do it."

"Good job, Mark. Let's talk again after her next hearing."

"Yes, sir," Zimmerman says, before hanging up.

# – CHAPTER 25 –

Hope returns to California to finish her studies. When she explained the situation, they welcomed her back so she could graduate from Stanford. Her perfect GPA didn't hurt.

Three weeks later, she calls her dad and Grace to catch up. She's so happy she's practically giddy. Blake moved up from Los Angeles and now they're living together. Hope knows nothing about Hannah's case. After talking with Grace for a while, Ryan gets on the phone.

"Hey, baby," Ryan begins. "How you doing?"

"Good."

"How was your flight back?"

"Not bad. We made pretty good time."

"Good. How's Blake?"

"He's wonderful! Dad, he's so sweet. He picked me up at the airport and we're planning our wedding."

"How long have you guys been together now?"

"Almost four years. We're going to get married right after I graduate."

"Four years…well that's good. You're a smart girl and I hear he loves you. You obviously love him, too."

"He wants to meet you. You'll be at my graduation, right?"

"Of course."

"Then you can meet him there."

"What about his parents? Do they approve?"

"They love me."

"Of course they do."

"They're not too hot on us living together. They're Catholic and look down on it. I think they're looking the other way since we're about to get married."

"What about kids? Have y'all talked about this?"

"Oh yeah. We both want two or three kids, but not right away. Right now, we're free. We want to travel. We want to get to know each other first. Then we'll think about kids."

"Sounds great, as long as you're on the same page. Hope, you have to talk about these things. I know you're in love, but you must have the same interests, like the same things, want the same things out of life. Be true to yourself."

"I know, I know, Dad. Don't worry. You don't have to keep saying this."

"I know, but it's important. Ask the tough—."

"The tough questions," she repeats at the same time.

"He's about to graduate too…right?"

"He got a degree in environmental science. Now he's graduating with a master's in environmental engineering. He's applied for a job at the EPA and the California Environmental Agency. I love hearing him talk about it all. He really wants to make a difference."

"And what about you? You're going to continue your studies, right?"

"You know, I've been thinking about that. I wanted to go to grad school, but now I've been thinking about law school."

"Law school? Where'd that come from?"

"I wonder," she laughs. "You know, I want to make a difference too. I think the best way to do that is as a lawyer."

"I hoped all the work and stress you kids saw me go through scared you away from law school. It's a hard way to make a living."

"You don't think I can do it?"

"Of course you can. With your grades at Stanford, you'll probably get into any law school you want. I think you'll be an awesome lawyer. It can be rewarding, but living with everyone's most difficult problems on your shoulders is tough."

"Well, I'm taking the LSAT in two months. We'll see how it goes."

"Let me know," Ryan says.

"Of course."

"How are you doing for money?"

"The money you gave me is more than enough. With Blake paying half the bills, it will last awhile."

"Sounds good, Sweetie. I'm really proud of you."

"Okay, Dad. I better let you go."

"Hey, Hope," Ryan says, trying to catch her.

"Yeah?"

"How's your back?"

"I don't know what's the matter. I must have pulled something. The whole ride home, it was killing me."

"I think you need to get it checked out."

"I don't have health insurance."

"Don't worry about it. Put it on your credit card."

"I just got some ointment for sprains at the pharmacy and some pain medicine they recommended. Let me see if this medicine helps. If it doesn't go away, I'll get it checked out."

"Good deal. Okay, Sweetie, have a good day. Love you."

"Love you, too."

# CHAPTER 26

Three weeks after Grace started staying with her dad, she finally meets Pam. They're eating lunch in the kitchen when she drives up and rings the doorbell. Ryan answers the door to her smiling face.

"Ryan," she says, jumping forward, wrapping her arms around his neck, and giving him a kiss. "How you been?"

"I've been good," Ryan says, holding each side of her slender waist and moving her back a step. He turns to the kitchen and says, "My daughter and grandbabies came to visit."

She looks around Ryan and spots Grace and the children sitting at the table. She gives them a wave and a big smile. In the most beautiful British accent, she says, "Hey, guys. So nice to finally meet you. You're all your dad talks about."

Pam looks younger than Grace. She has on a pink tank top, tiny white shorts, some pretty leather sandals, and she's holding a large beach bag. It's all pretty normal dress for around here.

She leans in to Ryan's ear that's facing away from the kitchen and whispers, "I've been calling and texting you, Sweetie."

Ryan smiles, and says, "We took a little trip. We went down the Amalfi coast."

She lifts up on her tiptoes, claps her hands with a smile, and says, "I just love the Amalfi coast."

Grace raises her eyebrows and gives a closed smile as if to say, *"Well, isn't that wonderful!"*

Pam turns back to Ryan and asks, "Are you going to introduce me, silly man?"

They walk to the kitchen. Ryan points to Grace and says, "This is my oldest daughter, Grace. Grace, this is Pamela. She goes by Pam."

Grace extends her hand and they shake. "Nice to meet you, Pam"

Pam gives her a full smile, and says, "So, you're a nurse?"

"A doctor," Grace answers.

Without correcting herself, Pam turns to Bonnie and says, "And this beautiful little angel must be Bonnie." She reaches down, tapping Bonnie on her nose. "I've heard so much about you!"

Ryan looks at Grace, who's watching in amazement. He ruffles Wesley's hair and says, "And this is Wesley."

Pam reaches down to Wesley, who's eating in his high chair, pinches his cheeks, and says, "Oh my God. You look just like your grandpa. You're just the cutest thing I've ever seen."

Wesley starts to cry but stops when Pam pulls away. They stand for a second and Ryan asks, "So….would you like to join us for lunch?"

"Ahh," she says with a smile. "I'd love to, but I just ate. Can I lay out by the pool while you guys finish?"

Ryan stammers for a second and says, "Uh…sure."

She walks right into Ryan's bedroom and comes out a second later in an all-white bathing suit that leaves very little to the imagination. It's obvious looking at her beautiful brown skin that she's spent plenty of time in the sun.

"I like your bathing suit," Bonnie says. "It's so pretty."

With a big smile, she twirls around and says, "Thank you, love."

She walks out the back door, and Ryan sits down to finish his lunch.

Grace breaks the silence by smiling at Ryan and says, "Boy, she sure has a lot of energy."

"I like her," Bonnie chimes in.

Ryan picks up Bonnie's fork, puts some macaroni and cheese in her mouth, and says, "Eat your lunch, Sweetie."

When her food is almost gone, Bonnie says, "I want to go swimming, Grandpa."

Ryan helps her down from the table. She runs into her room and comes out in her pink, one-piece bathing suit with mermaids across the front and ruffles above her waist. Very different from the bathing suit Pam just modeled.

They walk to the glass wall overlooking the pool down below and see Pam lying in a lawn chair with big sunglasses and earbuds in her ears. She has one leg slightly above the other, tapping to the rhythm of the song in her ears. Her long dark legs match her flat, tanned stomach and small breasts. Even Grace is captivated by her beauty. Sitting beside her is a bottle of tanning oil and bottled water.

Ryan starts to unlock the door but sees Pam has left it unlocked. He'll talk with her about that. Bonnie waits beside her grandpa, ready to go swimming. Before he opens the door, Grace looks at Pam and says, "Smart girl."

"Stop it," Ryan says with a laugh, taking Bonnie by the hand and leading her out to the pool.

"Well," Grace continues. "If she takes off her top, we're out of here."

## – CHAPTER 27 –

Over the next two months, Hannah's case moves pretty quickly. The judge got the motion for a speedy trial and set the case four months away. The investigator spent two weeks in Aspen talking to everyone. He got in Jackson's car and searched for anything, taking swabs of every speck of dirt, dust, and flake of skin. There were two blood samples that came back as Jackson's.

"I've been good," Zimmerman responds.

"How's our case down there?"

"The prosecutors think it's open and shut. At the last hearing, they offered forty years. She'll be eligible for parole in twenty-five. They have a little sympathy for her since her husband was such a shit."

"Not bad," Ryan says, wanting encourage him.

"That's what I do," Mark says. "I told Hannah, and she asked what I thought."

"What'd you tell her?"

"I told her it was a great deal for murder."

"And what'd she say?"

"You know, she's scared. Really, she doesn't know what to do. If she takes this deal, she'll be fifty-five when she gets out. Her daughter will be a grown woman. But if she gets life, she'll never see her again. She asked me what you think."

Ryan gives it some thought and says, "As you know, in the end, it's her decision."

"Yeah, I told her that."

"But tell her my advice is to refuse the deal."

"Refuse the deal?" Zimmerman asks. "I don't think they'll go down any further. I've done everything I can."

"Mark, there are considerations you don't really know about. I'll have to try this one."

"You're kidding. You're still going to try this case? What have you got? Did your investigator find the smoking gun?"

"Not really. I was hoping for more. The witness isn't quite as strong as her statement seems. The prosecutor pressed her to narrow down the day she saw Hannah and Jackson together to that weekend. After all this time, she can't be certain. I think she'll back down at trial. Otherwise, there wasn't a lot."

"Then you got nothing?" Zimmerman asks.

"I didn't get much, but sometimes nothing is our best friend. You just gotta present it that way."

"What way?"

"Mark, too many lawyers get hung up on some evidence in the case and it scares them away—especially if it's strong. They focus all their attention on what's there. I usually make more points on what's not there."

"I don't follow you."

"Keep in mind, the evidence you find is limited by reality. The evidence you don't find is limited only by your efforts and your imagination."

"Ohhhh," Zimmerman says like he gets it when, in truth, he has no idea what Ryan's talking about.

Sensing this, Ryan says, "Mark, these people are putting their lives in your hands. They're counting on you. *Think, think, think.* Have you ever heard the story about the kid who wanted a new bike for Christmas?"

"A bike for Christmas?"

"Sometimes I use this when I'm talking to jurors. This kid wanted a bike for Christmas that his dad couldn't afford. So, his dad took the newspaper he was reading and found a long, boring financial article that his son could never understand. His son could barely read. He tore it into a bunch of small pieces and told his son he'd give him the bike if he can put it back together in less than five minutes."

"That's cold," Zimmerman says.

"This boy picked up the pieces, grabbed some tape, and sat them on the kitchen table. Four minutes later, he came back and the whole article was taped together in perfect order."

"What?" Zimmerman laughs.

"Exactly! His dad looked at the article and said, 'How'd you ever do this?'"

With wide eyes, Zimmerman says, "I can't wait to hear this."

"'It was easy,' his son says with a big smile. He flips the paper over and says, 'There was this picture on the other side. I put the picture together so you could read your story.'"

"Son of a bitch!" Zimmerman laughs.

"That's what you gotta' do," Ryan says. "Never stop looking. Never give up. Flip things over. Look at the other side of things. You'd be surprised at what you find. They say what's there…you say what's not there."

"So…you're trying the case?" Zimmerman asks again.

"I am," Ryan confirms.

"And you think you can win?"

"That's a different question. That's a question I can't answer."

"You don't think she's innocent, do you?"

"Mark, have you had clients you think were innocent?"

"A few," Zimmerman says, "That's why I work to get them a good deal."

"After that hung jury you told me about, when they put handcuffs on your guy and led him away, how'd it make you feel?"

Zimmerman thinks about it for a second and says, "How'd I feel? I don't know. I was doing my job. I didn't think anything about it."

"Mark, I was in court one day, watching a trial and really thought the guy didn't do it. His lawyer missed so many things that I saw just watching the trial. His closing argument was so mechanical and impersonal—no passion or feeling. When this guy was found guilty, I almost cried. I'll never forget it. He got fifty years. If I had a guy I thought was innocent go to prison, it'd haunt me for the rest of my life. I'd probably give up my law practice and spend all my time trying to get him out."

"Damn," Zimmerman says.

"It's that serious. Their life is in your hands. Do I think she's innocent? I do. Do I think I'll win? I can never guarantee that. Do I think I'll kill myself and do everything possible to make sure she doesn't go to prison? You bet your ass I will!"

# – CHAPTER 28 –

Two weeks later, Ryan and Pam are relaxing by the pool when Ryan's cell phone rings. He almost doesn't take the call because he doesn't recognize the number. Since it's from the San Francisco area code, he picks it up and gives the caller a puzzled, "Hello?"

"Mr. Brunick?"

"This is him."

"Mr. Brunick, this is Blake. Hope asked me to call you."

Ryan can hear the fear in his voice. "Is everything okay?" he asks.

"I don't think so, Mr. Brunick. Hope is in the hospital."

"What!" Ryan says, sitting up on the edge of his pool chair.

"She's been having this pain in her abdomen. Last night, it got pretty bad and she had a fever. I didn't know what to do. I rushed her to the hospital."

"You did right, Blake."

"I told her weeks ago to go to the doctor. She said she was too busy with school."

"So what's wrong?  What's the doctor saying?"

With his voice starting to crack, Blake says, "They won't talk to me, because I'm not a relative. They say it's her kidneys. She has an infection or something. They're talking about surgery. I don't know what to do, Mr. Brunick. I don't know—"

Ryan jumps up and says, "I'm on my way, Blake. Tell Hope I'll catch the next plane out."

"Thank you, Mr. Brunick."


The next day, Ryan, Grace, Bonnie, and Wesley walk into Hope's hospital room. Hope is lying there in bed, holding Blake's hand and looking miserable.

"Hi, Daddy," Hope says, when her dad peeks in.

Ryan walks closer with a reassuring smile and says, "Hi, Baby." When Blake stands up, Ryan extends his hand and says, "So, you must be Blake. I've heard so much about you."

Taking his hand, Blake says, "It's nice to finally meet you, Mr. Brunick."

Bonnie is holding Ryan's hand. Hope looks down at her, opens her arms wide, and says, "Bonnie! I miss you."

Seeing Hope lying there in the scary hospital bed, Bonnie cups her hands just below her mouth and asks, "Are you sick, Aunt Hope?"

"Just a little," Hope says, showing Bonnie a tiny space between her thumb and pointer finger. "But I'll be okay."

Grace takes Hope's hand, and says, "How you doing, sis?"

With a subtle shrug, Hope says, "Not too good."

"So, what's going on?" Ryan asks.

Wincing from the pain, Hope says, "It's my kidneys. I guess all my back pain was from a kidney infection."

Ryan touches her face and says, "So, you never went to the doctor?"

Hope shakes her head. "The back medicine was helping some. I thought it was going away."

Grace, looking concerned, asks, "Why didn't you tell me about this? How long have you had this pain?"

"A couple of months, I guess. I didn't make the connection. Like I said, I was hoping it was getting better."

The doctor comes into the room and says, "You must be Dad. I'm Dr. Carson."

They shake hands and Ryan asks, "What's wrong with my baby?"

The doctor takes a deep breath and says, "Well, she's had a kidney infection for quite a while. The kidneys are so important because they remove waste from the body. They filter about forty-five gallons of blood every day. So, when they stop working, waste and fluids build up. Then you get an infection."

"Okay," Ryan says, wanting to know more.

"It looks like one of her kidneys has shut down, and the other is also infected. At this point, we need to discuss our options."

"Of course," Ryan says. "And what are her options?

"We need to consider dialysis or a kidney transplant."

"Okay, and what's the considerations?"

"Hope is young. If we go with dialysis, it could hold her over for the next ten or fifteen years."

"And the transplant?"

"The transplant is more permanent. If everything goes well, and her body accepts the kidney, she should be okay for a long time—maybe for the rest of her life. Not only do people who get transplants usually live longer, they also tend to have a better quality of life. They don't have to worry about dialysis, and they have fewer long-term health problems from the transplant than people have with dialysis. They tend to have more energy. Also, dialysis is hard on the body. It can cause problems ranging from anemia, where you have fewer red blood cells, to heart disease."

"And the transplant?"

"Any surgery has risks, like bleeding or an infection. Not common, but you need to know about it. The biggest problem is finding a donor kidney. The body could reject the kidney, which will put her back on dialysis. Hope will be on medicine, probably for the rest of her life, to prevent this. The medicine we have today is great. She should be fine."

"Then why do so many people have dialysis?"

"Mostly, because there are more people needing kidneys than there are donors. Many people go on dialysis because they have to. They have no other choice while they're on a waiting list for a donor kidney. For them, dialysis is a lifesaver."

Ryan nods his head and says, "Then it sounds like a no-brainer."

Hope and Grace each nod in agreement.

"So, how do we find a donor?" Ryan asks.

"We test for what we call an antigen match. The best match is someone who matches twelve out of twelve. It's pretty simple. We test blood and do additional saliva tests."

Ryan shakes his head while asking, "Do we have to test for a donor? Are there kidneys already out there that could be a match?"

"It doesn't really work like that. We first try to find a donor. Siblings have a twenty-five percent chance of being an exact match, and a fifty percent chance of being a half-match."

Grace jumps up, wanting to lighten things up, and says, "Well, let's go! I'm ready to donate!"

Doctor Conner smiles and says, "Data shows that a living parent is the optimal match. Because of the way chromosomes are inherited or passed down in a family, a parent and child would have at least a 50 percent chance of matching, especially if the parent is in good health. Whenever possible, we test the parent to find a matched donor."

Grace turns to Ryan, and says, "Well, let's go!"

Dr. Conner steps back and says, "Great, let's get that set up."

## – CHAPTER 29 –

After Dr. Conner walks out, Grace turns back to Hope. Squeezing her hand, she says, "Don't worry, sis. Everything's going to be okay. We got you covered."

Bonnie asks to get up on the bed, so Grace lifts her up and sits her beside Hope. She taps on Hope's cheek and says, "I got a new bathing suit, Aunt Hope."

Hope smiles and says, "Oh, wonderful. What color is it?"

"Yellow."

"Oh, I love yellow. What's it look like?"

"It's two-piece!"

"Two piece…two piece!" Hope teases.

"It's just like Pam's."

Hope looks at Grace and asks, "Who's Pam?"

Grace leans over and whispers, "We'll have to talk about Pam."

As they wait to hear back from Dr. Conner, Ryan goes over to the window and looks out. After a few minutes, Hope asks, "Are you okay, Dad?"

Still looking away, Ryan nods his head.

"Hope's going to be okay," Grace says. "Between you and me, we'll find a match."

Ryan turns around. His eyes are red and filled with tears. He leans back against the windowsill and says, "Grace, can we talk outside for a minute?"

"Sure," Grace says, standing up.

"Wait," Hope says, sitting up in the bed. "What's the matter?"

"It's nothing," Ryan says, putting his hand on Grace's shoulder for her to follow him out. "I just need to talk to Grace in private."

"In private?" Hope says with a scowl. "If it involves me, I want to hear it."

"It's nothing," Ryan repeats. "She's a doctor and I have a few questions. Bonnie doesn't need to hear everything….if you know what I mean."

Feeling something isn't right, Hope reaches both hands down to the bed, pulls herself up, and says, "Stop it, Dad!"

Ryan looks away and says, "Okay….it's stupid really. I just think Grace will probably make a better match since she's your sister. Let's test her first and see if she's a match."

Hope gives Blake a quick glance and then looks over at Grace, as if to say, *Am I going crazy?* She shakes her head at her dad and says, "What the hell are you talking about?"

"Nothing," Ryan says, "Let's just test Grace and see."

Hope looks back at Grace and tears up. Wiping her tears away, she says, "So, you don't want to help me? When I need you the most, you don't care?"

"It's not tha—"

Visibly shaking and about to cry, she screams, "Just go! Just go and we'll test Grace. Don't worry about it. If Grace isn't a match, I'll find someone else."

With his eyes tearing up and his chin quivering, Ryan walks over and picks Bonnie up from the bed. Holding her in his arms, he kisses her cheek and walks out of the room.

Once the door closes, Hope really lets go. With tears streaming down her cheeks, she shouts, "What the fuck. I stood by him. After all this…this *shit*, I stood by him."

Grace holds her hand and lets her cry. Blake sits in his chair with his head covered by his hands, doing his best to understand it all.

"The last day I was there, I told him I loved him. No matter what he did, I told him I'll always love him."

Grace looks up, shakes her head, and says, "I don't get it."

"Well, I've had enough of this crazy shit," Hope says. "I'm done."

Grace takes a deep breath and says, "Right now, you just need to get better."

"I'm sorry," Hope says. "I'm done with him. When I get out I'll never talk to him again."

Ryan walks back into the room without Bonnie and looks at Hope who's in tears.

"What?!" Hope asks like she's disgusted at the sight of her dad.

Ryan pulls up a chair beside Grace and looks down.

"What?" Hope repeats a little softer. "What do you want?"

Ryan sits down and says, "Hope, I don't know how to say this."

"What have you done now?" Hope cries out. "Just say it!"

"Hope," Ryan says slowly, before stopping.

"Oh my God," Hope continues. "I'm sick of all these lies. Please get out of my room."

"Hope," Ryan continues, "I don't think I'll be a suitable donor."

Grace looks over with her eyes open wide. Blake looks up with a puzzled look.

"Then don't," Hope yells. "I told you….I don't give a damn. I'd rather find some stranger out there to donate his kidney."

Ryan lowers his head and starts crying. He looks back up and says, "Hope….I thought this day would never come. The truth is, I know I won't be a suitable donor."

Hope starts to shout back for him to get the hell out of the room, but she stops herself in shock. She covers her mouth with her hand. You can see her fingers shaking. Grace takes hold of her other hand to steady her. Brushing one tear away after another, Hope asks, "What are you saying?"

Seeing his daughter crying breaks Ryan's heart. He bends over and cries out loud. Gasping for breath, he says, "I love…I love you, Hope. I've always loved you."

"You're not my—"

Still crying and looking down, Ryan shakes his head in his hands.

"Oh my God," Hope whispers. Then she shouts, "OH MY GOD!"

Blake leans over Hope and holds her in his arms. Grace lets go of Hope and wraps her arms around her crying dad. Doing her best to comfort him, she starts crying too.

Wiping her eyes, Hope asks, "How long have you known?"

It takes a minute for Ryan to talk again. "Three months after we split up. I was so broken. I spent all my time going over our whole marriage in my mind—the arguments, the good times, the bad times, all the things I wish I could change. About the time she got pregnant with you, we had been arguing and were a little distant. I was in a trial out of town that lasted weeks, and we didn't talk the whole time, which wasn't normal. We hadn't had sex in weeks. So after we split up, I started wondering about it all. Then I did it. I swabbed your mouth and found out."

"Oh my God," Hope repeats. "Did mom know you found out? Did you ever tell her?"

Ryan shakes his head. "I could never let her know. I didn't want anyone to know. I wanted to pretend like it wasn't true."

"Why?" Hope asks.

"I was so afraid if you found out, it'd ruin everything between us."

Hope looks down and wipes her nose. Still crying, she looks up, and says, "I'd never do that."

Ryan gets up from the chair and puts his arms around Hope. They're both crying when Ryan says, "You're my baby. That will never change."

"I love you, Dad," Hope gets out. "I love you so much."

After holding each other until everyone stops crying, Ryan sits back down and wipes his eyes.

"So that's why," Hope says, "That's why you—"

Ryan shakes his head and says, "I can't go back there. It's too painful."

Hope turns to Grace and asks, "So, you didn't know?"

Grace shakes her head.

Hope turns back to her dad and asks, "Why didn't you say something? All this time, you held it inside. Why didn't you tell us? If I knew, I wouldn't have been so—"

Ryan takes a breath and says, "You kids mean more to me than anything else in the world. I didn't want this divide between us. There was one other person who knew—my lawyer who represented me in my divorce case. There was a moment in our custody trial when he wanted to use it, but it wasn't so simple. If I wasn't your father, I could never get legal custody of you. I was actually afraid your mom would reveal everything in the middle of the case just to win custody. If I wasn't your father, I might win the other kids, but I'd lose you. I couldn't do that. I told my lawyer to stop, even if it meant losing *all* you kids."

Still in pain, Hope climbs down from the bed and sits on her dad's lap. She puts her arms around his neck, and they hold each other for a few minutes. Grace and Blake stand there looking on, not sure what to say.

Hope looks at her dad and asks, "Do you know who my dad is?"

"I have no idea," Ryan lies to his daughter.

The truth is, he does know who her dad is. After finding out this horrible truth, he searched through all of Faith's phone, email, text, and credit card records from the time when he was out of town. There were calls going back four months to Houston, Texas. Faith's credit card had charges for an expensive downtown hotel room for the weekend and charges for dinner at a fancy restaurant. When Ryan asked the hotel for the room charges, it showed a man named Jake Walker also stayed in the same room. This is how Ryan learned the last name of Faith's first boyfriend. The driver's license Ryan had his investigator pull showed his hair was dark black and his eyes were green.

Beginning to cry again, Hope says, "I'm glad I know. I'm glad I know what you've been through. It only makes me love you more. You raised me. You've always been there for me. That's what matters. No matter what, you'll always be my dad."

Gently touching Hope's face, another tear falls down Ryan's cheek. With trembling lips, he says, "You'll always be my daughter."

Wiping her eyes clear, Hope says, "Nothing's changed. I only love you more."

# – CHAPTER 30 –

The tests show Grace to be a match for Hope's transplant. Not a perfect match, but her blood and tissue type is compatible with Hope's. The procedure goes well, and Hope's hospital stay is pretty short. Five days later, she's back home resting.

She can't lift things for a few weeks, but otherwise she's back to her normal activities. The doctor made it clear she wouldn't have any fertility problems. After her body has plenty of time to heal, she should be able to have a healthy baby.

Ryan stays in an Airbnb with Grace, Bonnie, and Wesley in a little town just south of San Francisco called Carmel. It's this charming little town with cute little roads, cottage-style houses, beautiful restaurants, shops, and galleries all over town, and a beach with white sand that overlooks Pebble Beach. Clint Eastwood was once the mayor.

Ryan sets everything up under his new passport name, James Lincoln. He invites Blake down for a few days so he can get to know him better. They immediately hit it off. Blake tells the story about that first day when he met Hope—well, not the whole story. Ryan has no doubt Blake loves his little girl. He gives his full approval.

Grace put her house up for sale, since she no longer has a reason to be in Dallas. She sold the Aspen house long ago. Now she spends all her time with Hope, helping her get ready for her wedding.

Six weeks later, Hope graduates from Stanford University with Blake, Ryan, Grace, Bonnie, and Wesley cheering in the stands. She walks up the stairs, takes the diploma in her hands, and raises her diploma in the air to the crowd.

Two months later, Ryan is wearing a tux, standing at the front of the church, waiting for Hope to make her appearance in the entryway. Grace is her maid of honor and Bonnie's her flower girl and holds an enormous bouquet of flowers. A tear falls down Ryan's cheek as the entire crowd looks back, and the most beautiful bride walks up to him, kisses him on the cheek, and wraps her arm through his arm.

They walk together down the aisle and stop in front of the preacher. Blake is standing tall to the right with all of his friends beside him. The preacher looks at Ryan and says, "And who gives this bride away?"

Wiping the tears from his eyes, Ryan says, "Her father. Her father gives her away."

# – CHAPTER 31 –

Ryan spends all of his time inside the rental home except when he goes to the grocery store. He made sure the house has a swimming pool to keep the kids busy. As far as he's concerned, he never needs to leave. He has a lot of catching up to do.

Once Hope and Blake leave on their honeymoon, Grace comes back to Carmel. Sitting out by the pool, Ryan says, "I need to go visit Hannah."

"When?" Grace asks.

"I'll go next week. I'll just go for the day and come right back."

"I want to go with you," Grace says.

"It's probably better you stay here. Just stay here and watch the kids."

Grace shakes her head and says, "She's in jail because of me. I want to see her. I want to talk to her."

"Honestly, I'm afraid you might say something that will hurt what I'm doing."

"What would I say?" Grace asks.

"Well, for starters, don't say anything that would lead to your involvement with the murder."

"Of course," she says.

"We'll be with Zimmerman, and he's soaking everything up. So be careful."

"I will," she agrees.

"Then I guess it can't hurt for you to go. I'm sure it will be nice for Hannah to see you again."


Four days later, they meet at Mark Zimmerman's office. After all the introductions, Ryan lets Zimmerman know Grace will be going with them to the jail. "She's my legal assistant," Ryan says with a wink.

They drive over to the jail and through the metal detectors. No one even questions why Grace is there. Once inside, they wait for Hannah. Fifteen minutes later, she comes in wearing her prison outfit.

"Hannah!" Grace says, walking up and giving her a hug.

"Hi, Grace," Hannah says, not near as excited. "Thanks for coming."

It's sad seeing her in here. Before she was arrested, Hannah was so upbeat. She dressed classy; she looked classy. The months behind bars have taken their toll. She looks exhausted.

Grace pulls back and asks, "You okay, Hannah?"

Hannah bites her lower lip and shakes her head. "No, I'm not okay at all," she says, beginning to tremble. "They took Savannah away from my mom. They had the hearing and my mom showed up, but she didn't have a lawyer. They said she can come back in forty-five days with a lawyer. In the meantime, they issued an emergency order. They took Savannah away from me."

Grace steps forward and holds her again. "I'm really sorry, Hannah."

Hannah has cried herself out. She sits down at the table and says, "I can't believe they can do this. My daughter was fine with my mom. Now they'll put her with some stranger? It makes no sense at all." She lowers her head near the table and grabs a handful of hair in each hand. "Things have gone too far. I never thought this would happen."

Ryan comes around and sits beside her. He gently puts his arm against her back and says, "Hannah, my name is Ryan Brunick. I'm so sorry for everything you're going through."

Maybe it's the love in his voice, or the feel of his hand on her back that warms her to him. Maybe it's him calling her by name. Hannah looks up and embraces him in a hug. If Ryan had a dime for every hug he's received, he'd be an even richer man. Ryan can feel her crying and doesn't try to stop her. Grace comes around and kisses her on the head. Zimmerman watches it all.

Finally, Hannah looks up, wipes her nose, and says, "Hi, Mr. Brunick."

"I thought you hired a family law attorney," Ryan says. "I would have helped you if I knew."

"I thought I asked," Hannah says, looking at Zimmerman.

Zimmerman nods his head and says, "Yeah…I said you'd need a family law attorney."

Ryan takes both her hands in his and says, "I'm so sorry."

"Can you get my baby back?" she asks.

"Your trial will be over before the next custody hearing. Let's take care of that first, okay?"

Hannah nods her head.

"How's everything else?" he asks.

"Nothing else matters," Hannah answers. "The bank is foreclosing on my home, but it's the least of my problems."

"Okay," Ryan says. "I can help you there. Do you have the papers?"

She searches through her stuff and pulls out the foreclosure papers she was served months ago. Ryan hands the papers to Grace and says, "We'll handle this."

Hannah looks at Ryan and says, "I didn't kill Jackson. I know you hear this all the time, but you've got to believe me."

Ryan glances at Grace and says, "I believe you. We just gotta get a jury to believe you."

"Can you do that?" she asks.

"I'll sure try."

Hannah has lots of questions. "Is it true you've never lost?"

Ryan shakes his head and says, "That doesn't really matter, does it? All that matters right now is your case."

Grace sits on the other side of Hannah, and says, "No, he's never lost."

Now Ryan moves to the other side of the table to give him room to work. Zimmerman stays a few feet away watching Ryan work.

"I'm pretty up to date on your case," Ryan begins. "Mark has updated me on everything. We need to go over a few things."

Hannah sits up straight and says, "Good. I'm glad you came. I'm really afraid I might say the wrong thing and mess the case up."

Shaking his head, Ryan says, "You won't be testifying."

Hannah looks up pretty confused, and says, "But I want to testify. I want to tell them I would never kill anyone."

"Hannah, I know you're smart, but you're in something you've never been in before. It's not like a normal conversation. You don't get to tell your story like you're talking to a neighbor. These prosecutors have years of training and experience. They'll spend weeks going through every question to trip you up. It's not a fair fight. You have to answer their questions without really explaining. I've never had a client testify in a criminal case. How about you let me talk for you? I'll say everything you want to say. I'm pretty educated myself. I'll make sure they know."

Hannah nods her head and whispers, "Thank you."

"Now, how many times have you been to this vacation home in Aspen?"

"Gosh, too many times to count. Jackson loved it there. Maybe thirty or forty."

"Do you have any texts or emails where Jackson talked about how much he loved it there?"

"I think so. I'll try to find them if you'll get my phone."

"Don't worry about it." He pulls out an authorization and says, "Just sign here. I have an investigator who'll go through your emails and texts. He'll find them."

"Great," Hannah says, signing the paper.

Ryan continues. "How many times did Jackson hike those trails?"

"All the time," she answers.

"Any texts or emails about it?"

"I'm sure. He often told me to meet him there so he can hike or fish."

"Great…we'll get those too. Unfortunately, the prosecutor also has everything. They have some messages about an argument you and Jackson had right before he disappeared."

"I know," Hannah says, "I was—"

"It's okay," Ryan says, stopping her. "I've got it covered. I just want you to know what's coming. I see there was a million-dollar life insurance policy."

"It was Jackson who—"

"I know," Ryan says. "I got it. I just have one question. I see you never filed a claim on the policy. Did you ever write or go into the insurance company and ask them about it?"

"No…should I have?"

"Wonderful," Ryan says, "Now, in the six months before Jackson disappeared, tell me the most expensive things you bought?"

This comes out of left field. "Let me think," Hannah begins. "I bought a new couch for the living room."

"Great, when was that? Did you put it on your credit card?"

"That would be April or May and yes, on my Visa."

"What else?"

"In May, I ordered some pretty expensive workout equipment online —also on my Visa."

"Great, what else?"

"Oh, I ordered a couple dresses from Nordstrom sometime in May. It was on my Nordstrom card."

"Okay."

Hannah looks over at Grace and says, "Jackson bought me these diamond earrings for my birthday. They were pretty expensive."

"Also, on your Visa?"

"Probably," Hannah says. "We had the same credit card.

"Anything else."

"Not really," she says.

"Okay," Ryan says with a smile. "What about this money Jackson stole? Did you know about the money?"

"I knew nothing," Hannah says.

Ryan looks right at her and says, "You have to be honest here. Do you have the money? Have you spent any?"

Hannah looks right into his eyes and says, "I knew nothing about it. I swear."

"Okay," Ryan says, relaxing a bit. "Now tell me about Savannah."

Hannah takes a deep breath and says, "She's my baby. I love her more than life itself. I was so happy when I learned I was pregnant. She was always with me. I quit working to take care of her. When I'm with—"

"Do you have any photos of you together?"

"I have the one my mom gave me. The rest are at my house."

"Do you have a key hidden somewhere?"

"I don't think so."

"No problem," Ryan says with a nod. "My investigator can get in. He'll get everything we need for the trial." Ryan smiles at Hannah and says, "Okay, I think that's about it. That wasn't so hard, was it?"

Zimmerman looks quite puzzled. He thought he'd be there for hours, going over everything.

Before leaving, Ryan asks, "One last thing. Have you ever heard a picture is worth a thousand words?"

Hannah nods her head.

"Well, you're not going to testify, but your body language will say plenty. I know you're smart, but in court it won't help a lot. All I need you to do is look like a mommy, okay?"

With a smile, Hannah says, "I think I can do that."

"Great. We'll be there all week."

"Will it be over that fast?"

"Your case isn't really complicated. It should take maybe four days. I hope the jury comes back by Friday."

"And I'll be going home?"

"Well, we sure hope so, don't we?"

Hannah nods again.

"All you have to do is look sweet. The jury will be watching you closely. One outburst, or dirty look, and it can undo all my work. The jury has to like you. If a juror looks at you, give him or her a very subtle smile. When the court addresses you, always say, 'Your Honor.' When the jury gets up to go out, stand tall and smile their way. I want you to make a connection. The prosecutor will say a lot of things you disagree with. Some lawyers will tell you to ignore it. I disagree. I'll give you a tablet. It's really there for two reasons. If they say something you disagree with, simply write anything you want on the tablet and pass it to me. The jurors will understand you disagree."

"And the other reason?" Hannah asks.

"If you get bored, you can draw pictures or write poems or something. Just don't let the jury seeing you drawing pictures."

"I can do that," Hannah says. Everyone laughs a little.

Ryan gets up, walks around the table, and puts his arm around her. "I'll take care of all the rest."

When Ryan breaks away, Hannah asks if she can talk to Grace for a minute. Ryan taps on the window for the guard and walks out with Zimmerman.

Out in the hall, Zimmerman turns to Ryan and says, "That was quick. I thought you'd go over everything. There are a lot of questions that need answers."

Ryan shakes his head and says, "Sometimes I'll spend weeks with a client. In this case, she knows nothing. She doesn't have a lot to contribute."

"So, your investigator will do all the testifying?"

Ryan laughs a little and says, "You've never met my investigator. He's an ex-cop—a real bulldog. He's the last person I'd put on the stand. He doesn't put up with much. He'd probably get in an argument with the prosecutor and pull a gun on him or something."

"Then who are our witnesses?"

"I don't plan on calling any witnesses in this case."

"No witnesses?" he asks.

Ryan gets this look on his face and says, "There are four truths in a case."

"Four truths?" Zimmerman asks.

"There's the truth from the prosecutor; there's the truth from the defense; there's what really happened; and then there's the truth that the jury believes. All I care about is the last one. I don't think Hannah can come up with any better answers than I can. During the trial, I'll be the one telling her truth."

"So, you got it all figured out?"

"I think so. There's just one thing I can't figure out for the life of me. Why was his car found at that gas station? How was he lured there? It just makes no sense."

Back inside, Hannah spends fifteen minutes talking to Grace. First, they talk about Bonnie, Wesley, and Savannah. Then they talk a lot about Jackson. At the end, she looks at Grace and says, "Your dad seems nice."

"He is," Grace says.

"I don't know. I'm scared. He barely asked me anything."

"I don't know," Grace says, as confused by this as everyone else.

"I can't go to prison," Hannah says. "I don't care about me, but it will ruin Savannah. Promise me…promise me if I go to prison, you'll make sure she goes back to my mom."

Grace takes her hand and says, "Savannah isn't going anywhere. You're going home and Savannah is going with you."

Still not convinced, Hannah says, "I hope he knows what he's doing."

"Don't worry," Grace says. "All I know is he doesn't lose. I've seen him try cases that looked hopeless. If I were the one on trial, I'd be sure he knows exactly what he's doing."

"Then I'm okay?"

Grace pats her hand and says, "You're better than okay."

# PART FOUR

---

# THE TRIAL

*I've always loved movies about con men. I think con men
are as American as apple pie.*

*—Bill Paxton*

*You must always bear in mind that your past is never
quite as finished with you as you think you are with it.*

*—Kathryn Kennish*

# – CHAPTER 32 –

A month later, Ryan, Zimmerman, and Grace walk into the courtroom ready to get things started. This is the biggest trial in Aspen in several decades. It has all the twisted and sordid details. The reporters are packed outside the courthouse, which Ryan is used to. It's all new to Zimmerman.

Doing his best to stay out of the spotlight, Ryan turns to Zimmerman, and says, "Why don't you handle the press? It'll do you good. Just keep telling them our client is innocent—nothing more."

When Ryan walks into the courtroom, the prosecutors are already sitting at the best table next to the jury box. Both lawyers always want this spot. Ryan first walks up to Hannah's mom and dad. He extends his hand to her father and says, "Hello, Tom. I'm Ryan Brunick. I'm sorry we weren't able to meet earlier."

"Are you going to take care of our little girl?" he asks.

"The best I can," Ryan says.

He turns to face Hannah's mom and greets her with a hug. "Hi, Ann. So nice to finally meet you. I see where Hannah gets her good looks."

She squeezes him tight. "Thank you, Mr. Brunick. Thank you so much for taking our case. I've heard good things about you. I want you to know we believe in you."

"I'll do the best I can," Ryan says. "I'm glad you made it. I know you came a long way. Your support will be very important in this trial."

Ryan walks up and introduces himself to the prosecutors with a handshake. He is well aware that this prosecutor is very good. He has never lost a murder trial.

"Hello," he says with a smile. "I'm Ryan Brunick."

The younger lawyer doesn't give it much thought. The lead attorney whispers in her ear like he's stunned. He pulls away and asks, "Mr. Brunick, you're involved in this case?"

"Just a little," Ryan says.

"Have you filed a notice of appearance?" he asks.

"I filed that last month," Ryan answers.

They pull out another file from their boxes and rifle through the papers like they might rip them right out of the binder. They pull out Ryan's filing and read over it.

Grace takes a seat in the gallery on the front row beside Hannah's parents. A few minutes later, Zimmerman walks in and takes a seat on the other side of Ryan. An officer from the Sherriff's office comes in escorting Hannah in handcuffs. He frees her, and she sits down.

Ryan turns to her and says, "You look lovely. I bet it feels good to get this started."

She takes a deep breath, lets it out slowly, and says, "You have no idea."

At exactly nine o'clock, the judge and the court reporter enter and take their place. "Good morning, Counselors. How is everyone today?"

Ryan already did plenty of research on this judge. He called around and talked to a few attorneys to find out his quirks. He stands up, walks to the judge's bench, and extends his hand. "Good morning, Judge. I'm Ryan Brunick. Very nice to meet you."

This has never happened to the judge in open court. He's not sure what to do with it. Then, he recognizes Ryan's name from the past television coverage and some articles in the State Bar Journal. He shakes Ryan's hand and says, "Nice to meet you, Mr. Brunick. What brings you to our little courthouse?"

Before Ryan can respond, the lead attorney walks up to the judge and says, "Your Honor, I think we have a problem."

"And what's that, Mr. Crane?"

"Mr. Brunick just filed his notice of appearance. We object to his involvement in this case."

Ryan doesn't respond.

"So, he did file a notice of appearance?" the judge asks. "When was it filed?"

Like they were already aware of the filing, the prosecutor says, "Just last month, Your Honor. But he hasn't attended a single hearing. We thought he was simply a consultant. It's our understanding he's going to participate in the trial. Well, we object."

This is the lamest objection Ryan has ever heard.

The judge recognizes just how silly this objection is. Even more, he knows it will be a treat to see Ryan in action, and he doesn't get many treats on the bench. "Well, we wouldn't want to deny the defendant the attorney of her choice, would we? I'm not sure how the court of appeals would view that."

"I guess not," the prosecutor concedes, losing his first objection.

"Then I'm going to overrule that objection."

"Thank you, Your Honor," Ryan says.

"All right. Let's do a little housecleaning first," the judge begins. Picking up his pen to take notes, he asks both attorneys, "How long do you expect this trial will last?"

The prosecutors look at each other. The lead attorney says, "We anticipate maybe ten days."

Ryan gives a smile, and says, "I'm sure this court's docket is pretty backed up. I think we can finish this case by Friday. I'd like to free you up before next week. We might have to work late here and there but I think we can do it."

"Thank you, Mr. Brunick," the judge says. "Let's shoot for Friday." He turns to the prosecutor and says, "How many witnesses do you anticipate?"

"At this time, I think the State will call five witnesses."

"And who is that?" the judge asks, ready to write the names down.

"Uhm....we will call Officer Brandon, Larry Franks, Beth Windham, Jackson Kennedy's brother, and Grace Kennedy."

"All right," the judge says, writing each name down. "And Mr. Brunick, how many witnesses do you anticipate?"

"Just one, Your Honor."

"And who is that?"

"Just the defendant, Hannah Kennedy." He turns to Hannah and says, "Why don't you introduce yourself?"

This revelation stuns Hannah. She stands up trembling and says, "Good morning, Your Honor."

The judge smiles back, and says, "I think we've met already."

"Well, I ruled on all the pre-trial motions on Friday. Why don't we bring the jury in and get this trial started? I'm giving you each two and a half hours for voir dire."

When Ryan sits back down, Zimmerman leans over and whispers, "So Hannah is going to testify?"

"Not on your life. But if the prosecutor thinks she's going to testify, they'll save some of their points for her."

The jury panel pours in one after another. Both Ryan and Hannah stand up and give each one a smile. Once everyone takes their seat, the judge greets them good morning. He thanks them for their service and reads his initial instructions. He questions the potential jurors to make sure they are qualified to serve. Once he's finished, he turns to the prosecutor and says, "Mr. Crane, I believe you go first."

Crane walks up to the podium and introduces himself, his co-counsel, Mr. Zimmerman, Mr. Brunick, and Hannah. Each stands with a smile when their names are called. He's calm and smooth. It's obvious he's done this many times. He explains how he represents the State. He's one of them. He describes Jackson's terrible death, how the burden is on them to prove their case, and questions the panel to make sure we can get a fair jury.

After three hours, the prosecutor thanks the panel and sits down. Ryan is impressed.

"Thank you, Mr. Crane," the judge says. "Why don't we break for lunch."

By 1:30, everyone is back in the courtroom. The judge looks at Ryan and says, "Mr. Brunick, I believe it's your turn."

Ryan stands up and thanks both prosecutors and the judge. Immediately, he makes a connection. Just the way he stands, addresses everyone, and walks to the podium is impressive. Hannah closes her eyes and sighs with confidence.

"Good morning ladies and gentleman. I know you have many other things you'd rather be doing than coming to this courthouse today. I thank you for joining us. It may be the most important thing you'll ever do in your life."

The jurors smile and say, "Hello."

"This beautiful lady over here is Hannah Kennedy. She goes by Hannah." He turns to Hannah and says, "Why don't you introduce yourself to the jury?"

Hannah stands up and says, "Hello."

"How are you doing today?" he asks.

"I'm pretty nervous."

Hannah sits back down and Ryan turns back to the jury. "I'm sure she's terrified. You see, she's charged with murder. Could you imagine being charged with murder?"

Everyone shakes their head.

"Well, luckily for Hannah, she sits here an innocent woman. You see, under the law, she's presumed innocent."

Most jurors look over at Hannah.

"This is the part of the trial we call voir dire. Voir dire is a Latin word that means 'to tell the truth.' This is the only time in the case I get to ask you questions. More important, it's the only time you get to talk to us until the very end. There are no right or wrong answers. All Mr. Crane and I ask is that you tell the truth."

The jurors start to sit back in their chairs and relax.

"I have one question for you right off. If right now the judge turned to you and said, 'Go back. Go back right now and decide whether Hannah is guilty or innocent.' How many of you could decide this case?"

Not a single juror raises their hand.

"Thank you for being honest. But the truth is, Hannah is clothed with the presumption of innocence like a warm blanket on a snowy night. If the judge asked you to go back and render a verdict, it'd be easy. You should all proudly say, 'Not guilty.'"

Now the jurors nod in agreement.

"So if the judge asked you to go back and render a verdict without hearing a single witness, you'd all come back and say—"

All together, they say, "Not guilty."

"Doesn't that feel good? Again, you'd all say…"

"Not guilty," they repeat.

"Well done!"

Ryan walks over and pulls out a poster that simply says in large print, "BURDEN OF PROOF" and places it on the easel. He turns back to the jury panel and says, "Just like the prosecutor said, they have the burden of proof. I don't have to do anything. I don't have to put on a witness, question any witnesses, show you any documents, or do anything. Hannah doesn't have to testify, and under the Constitution, she's not required to testify. I can just sit here and say nothing. I know it's hard to imagine, but I could sit here the whole trial without saying a word. "

Most of the jurors laugh a little.

"How many of you are thinking, *if you want me to find Hannah not guilty, you better do something…she better testify?* "

All the jurors shake their head, no.

"The prosecutor also told you they have to prove their case beyond a reasonable doubt. I'd like to talk about that for a minute." Ryan puts another chart on the easel, and says, "This chart shows the different legal standards in a case." He points to the bottom of the chart and says, "Way down here we have "REASONABLE SUSPICION." We use that standard before a police officer can stop and detain someone. They must have a reasonable suspicion that a crime was committed. Is there anyone here who would find Hannah guilty based only on a reasonable suspicion?"

No one responds.

"Of course not," Ryan continues. He points back at the poster board and says, "Next we have probable cause. What does that mean? An officer has to have probable cause to believe someone has committed a crime before they can arrest them—just like they arrested Hannah. All they had to have was probable cause to bring her in here today. Some of you might think she must be guilty if they arrested her. Does anyone feel like that? Does anyone fell that she must be guilty if she got arrested?"

No one answers at first. Then, a man in the back slowly raises his hand. "Mr. Dumas," Ryan says. "You feel this way?"

"I guess," Mr. Dumas answers. "I don't think they would have arrest her if they didn't have the evidence to prove it."

"Thank you for being honest, Mr. Dumas," Ryan says. "But to arrest someone all they needed was probable cause to arrest her. The jury decides if she's guilty beyond a reasonable doubt—like is required in this case."

"Oh, I understand," Mr. Dumas answers.

Ryan looks across the room and asks, "How many others feel like Hannah must be guilty if she got arrested?"

All the jurors shake their head, no.

"Very good," Ryan smiles, returning to the board. Pointing a little higher, he says, "Next, we have 'PREPONDERANCE OF EVIDENCE.' Preponderance of the evidence means more likely than not. We use this when someone is suing someone else. To win, they must prove their case is more likely than not."

Most of the jurors nod their heads.

"All right," Ryan says, looking out at the jury. "Let's be honest here. How many people, being honest, would say, 'The bottom line is, if I believe it's likely she did it. . .if I believe she probably did it. . .then I will vote guilty—plain and simple?"

A handful of jurors raise their hands.

Addressing each one individually, Ryan asks, "Even if the judge instructs you that Hannah must be guilty beyond a reasonable doubt, if you think she probably did it, you'd vote guilty?"

Four of these jurors nod their heads. One says, "Yes sir, I think I would."

The judge calls them to the bench and excuses them as possible jurors.

Ryan turns to the board and says, "Next we have 'CLEAR AND CONVINCING EVIDENCE.' We use this standard in cases, like when you're terminating someone's parental rights. The standard is clear and convincing." Ryan looks across at everyone in front of him and says, "This is when things get a really tough. Who here is thinking, 'If I feel the evidence is clear and convincing that she's guilty, then I'm voting guilty."

Twenty-nine potential jurors raise their hands.

"So," Ryan continues, "in this case the standard is beyond a reasonable doubt. But being honest here, if it's clear and convincing to you, you're voting guilty even if you have a doubt. Is that right?"

They all keep their hands up high. After a few more questions, the judge dismisses most of them.

Ryan turns back to the first juror and confirms, "Ms. Ramirez, after hearing all the evidence in this case, would you be able to vote not guilty even if you believe it's more likely than not that Hannah committed the crime?"

She looks right at Hannah, back at Ryan, and says, "Yes, sir."

"And would you vote not guilty even if it's clear and convincing to you that she is guilty?"

"Yes, sir," she repeats.

"And why is that?"

Looking back at Hannah, she proudly says, "Because it's not beyond a reasonable doubt."

"Exactly!" Ryan says.

Ryan looks at everyone still sitting in front of him and says, "Okay, you're all under oath here. Can each of you commit to me, and to the judge, that you'll follow the law and find Hannah not guilty even if you think she probably did it…even if it's clear and convincing that she did it?"

They all make that promise.

"And you'll vote not guilty if you have *any* reasonable doubt about Hannah's guilt?

They all agree.

Next, Ryan directs his attention to a woman sitting on the second row. "Ms. Peterson, I see you have children. How many?"

"I have two boys," she says.

"And how old are they?"

"One is nine and one is eleven."

"What are their names?"

"My oldest is Clark and my youngest is Marshall."

"Wonderful," Ryan says. "I want you to imagine something for me. Imagine you come home, and a window is broken in your house. You call little Clark and Marshall down to find out who did it."

"Okay," she repeats, as the other jurors look on in anticipation. Hannah wonders how this has anything to do with her case.

"Now, assume you turn to little Marshall and tell him, 'Marshall, I want to start by saying I don't believe you broke the window and you don't have to do or say anything. You don't have to prove anything to me. You can just sit and listen. Oh, and I presume you're innocent from the get-go. Also, it will be incredibly hard for me to decide you're the one who broke the window. I might believe you did it. It might even be clear and convincing, but that's not enough. It will have to be beyond any reasonable doubt in my mind.'"

Mrs. Peterson nods her head.

"Next you turn to little Clark and say, 'Now you…you're a different story. Without hearing anything, I already believe you did it. You better speak up and prove you didn't. You will have the burden of proving me wrong. But I've got to warn you. I'm going to find you guilty and punish you if it's likely, or probable, that you did it."

Someone on the back row says, "That's not right." Everyone in the courtroom laughs.

"Exactly!" Ryan says. "You see, Mrs. Peterson, if this is how it was in your home, poor little Clark wouldn't stand a chance, would he? Marshall would probably win every time, wouldn't he?"

"Probably so," Mrs. Peterson agrees.

Ryan turns to the jury panel and says, "You see, folks, that's how serious all of this is. Hannah is presumed innocent; the prosecutor has the burden of proof; Hannah doesn't have to do or say anything; and the prosecutor must prove their case beyond a reasonable doubt. Hearing how hard it is, you'd think the prosecutor would never win. And that's not coming from me. It comes from the Constitution that protects you and me if we're ever, like Hannah, accused of a crime. The judge is going to instruct—actually order you—to follow these rules. Can all of you promise me, and the judge, you'll keep your sworn oath and never find Hannah guilty unless you are convinced, beyond a reasonable doubt, of all these things?"

He goes one by one to each juror makes that promise.

"One last thing," Ryan continues pointing at the back door. There are a lot of cameras and reporters out there. Hannah and I believe you're going to have to do something that may be pretty difficult. You're going to have to walk out of here after finding her not guilty. It won't be easy, because the people out there won't hear the evidence like you will. Will any of you feel intimidated by the people outside this courthouse. . .maybe your family, or neighbors?"

They all shake their heads no.

"You can all walk out of here after finding Hannah not guilty with your heads held high?"

A big "yes" echoes through the room.

"Thank you so much," Ryan says and sits back down.

Hannah was able to follow everything. When the prosecutor talked about the law, Hannah spent most of her time lost or confused. Now it all sounds so simple. These confusing legal words all make sense. The judge announces a recess and Ryan, Hannah, and Mr. Zimmerman go to a private room to decide who they will strike off the jury.

Once the door is closed, Zimmerman exhales loudly and asks, "Where do we start?"

"Now we pick who we want?" Hannah asks.

Ryan shakes his head and says, "Most people don't understand jury selection. The attorneys don't actually pick a jury—they strike jurors. These are called peremptory challenges or peremptory strikes. In Colorado, the state strikes ten, the defendant strikes their ten, and the first twelve people who didn't get struck are on the jury. People who talk the most are more likely to get struck. Those who say very little are more likely to be on the jury."

"Don't we want more women?" Hannah asks.

Shaking his head, Ryan says, "Not necessarily."

"Really?" Hannah says. "I thought women would vote not guilty?"

"Not always," Ryan says. "Women are usually harder on other women than men are. You're attractive and that will help. A man will be less likely to send a woman and mother like you to prison for the rest of her life."

The *rest of your life* part hits Hannah hard. After taking a deep breath, she says, "Whatever you think, Mr. Brunick. I trust you."

There were two black men on the first row and two black women on the second. They tend to be more distrusting of the police. Ryan puts a star by each of their names. From the county records, Ryan uncovered a divorce filing by two women that included a restraining order with some pretty terrible facts. Ryan puts stars by their name as well. There were also three stay-at-home moms. All these will be shocked by Jackson's deceit. Ryan puts a star by their names.

Two male jurors owned guns and were members of the NRA. They tend to be hard on defendants. One juror struggled with the whole presumption of innocence thing. When Ryan asked about "beyond a reasonable doubt," they didn't seem convinced. Ryan crossed them off his list.

He crossed off five women. One worked at a bank, one was an insurance defense lawyer, one was an accountant, one was a doctor and had never been married, and one seemed to nod at everything the prosecutor said.

Ryan used his last strikes to cross out a man on the second row who said he'd be more likely to believe a police officer over a normal witness and a woman on the third row who initially she would vote guilty even if she had a doubt, but reluctantly changed her mind.

Once they are finished, Ryan and the prosecutor turn in their lists of strikes to the bailiff. One by one, the judge calls each juror who was not struck by either side. They take their seat in the jury box.

Of the four black people on the first two rows, only one is on the jury. Two of the three stay at home moms who seemed very favorable to Hannah are gone. Ms. Ramirez, with the two boys, is on the jury. One man, who Ryan really liked but thought the prosecutor would strike, is also on the jury. Another man on the fourth row, who Ryan hoped wouldn't get reached, is called forward to the jury box.

Some say picking a jury is the most important part of a trial. Seven men and five women wind up on the jury. For better or worse, this is Hannah's jury.

# – CHAPTER 33 –

After a late lunch, the State calls their first witness. They call the lead investigator in the case, Detective Victor Stowe. He walks through the courtroom wearing a blue suit and tie, a badge attached to his belt, holding a portfolio briefcase, and looking real professional. He's testified many times through the years and it shows.

He begins by telling the jury how he was first called to the home of Grace Kennedy after her husband, Jackson Kennedy, never came home after she returned from Thailand. After getting down the basic facts, they opened a missing person investigation. They first ran a check on Jackson's cell phone and credit cards in an attempt to locate him. Both turned up nothing. There were no calls made on his cellphone and no charges by him on his credit cards since the day after Grace left for Thailand. They discovered his car near the airport, but everything looked pretty normal. They checked with the airlines and there was no ticket issued in his name. They did, however, find something interesting. They discovered calls and texts to and from the defendant going back several years, right up until the date Jackson went missing. After a brief follow-up with Grace Kennedy, they traveled to Colorado and spoke with Hannah Kennedy.

"Mr. Stowe, was the defendant cooperative?"

"Well, yes and no. At first she was cooperative. She came down and talked with us, but soon terminated the interview."

"So, what did you learn in your brief interview with the defendant?"

"Our investigation revealed Jackson Kennedy was having an affair with the defendant."

All jurors look over at Hannah with surprise. She writes, "NOT AN AFFAIR!" on her tablet and hands it to Ryan. He nods and hands it back.

Mr. Stowe testifies that Hannah denied having anything to do with Jackson's disappearance. She said they were supposed to meet, but Jackson never showed up. That's all she knows about it.

"And what was the date when she said she waited for Jackson but he didn't show up?"

"Stowe looks at his report and says, "That would be June fifteenth."

"Can you tell the jury if you had any concern when she told you this?"

"I did. There was something about the way she talked that seemed suspicious. I'm trained to not only hear the words but to watch the way she says it. She seemed quite nervous...you know, fidgety. She was evasive and didn't really make eye contact. Her whole demeanor raised suspicion. Then she suddenly terminated the interview."

"Now, earlier you said Jackson was having an affair. Actually, he was married to both women, wasn't he?"

"Oh, yes sir. He was married to both women at the same time."

The jurors look puzzled at this. A couple look over at Hannah again.

"Did you ask the defendant if she knew Jackson was married to another woman?"

"I did, and she said she was aware he was married."

Again, Hannah writes on her tablet while all jurors look on. Ryan returns the tablet and whispers, "I know." It's just loud enough for the jurors to hear.

"And why is this important?"

"Well, if he was married to two woman—which he was—and the defendant knew about it, it would give her a motive for the murder."

"And she had that motive?"

"She did."

"Anything else?" the prosecutor asks.

"Well, she ended the interview pretty quickly. But she did say one thing I thought was important."

"And what's that?"

"She told me I wouldn't find Mr. Kennedy."

"She said you wouldn't find him!?"

"Yes, sir."

"And why is that important?"

"I wondered how she'd know this. How would she know where he is?"

"What happened next, Mr. Stowe?"

"Not a whole lot. We kept searching but didn't find him. We kept checking his cell phone and credit cards, but there were no calls or charges.

Then, almost two years later, a hiker was going through the Maroon Bells and found his body."

The prosecutor picks up a stack of emails and text message and introduces both without objection. She walks up to Stowe and asks, "Why was the location in the Rocky Mountains important?"

Stowe reads the email and text message and testifies, "We had an email and these text messages where the defendant and Jackson agreed to meet at the vacation home, but his car was still in Austin. The defendant denied he ever arrived. Well, now we knew he did, in fact, arrive in Aspen."

"This proved the defendant wasn't honest with you?"

"Yes, sir. She lied to us."

"So, how is the car still in Austin?"

"It's clear that he drove the car to Colorado. After the defendant murdered him, she drove the car back to Austin to make it look like he never arrived in Colorado."

"What condition was Jackson's body in after two years?"

"He was pretty decayed. The winter snow helped preserve his body some, but he was in pretty bad shape."

The prosecutor introduces the photos of Jackson—mostly for shock value and the shock value was huge. Most jurors had to look away. With a stunned look, Hannah looked down and cried.

"Did you find anything interesting about the body?"

"It appeared from the location he had fallen a pretty good distance. We discovered he had a wedding ring on his finger. We learned it was the wedding ring from his marriage to Hannah."

"And why is this important?"

"Well, Jackson's car was found in Austin. We weren't sure if he ever made it to Colorado. But the ring on his finger wasn't from his marriage in Austin. It was the defendant's wedding ring. It showed he must have arrived in Aspen and changed his wedding ring."

The prosecutor walks up to Stowe and hands him a paper. "Do you have any other reason to believe he arrived in Aspen?"

Stowe takes the paper and testifies, "On the day Hannah said Jackson never arrived, she received this text." Stowe reads the words Grace's old boyfriend Sean typed so long ago: "I'm here."

The jurors are stunned. Hannah writes on her notebook pad. Ryan listens with interest, not looking affected at all.

"Now, Jackson had a vacation home in the Rocky Mountains near these Maroon Bells?"

"He did."

"And did the defendant go to that home from time to time?"

"The defendant told me they'd go there quite often."

"Did you search the home?"

"Several times."

"What was important about that?"

"We didn't want to zero in on the defendant. We were concerned Mr. Kennedy might have been abducted by an intruder at the home and murdered, but the house was in perfect order. There was no sign of a break in, and no sign an intruder had been there. No signs of a struggle."

"In your investigation, did you find anything else important?"

"Oh, sure. We ran a check on the defendant's credit cards and discovered she had purchased a handgun three months before the murder. It was a 38 Special revolver."

All jurors write on their notebook pads. Hannah writes on her pad and hands it to Ryan. He nods his head and again whispers, "I know."

Feeling extremely confident at this point, the prosecutor asks, "What else did your investigation reveal?"

Stowe looks at Hannah and says, "We learned she had purchased a million-dollar insurance policy insuring Jackson's life."

"And who's the beneficiary on that policy? Who gets paid if Jackson dies?"

"The Defendant."

After four hours, the prosecutor passes the witness. It's now six thirty-five. The judge recesses for the day and all the jurors walk out of the courtroom. Hannah tries to make eye contact, but no jurors look her way.

Ryan stays in the courtroom writing on his pad. Hannah gets the attention of the bailiff, and asks him to take her to the restroom. She goes into an empty stall so she can't be seen and cries. Grace walks in a few minutes later and takes Hannah in her arms.

"I'm going. . .I'm going to prison," Hannah gets out.

The truth is, deep down inside, Grace is thinking the same thing. This all sounds overwhelming. She can't help but wonder if her dad is about to lose his first case. Instead, she shakes her head and says, "It's too early to say that. This is just the first day."

"You heard him. They got everything. I bought a gun, he texted me he's here, there's an insurance policy, I drove the car back, he had on my wedding ring. I look like a liar. I'm going to prison. I'm going to prison and I'll never see Savannah again. My life is over."

Hannah's mom comes in and puts her arm around Hannah. She doesn't feel any better about how things are going. She holds Hannah in her embrace and says, "Don't give up, Hannah. We're praying for you. You can't give up."

Hannah walks out of the courtroom holding her mother's hand with her father right beside her. All she can think about is Savannah.


When the trial resumes the next morning, Ryan addresses Mr. Stowe, sounding not the least bit worried. With a friendly smile, he says, "Good morning, Detective Stowe."

"Good morning."

"Officer Stowe," he begins, "when you testified yesterday you said Jackson was having an affair. Correct?

"Yes…I made a mistake."

"Sure, you're not perfect. You can be wrong from time to time, even when you're under oath?"

"Sure," he says.

"In fact, it wasn't an affair at all. He was married to both Hannah and Grace Kennedy, wasn't he?"

"Yes, sir."

"And it's not like he abandoned his first wife and went to the other. He was seeing them both at the same time, wasn't he? He had two homes, two wives, two whole lives."

"That's true."

"From talking with Hannah and Grace, you learned he would spend three, four, five days at one place, then go back to the other place."

"That's what they each told me."

"Can you imagine how difficult that must have been? Three days here, three days there; calling back and forth; having to raise two different families and children."

"I'm sure it was difficult."

"It must take a lot of lies to keep this terrible thing going?"

"I'm sure."

"His whole life was one incredible lie, wasn't it?"

"Yes, sir."

"Well, he also had to pay for two lives, didn't he?"

"I assume so."

"And how did he do this?"

"Well, our investigation revealed he was stealing from his company."

"Stealing? How much?"

"Over eight million dollars."

The jurors sit up and Ryan asks, "And you never mentioned this earlier?"

"I didn't think it was important."

"Eight million dollars? The defendant was in the middle of stealing over eight million dollars and you didn't think that was important?"

"No, sir."

"Well, let me ask you. If you were stealing that much money, wouldn't you be looking over your shoulder?"

"I guess I would."

"Sure, you would. You steal that much money and someone might be out for you. And that makes a lot of motive. How many people did you interrogate at his work over his disappearance?"

"We didn't investigate anyone."

"I mean, this is real money. Someone is out a whole lot of money, right?"

"Yes, sir."

"Eight million dollars, and this jury will never know the person or persons who lost all that money? We'll never know what that person or persons was doing on the day Jackson disappeared?"

"I guess not."

"Now, you testified Hannah confessed to knowing Jackson was married to another woman, right?"

"She did."

"This interrogation was videotaped and recorded, right?"

"Yes sir."

Ryan pulls out a transcript and says, "Well, let's look at the statement from the videotaped interrogation." Ryan hands him the paper and says, "Read this highlighted part to the jury."

He reads: "Mrs. Kennedy, how was your marriage to Jackson?

"I don't know. I guess, like most marriages."

"Were you having any difficulties?"

"No sir."

"Were you aware if he was having an affair?"

"He probably was."

Ryan looks up and says, "I don't get it. Where did she admit to knowing Jackson was married to another woman?"

"Right here," he says, pointing at the paper.

"But you never asked Hannah if she was *aware* Jackson was married to another woman, did you?"

"Not in those words."

"You asked if he was having an affair?"

"Correct."

"So, you really deceived this jury when you testified, under oath, that she admitted to knowing Jackson was married to another woman, right?"

"Not intentionally."

"And she said he *probably* was. Not that he *was.*"

"Correct."

"Have you ever heard the expression, go with your gut or believe your instincts?"

"Sure."

Ryan looks at Hannah, and says, "At this point, this poor woman is married to, and has a baby with, a man who has been coming home, leaving for no reason for days at a time, and telling one lie after another. I'm sure her gut instincts kicked in by now. Is it any surprise she would think he was *probably* having an affair?"

Stowe pauses for a minute before saying, "I see your point."

"Now Jackson was found with Hannah's wedding ring on his finger, right?"

"Yes, sir."

"But you have no idea *when* he put that ring on, do you?"

"Not exactly."

"For that matter, you can't even tell this jury when Jackson died, can you?"

"Well, it's a little difficult after two years."

"All we know is the date he was last seen and when Grace Kennedy returned from Thailand."

"That's true," Ryan agrees, "but for all we know, he could have been held for weeks or months before he was killed. You really have no idea when he was killed, do you?"

Stowe looks stumped when he says, "When you put it that way, no."

"And for all you know, he could have put that ring on his finger the day Grace walked out the door to go to Thailand."

"That's possible."

"I mean, to make sure he didn't forget, he would want to put that ring on as soon as possible, right?"

"Could be."

"So, the ring really proves nothing. We don't know if Jackson ever arrived in Aspen before his death or not."

"Well, we know he did arrive. He text the Defendant that he arrived."

"Well, let's look at that text. It says, 'I'm here.'"

"Correct."

"He doesn't say, I'm here in Aspen."

"Where else would he be referring to?"

"He could be letting her know he's at the airport or at the gas station. You really have no idea, do you?"

"Well, he was found in Aspen."

"He could have flown. Did you check all the flights out?"

"Yes, sir."

"And every private flight out."

"Yes, sir."

"Well, that really narrows things down, doesn't it?"

"In what way?"

"Well, it's possible he was killed by someone who knows he had a home in Aspen—maybe someone he stole all that money from—and took him to the mountains near his vacation home to make it look like he fell while hiking."

Sounding sure of himself, Stowe says, "Or he drove to Aspen, the defendant killed him, and then drove his car back."

"So there really is no other explanation. Either he was killed in Austin and dumped in the mountains by someone else, or he was killed in Aspen by Hannah and she drove his car back to Austin."

"I guess so. I can't think of any other explanation."

"And if he never drove to Aspen, Hannah can't be the murderer, right?"

Stowe stops for a minute to consider this, then says, "I'd agree with that."

"Well, I think we can tell which is true."

"How's that?"

Ryan first pulls out a report, and then shows a map of the highway between Austin and Aspen on the large screen sitting in front of the jury. Directing everyone's attention to the map, Ryan asks, "It's a pretty straight shot from Aspen to Austin, isn't it?"

"Yes, sir."

"And looking at this report, there's a toll road here, here, and here, right?"

Stowe pauses a second and says, "Yes, sir."

"These toll roads take a photo of every car going through, right?"

"Yes."

"And did you check those three tolls to see if Jackson's car came back from Aspen?"

Surprising everyone, Stowe says, "Actually, we did."

"For all these weeks?"

"Yes, sir."

"And did Jackson's car ever come through those tolls back to Austin?"

"Actually…no."

"And you never turned this over to Hannah's attorney?" Ryan asks.

"I don't know what you received. But the defendant might have been thinking ahead. She might have taken another route and avoided all these tolls."

"That's true." Ryan agrees. "Hannah might be incredibly brilliant. But that drive back to Austin would have taken a lot longer, right? By my calculation, it would have taken three hours longer for her to avoid these tolls."

Smiling a little because he knows he just stumped Ryan, with a little shrug Stowe says, "She sure had a reason to do that if she just murdered her husband."

"Sure," Ryan agrees again. "But Jackson didn't murder anyone. He had no reason to take the long way there. In fact, he was probably in a hurry to get back home."

Now the jurors look on with interest.

"And did you show Jackson's vehicle pass through any of these tolls going from Austin to Aspen?"

"No, his car didn't register on those tolls either."

"Not at all during this time."

"Actually, no."

"Didn't you think this was an important fact to tell this jury? You sat up there and swore, under oath, that Jackson drove to Aspen, Hannah killed her husband, and then she drove all the way back to Austin to cover it up. You never said, 'Oh, to be honest, we checked the tolls and never saw his car drive either to Aspen or back again.'"

"Truthfully, I forgot all about this."

"So, this was really dishonest, wasn't it?"

"Not dishonest…I just forgot."

Ryan continues, "You said you checked his credit card charges. Did you find a single credit card charge in Aspen?"

"No, sir."

"It's a long drive. Surely, he stopped for gas or something to eat. Any charges along this highway?"

"No, sir."

"And you read those emails to the jury proving Jackson and Hannah were arguing right before he disappeared. Do you even know what they were arguing about?"

"It's not really clear."

"Well, let's look a little closer." Ryan approaches with the same stack of emails that were admitted earlier. Again, he asks Stowe to read the highlighted text from Hannah to Jackson."

Jackson

------------------------------------------------------------

February 22: 6:44 p.m.

> I have family and friends here and you expect me to just leave?

"Obviously, they were arguing about Jackson expecting her to go somewhere, right?"

"It looks like it."

"Well, let's go back just two weeks earlier. Look at this text from Jackson to Hannah.

Jackson

---

February 8: 1:20 p.m.

> I think you'd love Paris or Australia. Just give it a chance.

After reading the texts, Ryan says, "So now we know. After months of going back and forth, driving this woman crazy; Jackson has stolen eight million dollars and wants this poor woman to move away from her family and friends and go to the other side of the world."

Stowe nods his head and says, "Maybe."

Ryan then introduces a stack of receipts and credit card charges with attached affidavits. "I want you to look at these for a minute," Ryan says, going from one to the next. "In the months before and after these arguments, Hannah bought a new couch, exercise equipment, an outside pool for the baby, two lamps, a new bedspread, and new pots and pans for the kitchen. It's pretty clear Hannah has no intention of going anywhere."

"Maybe not."

"And Jackson bought Hannah some pretty expensive earrings."

"I see that," Stowe acknowledges.

"This doesn't sound like two people on the outs, does it?"

"I can't answer that," Stowe mumbles.

Ryan directs Stowe back to the emails. "I want to show you these…one, two, three, four, five, six, seven, eight….eight emails Hannah sent Jackson *after* the email you read earlier, where they're arguing. Again and again, she tells him how much she loves him."

Stowe reads the emails to himself.

Ryan puts a text up on the television screen and says, "Let's look at this one she sent a week before Jackson disappeared:"

Jackson

--------------------------------------------------------------

June 7: 9:21 p.m.

I love you honey. We can get through anything as long as we're together. I can't wait to see you again.

Ryan then shows Stowe a card Hannah gave Jackson. "When you searched Hannah's home, did you see this card sitting right there on Jackson's nightstand?"

"I think I remember seeing it."

"Did you know it was sent just weeks before he disappeared?"

Hannah knows this was sent six months previously, but this time she doesn't write any notes on her tablet.

Ryan hands the card back to Stowe and says, "No, sir."

"Does this sound like a woman who's about to kill her husband?"

Stowe looks up at the email and then back at the card. He looks at the prosecutor and says, "I don't know what she was thinking."

"Exactly," Ryan says. "You just don't know. Then you testified Hannah told you that you'd never find Jackson, right?"

"She sure did."

"And when Hannah said this, you just assumed she said it because she killed him?"

"How else can you take it?"

"Again, it's clear from the texts, Jackson was talking about leaving to the other side of the world, right?"

"Yes, sir."

"And he had eight million dollars to help him stay hidden, didn't he?"

"Evidently."

"So, it's pretty clear why she thought you'd never find him. Not that she killed him; but he was gone—long gone—with plenty of money to stay hidden."

Stowe again looks at the prosecutor, who shakes his head, and says, "It could be."

Hannah now listens in amazement. She glances over at the jury, who's paying close attention. One juror looks over at Hannah and they exchange a quick smile.

"I want to talk about that gun that you testified Hannah must have bought to kill Jackson."

"Okay."

"Do you have anything to indicate Jackson was actually shot?"

"Well, the body was in pretty bad condition."

"Right, but the bones were intact. Was there a bullet hole in his skull?"

"No sir."

"Did any of the bones have bullet holes?"

"No, but he could have been shot in the soft tissue."

"Right, and did you find a bullet in any of those decaying soft tissues?"

"I don't believe so."

"Or on the ground under him?"

"No sir."

"So, we have no evidence Jackson was *ever* shot. And you assumed it was Hannah who bought the gun because it was on her credit card?"

"That's right. She charged it on her card."

"Did you know they shared a card?

"I'm not sure."

Ryan walks up with a credit card receipt, and says, "I'd like to show you the actual credit card receipt for the purchased gun. Tell the jury who signed for the card."

"It says, Jackson Kennedy."

"And you assumed this gun was bought to kill Jackson?"

"Well, it's a heck of a coincidence."

Ryan nods his head and says, "And there might be another coincidence." He hands Stowe a document to review. "Were you aware of this police report?" he asks.

"I've never seen this before."

"According to this report, two days before this gun was purchased, someone broke into Jackson's Aspen home and stole some things, didn't they?"

He takes his time reading and finally says, "I see that."

"Mr. Stowe, do you have a gun to protect your family?"

"Yes, sir."

"So it's not real surprising Jackson bought a gun to protect his family."

Ryan nods his head and says, "No, sir."

"Detective Stowe, the truth is, the area where Jackson Kennedy was found is quite dangerous, isn't it?"

"Yes, it is."

"And Jackson hiked those trails all the time, didn't he?"

"He did."

"Many people have been killed hiking those trails?"

"I don't know how many, but yes, people are killed."

"In fact, it's all speculation. You cannot rule out the possibility that Jackson went for a hike and fell down those trails or someone else killed him."

"Anything's possible."

"And you have no gunshot wound, or a bit of other proof that Jackson was actually murdered."

"I think we do have proof."

"This proof you came in here with? The proof the jury just heard?"

"That's our proof. But there's more. I think another witness still has to testify."

"Let me ask you, did you check Jackson's house for blood or signs of a struggle?"

"Sure."

"Did you find anything?"

"No sir."

"People often use bleach or some cleaner to clean up blood after such a messy murder, true?"

"Yes, sir."

"Did you find evidence of bleach or anything that was used to clean up after this horrible murder?"

"Not in the home."

Ryan approaches Stowe and says, "While we're at it, I want to show you these photos of two blood samples found in Jackson's car back in Austin, far, far away from Hannah in Aspen. Did you find these?"

Stowe looks at the spot of blood on the seat and the gearshift. "We never saw those."

"So, you never tested them?"

"Obviously not."

Knowing the blood came back as Jackson's, Ryan says, "It could have been the killers, but this jury will never know who that blood belongs to?"

Stowe just keeps looking at the photos without responding.

Ryan was quick as he moved from one question to another. Five hours after he started, Stowe is mentally and physically exhausted. With a warm smile, Ryan says, "That's all I have. I thank you, Detective Stowe, for coming in here today."


The prosecutors comes back from lunch not nearly as peppy, but his case isn't over by a long shot. The real evidence is coming. When the jurors all return from lunch, the female prosecutor stands up. She is quite lovely, with brown hair, brown eyes, and a slender figure. She's wearing a nice business suit with heels. She has a beautiful voice and speaks with a southern accent.

She calls Larry Franks, an expert witness, to testify about cell phone towers. After introducing him to the jury, the prosecutor asks, "Can you explain to this jury how cell phones ping off cell phone towers?"

"Certainly. All cell phones operate off of cell phone towers. A cell phone 'ping' is the process of determining the location, with reasonable accuracy, of a cell phone at any given point in time. It is very similar to the GPS used by vehicles. To 'ping' means to send a signal to a particular cell phone and have it respond with the requested data. The term is derived from SONAR, when a technician would send out a sound wave, or ping, and wait for its return to locate another object. New cell phones are required by law to be GPS capable, so a 911 operator can locate who is making an emergency phone call. When a new digital cell phone is pinged, like when we have a missing person, their cell phone can locate them within a geographic area—sometimes within several feet of the cell phone. As you go from one location to another, it will register on the next cell phone tower."

"And how far are towers located away from each other?"

"The cell towers are typically 6 to 12 miles apart—less in cities. By comparing signal strength and time lag for the signal to reach each tower, we can triangulate the phone's position."

"Does the person have to be using the phone at the time?"

"No ma'am. The phone just needs to be on."

"Can you tell the jury, on the day the defendant was supposed to meet with Jackson, what did you find?"

The witness points to the aerial photo and says, "This is an aerial view of the Rocky Mountains." Pointing at a specific location, he says, "On the day Jackson was supposed to meet with the defendant, the defendant's cell phone pinged off of this tower right here."

"Right in this area of the Rocky Mountains."

"That is correct."

"And how long was she there?"

"Approximately two hours."

"Thank you. Pass the witness."

Ryan picks right up. "Mr. Franks, this data you recovered can only tell where the phone was located, correct? It can't tell who was using the phone."

"That's correct."

"And it cannot tell who's with the person who used the phone."

"No sir."

"So, in this case, all it showed us is that Hannah's personal cell phone pinged…or was located…at that tower from about 5:42 p.m. to 7:33 p.m., right?

"Correct."

"If Hannah already told the investigator she was in this area in the Rocky Mountains around that time, then this proves how honest she is. Otherwise, it gives us nothing new, right?"

"I guess not."

"Well, I'd like to see what it *doesn't* tell us. That cell phone tower you talked about earlier…can we put that back up." When the aerial photo is back on the screen, Ryan circles the one he testified about. Pointing at the map, he says, "Now, this *is* the closest cell phone tower to the vacation home, correct?"

"Correct."

"But Mr. Kennedy's body wasn't found at the vacation home. It was found over here." He points to another tower and asks, "Wouldn't this cell phone tower over here be the closest cell phone tower to the place his body was discovered?"

He looks up and says, "You know, I think it would be."

"And did you check that cell phone tower?"

"To help triangulate the location where Mrs. Kennedy came from and returned to, we checked all the nearby towers."

"And did Hannah's cell phone ever ping off the tower where the body was discovered?"

"No, it didn't."

Already knowing the answer because he has the same report, Ryan asks, "By the way, where did Hannah come from?"

"She came from her home."

"And where did she return to?"

"She returned to her home."

"She never drove where Jackson was found."

He shakes his head and says, "No, sir."

"Oh," Ryan says dramatically. "And she never drove to Austin?"

"Austin….no sir."

"Thank you."

The second day ends the same way it began—with the prosecutors back on their heels. Quite frankly, they were prepared for the run-of-the-mill court appointed trial where evidence is simply accepted as true. Most defendants don't hire investigators to find credit card bills, receipts for guns, or some damn police report from some damn robbery. Lawyers don't pour over hundreds of pages of texts and emails. That takes a lot of time, a lot of money, and someone who can get a jury to understand it.

After the jury walks out for the day, the lead prosecutor looks over at the smile on Hannah's face as she hugs her mom and dad and thinks: *That's okay. Tomorrow is another day. His first witness will be the nail in her coffin. You can forget everything else. This one witness will be her undoing.*

# CHAPTER 34

Day three starts with the prosecutor calling Beth Windham. She goes by Beth. She and her husband have lived next door to Jackson's vacation home for over twenty years.

Crane spends a lot of time building her up as a sweet, credible witness. Ryan knows why. His whole case hinges on this one woman and her testimony will be shaky at best. Mr. Crane finally gets around to the reason we're here.

"I want to direct your attention to June fifteenth. On that day, did you see the defendant at her vacation house?"

"Oh, yes, sir. I was leaving my house at approximately six forty-five. You see, I have this lovely driveway leading to the road. There's rose bushes on each side. They're my prize. They alternate yellow and red. Anyway, I stopped at the end of the driveway and waited for another car to go by."

"And did you see who was in the car?"

"It was Jackson and Hannah Kennedy."

"How do you know it was them?"

She gives a little laugh and says, "Well, their house is right next to mine. I know them pretty well. Right after they passed my car, they pulled into their driveway and got out."

"And you saw them get out?"

"Yes, I saw them get out."

"So, if Hannah Kennedy told Detective Stowe that Jackson never arrived that day, would that be true?"

"Well, heavens no! I saw them together with my own eyes."

"Thank you….pass the witness."

Ryan looks at Beth and says, "Hello, Ms. Windham. I'm Ryan Brunick. You and I have never met before, have we?"

"Ryan Brunick?" she repeats. "Aren't you the one who sent that investigator to my house?"

"Oh, you spoke with my investigator?"

"Yes. I thought he was a little pushy."

"Now this all happened a long time ago, right?"

She nods and says, "It has been quite a spell."

"It's probably hard to remember everything after all these years, right?"

"Oh, no!" she says. "I remember this very well."

"Now, the day Hannah told the investigators that Jackson never showed up was a Wednesday. After so long, is it possible you got the day wrong? Maybe you saw them together on, say another day?"

"Oh, no sir."

"And how can you be so sure?"

"Because I have my Bible study every Wednesday at five o'clock to six o'clock. I just finished my Bible study, straightened up a bit, and left to go out for dinner."

Knowing the answer, Ryan asks, "Where did you go to eat dinner that evening?"

She crosses her arms and says, "I already told your investigator."

"Do you mind telling the jury?"

"I went to eat at the Olive Garden restaurant in town."

"Were you alone?"

"I was with my friend Shirley."

"Maybe it was somewhere else. How do you remember it was the Olive Garden?"

"I thought it was the Olive Garden, but after your investigator left, I asked Shirley, and she remembered the same thing."

"Maybe she was wrong?"

"Oh no, she was positive."

"Maybe this was another time y'all ate together."

"No, Mr. Brunick," she says, a little testy. "It's the only time we've ever eaten together."

"And do you like the Olive Garden?"

"Well, I like those breadsticks they have."

"Do you eat there often?"

"Heaven's no," she says with a wave of her hand. "I don't eat anywhere often. I can't afford it on my social security. I hadn't been to the Olive Garden in more than a year."

"What about after this time?"

"I haven't been back since I ate there with Shirley."

"Well, maybe it was another Wednesday. Maybe it was a week earlier or a week later after the Bible study?"

She shakes her head and says, "Oh no, it was on that Wednesday?"

"How do you know?"

"Because I remember we studied the Prayer of Jabez that day. It's a beautiful prayer in the Old Testament." Beth gets all animated like she loves talking about this stuff. She turns to the jury and says, "You see, Jabez asked God to bless him, and enlarge his territory, and keep him from evil so he doesn't cause no pain. And you know what God did? The Bible says God honored that prayer. He thought Jabez was an honorable man who prayed a righteous prayer."

Ryan lets her finish. "That's a wonderful story, Beth. But what does that have to do with Hannah?"

"Well, I keep all my Bible study material. I looked back over my workbooks to find out when we studied the Prayer of Jabez. It was on Wednesday, June fifteenth. That's how I know the day."

"And you're certain about that?

"Oh, yes."

This does not seem like the same woman who met with the investigator. Just two months ago, she wasn't sure at all. Now she testifies like there's no doubt in her mind. Ryan figures the prosecutor must have gotten to her.

Hannah starts to feel hopeless again. This woman is good. She looks so sweet, and now she's using the Bible to back her up. Even Ryan can't shake her. Hannah starts thinking about prison again.

"Mrs. Windham, did you meet with the prosecutor before the trial?"

"I met with him, just like I met with your investigator."

"And did he suggest that it was the fifteenth?"

"Oh no! I told him I had a Bible study that day. He told me to look back over my stuff and find out what Bible study we did that Wednesday."

This is surprising. Pointing at the prosecutor, Ryan says, "So, you didn't tell him all about the Prayer of Jabez, and he asked you to find the day. He asked you to find the Bible study you did on the fifteenth."

Crane jumps up and says, "Objection! He's confusing the witness."

"Overruled."

"Then he's badgering the witness."

"Overruled."

Mrs. Windham looks completely confused. All shook up, she waves both her hands in front of her, and says, "Oh, Mr. Brunick, you got me all mixed up and I don't appreciate it. I'm a woman of God. I swore to tell the truth. It was the fifteenth....the Prayer of Jabez....please don't try to trick me."

"It's okay," Ryan says. "I think we get the idea of what went on between you and the prosecutor. Mrs. Windham, you've known Jackson Kennedy since the day he bought the home next to yours nine years ago, correct?"

"Correct."

"And you even met his other wife, Grace Kennedy, who's sitting behind me, didn't you?"

She gives Grace a smile, and says, "I did. They came over for lunch a few times."

"Did you like Grace?"

"Oh yes. I thought she was lovely. She believes in God, just like me. She even came to my Bible study once."

"And what about Hannah? Did she come to your Bible Study?"

"No, she didn't."

"What did you think when you saw Jackson showing up with another woman?"

She puts her hand over her chest and says, "Well, I didn't know what to think. First, I thought he must have divorced poor Grace, but three months later, he was back at his house with Grace again."

"And did you ever see Hannah again?"

Quite entertaining, she nods her head and says, "I sure did. They started bouncing back and forth, back and forth. I saw this Hannah girl over there more than I saw Grace."

"And how'd that make you feel?"

"Mr. Brunick…I told you, I'm a Christian woman. I just don't understand all these kids just blatantly living in sin. It's not right. Well, I can love the sinner, but I hate the sin."

"So, I guess as a good, God-fearing woman, it's fair to say you didn't care too much for Hannah."

She shakes her head, crosses her arms and says, "I guess not."

"Thank you, ma'am."


The prosecutor is feeling better. Ryan pressed hard, but she stuck to her story. He looked lame, trying to shake her. Once Mrs. Windham steps down and walks out the door, Hannah writes on her tablet, "She killed us!"

Ryan approaches the judge and asks, "Your Honor, I have a request of the court. Given Mrs. Windham's testimony, I have a witness I need to call. He flew a long way, and he's waiting outside. I expect his testimony will be quick. I'd ask permission to call him now so he can return home."

The judge turns to the prosecutor and asks, "Any objections?"

"Who's this witness?" Crane asks.

"It's the designated corporate representative for Darden Restaurants."

"Darden Restaurants?" the prosecutor scowls. He turns to the judge and says, "Your Honor—"

"You know," Ryan chimes in. "He's going to testify anyway. Let's hear what he has to say and let him go home."

The prosecutor lifts his hand and says, "Okay…no objection."

The judge writes it on his docket sheet and says, "Wonderful…I like to see attorneys working together."

The witness walks through the back doors holding a manilla folder. He's sworn in and introduced as the designated representative for Darden Restaurants.

After a brief introduction, Ryan asks, "Did you receive the subpoena I served on Darden Restaurants?"

"I did, and I have it here."

"And what is Darden Restaurants?"

"It's the corporation that owns The Olive Garden."

"And did you locate the documents I subpoenaed from your company?"

"I did."

"And did you bring them here today?"

"Got em' right here," he says, raising the papers.

"So, tell the jury…what did you bring?"

"With an exhaustive and costly search," he says, looking right at Ryan, "we located all credit card charges involving Ms. Elizabeth Windham."

"And were there such charges?"

"Only three."

"And how many occurred within the year in question?"

"Only one. I have it here."

Ryan takes the document showing no emotion, returns it to the witness, and says, "Tell the jury the date that Mrs. Windham ate at The Olive Garden."

"That would be Wednesday, June second."

"Two weeks *before* Wednesday, June fifteenth."

"Correct."

"Thank you…pass the witness.

Crane jumps up and says, "But she could have eaten there and paid cash….correct?"

The witness nods his head and says, "Sure."

"Pass the witness."

Ryan simply says, "But if the witness testified she rarely eats at the Olive Garden—in fact she never ate there again after this one time, then we don't have to worry about any cash purchases, do we?"

Confused, the witness says, "I have no idea."

"Pass the witness. You can step down."

Hannah can't help but smile.


This morning couldn't have gone any better. When the jury walks out for lunch, each one smiles at Hannah, who's watching politely as they walk by. Once the door is shut, Hannah puts her head down and cries. She turns to Ryan and says, "Thank you, Mr. Brunick. I owe everything to you. I owe you my life. I owe you my daughter's life."

Ryan hugs her and then her mom and dad. Grace stands beside them, waiting to leave. Ryan starts to put his things away, glances up, and is frozen in shock. Not sure what just happened, Grace looks back and also freezes in shock. Ryan's wife, Kate, is standing at the back of the courtroom!

## – CHAPTER 35 –

Ryan….is….utterly….dumbfounded.

Kate is standing at the back door, holding her hands in front of her. She's dressed in a pretty dress that Ryan once bought her. Her hair is straightened, and she's wearing makeup, but she looks ten years older than she did the last time Ryan saw her. Ryan's not sure how long she's been standing there, but her eyes are full of tears.

Ryan's not sure why she came. He puts everything back in the boxes, taking as much time as he can. Grace helps him pack, unsure what to say. Ryan hopes Kate will simply walk away.

When he can't delay any longer, Ryan, Grace, Hannah, and her parents all walk to the door. When they get close, Kate gives Grace a teary smile.

"Hi, Grace," she says.

Grace nods and says, "Hi, Kate."

Kate then smiles at Ryan. When he doesn't smile back, Kate says, "Ryan, can we talk for a minute?"

Ryan shakes his head and says, "I don't think so."

Showing the years of pain on her face, she begs, "Please, Ryan."

Ryan looks at Grace, who says, "Just talk to her, Dad."

Ryan stands for a moment before handing Grace his briefcase. "Hold this for me," he says.

They walk into the hallway and Ryan turns to Kate, wanting this to be as brief as possible. Kate's eyes are full. The first tear falls down her cheek, so she wipes it away and says, "Can we go somewhere private?"

Ryan closes his eyes and says, "Kate?"

"Please," she pleads.

Since the jurors have all left the courthouse, Ryan walks to the jury room with Kate following right behind him, still wiping her tears. He takes a seat thinking Kate will sit across the table. Instead, she sits down right next to Ryan and puts her hand on his arm.

"You looked good in there," she says with a sympathetic smile. "You are really incredible."

"Thanks," Ryan says looking straight ahead.

"There's nobody like you."

Ryan takes his free hand and rubs his face, concealing his eyes. When he puts his hand back on the table, Kate starts crying again. With trembling lips, she says, "I'm so sorry, Ryan."

Ryan closes his eyes and slowly shakes his head. He tries to pull his arm away, but Kate holds on tight. Squeezing his arm a little, she says, "Ryan, please listen to me. These past years have been so hard on me."

Seeing Kate up close with her face covered in tears, Ryan thinks she actually looks fifteen years older. It's plain to see that she hasn't been taking care of herself.

Kate wipes her eyes and says, "That wasn't me. I swear to God that wasn't me. My lawyer did it all. He told me what to say. He hated you, Ryan. He prepared the papers and told me to give them to you."

Ryan can smell the years of smoke in her hair and on her clothes. It repulses him. No longer fooled by the sweet lies a beautiful woman can make you believe, he shakes his head and says, "No…that was you. That was you at the house who threatened to call the police. It was you, not your lawyer, who met me at the hotel that day. I tried to talk to you, but you shut me down. You practically threw those papers at me with a look on your face that could kill. I watched a stranger…no, an enemy, walk out of that restaurant."

Scrambling for something to say, Kate grabs Ryan's hand again and says, "Ryan, I really think I was in shock. When I heard about everything, I was stunned. I knew you. I knew what a great man you were. When I heard everything, I couldn't believe it."

"I understood. I told you I understood."

Gasping for breath, Kate cries, "I…I…love you, Ryan.

Kate hopes Ryan will hold her and confess his love She wants to walk out together; but he just sits there looking stoic.

"Ryan, it all happened so fast. I didn't have time to think things through."

Softening just a little, Ryan takes his free hand and puts it on Kate's. He looks into her eyes, and says, "But I tried." Shaking his head, he says, "I tried to give you time."

Kate puts her head down so her lips are against Ryan's hand. She nods her head in agreement and whispers, "I know….I know."

Ryan squints his eyes shut and says, "I would have done anything for you."

Kate kisses Ryan's hand and looks up. "I loved you, Ryan. You have no idea how much I loved you. You were my whole life."

Finally, Ryan says it. He says the words she's been wanting to hear. "I loved you too. You were *my* life. But you asked me to leave, and I did. It was so hard, but I left."

As a tear drops on Ryan's hand, Kate says, "I know. I'm so sorry." She kisses the back of his hand again. "Ryan, we had something so good. Do you know how hard it is to put two families together? But we did it. We did it together. For all those years, we almost never argued. I knew what you'd been through. I knew the hell Faith put you through. You were the head of the family, and I respected that. You have no idea how much I looked up to you. You were my Prince Charming. Ben loved you. God, he loved you so much."

Ryan's eyes tear up and he says, "I loved him too. How's he doing?"

Kate shakes her head and says, "He's not good. He hates me for leaving you. He won't listen to me. Every time I tell him anything, he says how much he hates me. He says I killed you. He blames me for everything. He needs you, Ryan. He's in so much trouble. He hangs around these kids and does drugs. He won't go to school. He sometimes leaves and doesn't come back for days. Every time I turn around, he's getting arrested. I'm afraid. I'm really afraid he'll spend the rest of his life in prison."

It's hard to think of Ben like that. Ryan looks down and shakes his head.

"Ryan, I've tried to move on. I've been with other men, but it's so shallow. They mean nothing to me. How can I be with anyone else after you? Men are stupid. They only want one thing. I feel so dirty. The whole time I'm dating someone else, all I do is think of you."

Kate moves close and kisses Ryan's face again and again. When Ryan pulls back, Kate whispers, "Kiss me. Please…kiss me."

Ryan looks down and says, "I can't."

Looking into his eyes with her lips close to his, Kate says, "Ryan, you loved me once. I know you still love me. We can get it back. We can put everything back like it was."

Ryan shakes his head and says, "It doesn't work like that."

"It can," Kate interrupts. "You don't have to do anything. I'll do it. I'll do it all. I'll spend the rest of my life making you happy. Just give me one more chance."

Feeling Ryan about to say no, Kate puts her hand over Ryan's mouth and says, "Don't say anything. We don't have to do everything right now. Let's start over. Let's just date again. Let's go back to when we first met. Remember how great it was? We can have that again."

Ryan pulls back while holding Kate's face in his hands. She has the saddest look he's ever seen, and for a brief second he sees the beautiful woman she once was. Looking straight into her teary eyes, he says, "Kate, I loved you. I really did."

Kate presses her lips against Ryan's lips. A rush sweeps over her. When he doesn't pull back, she turns her face and opens her mouth to take the kiss he offers.

Suddenly, Ryan pulls away and his tone changes. Gone is any more talk about love. He shakes his head and says, "You talk about love and what a great thing we had. You could have left, but that wasn't enough for you. You tried to take everything. You wanted to leave me and the girls with nothing. I will never love you again, because I can never trust you. You tried to hurt me worse than anyone has ever hurt me. That's all I see when I look at you."

Hearing Ryan's words, Kate starts crying again.

Ryan stands up, covers his face with his hands, and then spreads his arms wide. Talking louder, he says, "Look at me. I'm not young anymore. I'll never be able to trust you again. Honestly, I'll never be able to trust any woman again." He turns around and says, "I've got to go, Kate, but I wish you the best. I'll send you some money. You deserve that much. Ben deserves that much."

"Please, Ryan," Kate begs.

Ryan walks to the door but turns around when Kate asks, "So....Hope got married?"

"She did," he says. "It was really beautiful."

"Can I see her again?" Kate asks.

With a smile, Ryan nods his head and says, "I'm sure she'd like that."

Ryan leaves the jury room and closes the door behind him. He can hear Kate crying as he walks down the hall.

Back at the entrance to the courtroom, Ryan walks up to Grace and takes his briefcase from her. "What did she want?" Grace asks.

Still a little emotional, he says, "Nothing really. She just wanted to say hi."


Three weeks later, Ryan walks into his bank in Montenegro and wires one million, one hundred thousand dollars into Kate's bank account in Waco, Texas. This is the money she would have received under the prenup.

# CHAPTER 36

After lunch, the prosecutor calls Jackson's brother, Alex, to the stand. Jackson's mother and father already passed away, so they want his brother there to pull at the heart and show Jackson's humanity.

He started strong, but breaks down talking about Jackson laying hidden in that mountain for two years. He testifies how Jackson was a good man, and now he's lost his brother and his best friend.

Ryan walks up to Jackson's brother, whom he met only once at Jackson and Grace's wedding. He first apologizes for his loss, and then he takes out a binder full of photos—photos of Hannah and Savannah, Hannah and Jackson looking happier than ever, and Hannah and Jackson with Savannah.

"Do these photos accurately depict their family?"

"At the time, yes."

"How did you feel about Hannah before you found out about his terrible death?"

"I loved her. She was like a sister."

He points to the picture of him, Jackson, and Hannah together and says, "This is a beautiful picture of you, your brother, and Hannah. When was it taken?"

Staying strong, Alex says, "Two weeks before he disappeared."

"They look pretty happy together, don't they?"

Wiping his eyes, Jeff says, "Yes, sir."

"Thank you…and again, I'm sorry for your loss."

The judge turns to the prosecutor and asks, "Any more witnesses?"

The prosecutors look at each other and back at the judge. After a brief pause, Crane says, "Uhm…we call Grace Kennedy."

This move surprises Ryan. He didn't believe the prosecutor would actually call Grace since they have no idea what she might say. Not showing his surprise, he stands up and says, "Very well, Your Honor, can we take a thirty-minute break and start fresh?"

With a smile, the judge says, "I was going to suggest the same thing."

Ryan, Zimmerman, Grace, Hannah, and Hannah's parents gather around the courtroom cafeteria table. Grace looks terrible.

"What the hell, Dad!" she says.

Ryan puts his hand on her arm and says, "This isn't a surprise. We knew they might call you when they issued the subpoena."

"But we have the case won…right?" Hannah asks.

Ryan takes a drink of his coffee and says, "We made our points."

"Made our points!" Hannah's dad says. "You've kicked their ass. Have you seen that jury? They went from thinking Hannah was a monster to looking at that Stowe jackass like he's an idiot. Two of the guys just smiled at me out in the hallway."

"That's a good sign," Ryan says.

"Then why don't they dismiss the case?"

"We're in the middle of trial. Prosecutors hate to lose. They want to win at all cost. They won't just dismiss the case. After they rest their case, I'll ask the judge to dismiss it."

With her stomach in knots, Grace says, "Then why are they calling me?"

Ryan addresses everyone and says, "Jackson is gone. He was probably killed. The jury will want to blame someone. The prosecutor is desperate. I'm sure the jury is wondering if you did it. They want to put you on the stand to prove you couldn't have been the killer. I don't blame them there. They want to show Jackson was playing you both and Hannah lost it. They're desperate—it's all they got. They probably want to ask about his two kids...how their dad was killed and now they must grow up without a father. They're hoping the sympathy card might sway at least one juror to convict, so they can get a mistrial and regroup for a second trial."

"A second trial? Can they do that?" Hannah asks nervously. "Can they try me again?"

"If the jury isn't unanimous, there's a mistrial."

"And I'm stuck in jail?" Hannah asks.

"Let's not think about that right now. All that matters right now is the jury sitting in front of us."

"Will it work?" Hannah asks. "Could some of the jurors vote to convict me?"

"Not the way I'm reading this jury." Ryan turns to Grace and says, "What I'm about to tell you is critically important. DO NOT LIE! Whatever he asks you, tell the truth. If the jury thinks we're lying, or trying to pull a fast one, it could be bad."

Ryan finishes his coffee, wipes his mouth with his napkin, and says, "Come on, let's go back in."

Everyone gets up and starts for the courtroom. Grace grabs Ryan's arm and says, "Dad, are you sure?"

"Absolutely," Ryan answers.

Grace moves closer and asks, "I can't do it. What about—"

Strong and firm, Ryan says, "Just tell the truth. I'll handle whatever comes."

# – CHAPTER 37 –

Grace takes her seat on the stand and swears she'll tell the truth. *Tell the truth....tell the truth.* She repeats in her head. She adjusts the microphone in front of her and prepares to testify.

The female prosecutor clears her throat with a cough and asks, "Could you please introduce yourself to the jury?"

Grace looks at the jury and says, "I'm Grace Kennedy."

"And you were married to Jackson Kennedy?

"Yes, ma'am."

"For how long?"

"Thirteen years."

"Can you tell the jury where you were when Jackson disappeared?"

"I was in Thailand visiting my mom's gravesite."

After establishing the day she left and the day she returned, she asks, "And after thirteen years of marriage, you found out your husband was married to Hannah Kennedy, right?"

Grace shows a hint of anger. She looks up and says, "Yep."

"How did you feel when you found out?"

"I was pretty upset."

"Pretty upset?"

Grace tears up a bit. She grabs a tissue and says, "Okay…I was furious. Is that what you want to hear? I was furious. I felt like a fool."

"I mean, he had another wife, another baby, another house, another life…everything. I bet that made you crazy."

"I don't know what you mean."

"I'll move on," the prosecutor says. "I understand you went to Aspen to visit the defendant."

Grace didn't expect this. She looks at her dad and says, "Yes, ma'am."

"How was the defendant about finding out her husband had another family?"

"I guess she was angry."

"You guess? Did she say she was angry?"

"I'm sure she did."

"What else did she say about it?"

"I don't know. She said she had plenty of time to get over it. She said she was ready to move on."

"Just like that? Move on?"

"You don't know. Everyone is different."

"Did she tell you she was in a sexual relationship with a man from her work?"

This takes Grace by complete surprise. She never expected it. *Tell the truth. Tell the truth.*

"I don't know about a sexual relationship. She said she was seeing someone."

"How long was this since Jackson disappeared?"

"I don't know…over a year later."

The prosecutor looks at the jury trying to be dramatic and asks, "If your sister, Hope, called Detective Woods *eight* months after Jackson disappeared and told him about your conversation, would that date surprise you?"

Grace shakes her head and says, "Okay…eight months."

*"Eight months* after her husband disappears, and she's already in a sexual relationship with another man?"

Hannah writes on her tablet. Grace says, "We thought he had left to Paris—"

"*You* thought," the prosecutor interrupts. "The truth is, no matter what she told you, you don't know what Hannah was really thinking. Maybe she knew he was dead in the Rocky Mountains."

"Well, she sounded like she believed he left."

"And that's when *you* found out. You don't know when Hannah actually started seeing her new lover. For all you know, she was seeing him *before* he disappeared?"

Grace raises her hands like she has no answer and says, "I guess. I don't know." Suddenly, she realizes she might be losing the case.

"How were you on this first visit?"

"I was upset. I was crying."

"And Hannah?"

*Tell the truth.* "She wasn't crying, but she was upset too."

"Didn't cry a tear?"

"I don't think so."

"I understand you saw her a second time."

Happy to move on, Grace says, "We met at the vacation house. I invited her."

"And was she still seeing this guy?"

"She said she was."

"What did she say about him?"

*This is bad.* She looks down and says, "She said she loved him."

The prosecutor looks at the jury and says, "She loves him!"

"I guess."

"Was she happy about it?"

"I guess she was."

"Her husband is dead and now she's happy?"

Everyone can see that Grace is getting frustrated. "No," she says shaking her head. "You're changing what I said. She was happy about her new relationship."

"So, the defendant's husband is missing, she's having sexual relations, she's in love with another man, and now she's happy. Did the defendant ever tell you she was trying to find her husband?"

"We didn't talk about that."

"So, no?"

Feeling like she's in the middle of sending Hannah to prison, she shakes her head, and barely louder than a whisper, she says, "No."

"Or that she tried to call him?"

"No."

"Or that she once emailed him?"

"No."

Getting all she can, the prosecutor moves on.

"Mrs. Kennedy, you have two little children, correct?" She pulls out two large photos of Bonnie and Wesley. "Do these photos show your precious children?"

"Yes."

"It must have been hard to tell them their father is gone."

Grace starts to cry, so the bailiff hands her another tissue. Wiping her eyes, she says, "It was the hardest thing I've ever done."

"I bet they took it pretty hard."

"Wesley was little. Bonnie was pretty upset."

"I'm sorry Ms. Kennedy. I can see how hard this is for you. She cried?"

"Yes, she cried."

"I bet she's still pretty upset about everything."

"Sure…she misses her father."

Feigning real empathy, the prosecutor clears her throat again and asks, "It's probably going to be really hard on them growing up without a father?"

Grace wipes her tears and says, "I'm sure it will be."

"And what about you?"

"What about me?" Grace repeats.

The prosecutor says, "I know you aren't happy about Jackson cheating on you, but it must have been pretty hard on you when you found out he was killed."

"I don't know. I felt everything."

"Sad?"

"I was sad."

"Hurt."

"Sure."

"It was really hard on you, wasn't it?"

"It was pretty hard on me."

"And eventually you found out the defendant was arrested for Jackson's death."

"Yes."

"Where were you when you found out the defendant was arrested for the death of your husband?"

"I was in my home. I learned about it like most people. I saw the news on television."

"And what did you think?"

"I was shocked," Grace says. "I was totally shocked."

"Why were you shocked?"

"Why was I shocked?"

"Yes, ma'am."

*Tell the truth.* "I was shocked because I know she's innocent."

Up to this point, the prosecutor has been running quickly through her questions, just as she'd written it out on her legal pad. Question after question, everything was going according to plan. This was the end of the case, and she made some strong points. Hannah was having an affair and the jury heard the effect Jackson's death will have on so many people—especially his wife and children. Suddenly, the prosecutor stops and looks up with a puzzled look. "You know she's innocent?"

"Yes, ma'am."

"And why do you believe she's innocent?"

"Because I know who killed Jackson."

Suddenly, Grace has the full attention of the prosecutor, the judge, the jurors, Ryan, and everyone else in the courtroom. The prosecutor looks over at Ryan, who's rubbing the rim of his nose. Ryan meets her gaze and shrugs his shoulders like this is all new to him.

At this point, the prosecutor is stuck—she has no choice but to press forward. She turns back to Grace and asks, "And how do you know who killed Jackson?"

Grace looks over at Hannah, who looks as shocked as everyone else in the courtroom. She takes one last deep breath and says, "Because I'm the one who killed him."

One collective gasp fills the courtroom. The jurors are staring at Grace like they just witnessed an explosion or something. Someone on the front row yells, "Oh my God!"

Jackson's brother stands up and yells, "You murderer!"

The judge starts banging his gavel on his bench, yelling, "Order.... order....order."

When it's obvious that all the banging in the world won't quiet things down, he turns to the bailiff and says, "Call security." He then points across the courtroom and shouts above the crowd, "There will be order in my court! The next person who speaks out will be removed from the courtroom. I'll clear everyone out of here if I have to."

As soon as he's done, a hush fills the room—except for the sound of Hannah crying next to Ryan.

The prosecutor, barely able to talk, says, "Are you telling this court, under oath, that you killed——"

Grace looks down and whispers, "Yes, I killed Jackson."

"Excuse me?" the prosecutor asks.

Grace looks up and says, "I said, yes. I killed Jackson."

Again, the court erupts, and again the judge bangs his gavel. The judge turns to the bailiff and says, "Please escort the jurors back to the jury room."

Everyone stands as each juror, in single file, walks out of the hushed courtroom. When the bailiff returns, the judge says, "Please take Grace Kennedy into custody."

In a moment that rivals any Perry Mason movie, Grace steps down from the witness stand. The bailiff approaches Grace and says, "Please put your hands behind your back."

Grace turns around, and the bailiff clicks handcuffs on each of her wrists. He takes Grace by the arm, and they walk out the side door.

# – CHAPTER 38 –

This is beyond anything the judge has ever faced in his courtroom. When does a witness, under oath, confess to murdering the victim in the middle of the murder trial? Once Grace is out of the courtroom, the judge turns to the prosecutor and says, "Counselor, in light of the testimony we just heard, is it your intent to proceed with this trial?"

The prosecutors both lean into one another and whisper something back and forth. All you can see is the moving of lips and the shaking of heads. Still understanding that right now he's representing Hannah, Ryan stands to his feet and says, "Your Honor, the defendant, Hannah Kennedy, moves the court to dismiss all charges against her."

The prosecutors break from their private discussions and stand to their feet. "Uh…yes, Your Honor. The state concurs. The state also moves to dismiss all charges against the defendant, Hannah Kennedy."

A case can be dismissed either with prejudice or without prejudice. If a case is dismissed *with* prejudice, it means the state can never refile or charge the defendant again for that crime. If the case is dismissed *without* prejudice, Hannah would always have the charges, as well as the rumors, hanging over her head. Wanting to protect his client, Ryan pushes further. "Your Honor, we would ask that the case be dismissed *with* prejudice."

The judge looks over at the prosecutor, who says, "The state would prefer a dismissal *without* prejudice to re-filing."

Ryan shakes his head and says, "Your Honor, at this point, the state doesn't really have a choice. Double jeopardy already applies, so any dismissal *must* be with prejudice."

The prosecutor, well aware that he doesn't really have another choice, says, "Yes, the case is dismissed *with* prejudice."

"Very well," the judge says. "The case against the Defendant, Hannah Kennedy, is hereby dismissed with prejudice to re-filing."

The judge writes it down on the docket sheet before telling the bailiff, "Bring the jury back in."

Once they're seated, the judge turns to the jury, who are all sitting in their chairs wondering what the hell just happened. He clears his throat and delivers an apology.

"Ladies and gentlemen, I apologize to each of you for wasting your time over the past week. I'm sure you have better things to do. In light of the recent developments, you are dismissed from any further service while I take care of this mess. Please stop by the district clerk's office and make sure they have your correct mailing address to send you your checks."

The bald-headed man closest to the judge, who spent the entire case watching carefully and taking notes, stands up and asks, "Am I free to stay?"

All the other jurors either nod their heads or also ask to stay.

"You are certainly free to stay if that's what you choose," the judge says. "While we're waiting, I'd like to ask each of you a question. You may refuse to answer if you choose. You heard the evidence in the case. Before Grace Kennedy's testimony, did any of you already make up your mind about the defendant, Hannah Kennedy's guilt?"

All the jurors look to their left and their right at each other before slowly raising their hands. With twelve hands raised for everyone to see, the judge asks, "And what were your thoughts regarding the Defendant's guilt?"

Each juror, one after the next, says,

"Not guilty"

"Not guilty"

"Not guilty"

"Not guilty, Your Honor."

"Not guilty"

"Not guilty"

"Not guilty, Judge."

"Not guilty"

"Not guilty"

"Not guilty"

"Not guilty"

"Not guilty"

The judge takes off his glasses, sets them on the table, and massages his temples with both hands while leaning over on his elbows. After taking a deep breath, he looks up at Hannah, who's standing beside Ryan, looking as confused as everyone else.

"Ms. Kennedy," the judge begins, "on behalf of the State of Colorado and Pitkin County, I want to give my sincere apology to you and your family. I know this hasn't been easy on you. The good news is *sometimes* the system works. All charges against you are dismissed, with prejudice. You are hereby released from custody and free from any further prosecution, or threat of prosecution. I wish you the best."

Hannah's eyes tear up a little as everything sinks in. She turns and gives Ryan a big hug. Both her mother and father are standing at the front of the gallery. She turns around and hugs them both at the same time. Hannah's mother is crying while holding her only daughter in her arms.

Now sobbing on her mom's shoulder, Hannah turns to the judge and asks, "What about my baby? When will I get her back?"

The judge, looking helpless, says, "I'm sorry, this is only the criminal case. You'll need to handle that in the family law courts. I'm sure your attorney will make sure that court knows about the judgment I'm about to sign. I pray your child is returned immediately."

Seeing Hannah cry and plead for her baby is emotional for everyone. A couple of jurors are dabbing their eyes. Even the judge is a little teary-eyed as he watches Hannah walk out with her mom and dad on each side of her. Once they walk out and close the door, the judge turns to the bailiff and says, "Bring Grace Kennedy back into the courtroom."

The bailiff walks out the door on the left. Not a single person gets up, walks out of the courtroom, or says a word. This is what everyone in the courtroom is waiting for. No one has any idea what's going to happen next. Given she just confessed to the crime, it's obvious she'll be found guilty and sent away for a long, long time.

Probably ten minutes go by before the door at the back of the courtroom opens again—but it's not Grace. Hannah walks back into the courtroom without either her mom or her dad. The judge, both attorneys, the jurors, and all the spectators in the courtroom watch as she walks down the center aisle and takes a seat on the front row.

Another five minutes go by as everyone waits for the bailiff to return. The judge leans all the way back in his chair and rocks back and forth, staring up at the ceiling. Ryan sits tall in his chair. Every once in a while, he writes who-knows-what on his legal pad. It seems like all the writing in the world can't fix this disaster.

## – CHAPTER 39 –

Grace started the day feeling so good about everything. No matter what the prosecutor threw at them, her dad had an answer. She had thoughts of Hannah flying to Montenegro with Savannah, where they'd relax for a few months and travel around Europe. Now here she is handcuffed to a bench about to be charged with murder.

Sitting in her blue dress, she realizes for the first time how cold it is in this courthouse. She looks down at her arms and sees her hair standing on end and her arms covered with goosebumps. She can't even cross her arms to warm up because her wrists are handcuffed behind her back.

Every once in a while, a court police officer walks by in his full uniform without saying a word. A sweet-looking lady holding a stack of files walks by and gives Grace a friendly smile. Grace wants to smile back, but she has nothing to smile about. Two attorneys come in, each holding a briefcase, and talk back and forth about their case. One looks over at Grace as he passes, and with a nod, he asks, "Hello, how's it going?"

*How's it going?* Grace puts her head down in her lap without responding.

Back in Montenegro, it was easy to talk about doing the right thing. Grace thinks back on that day at the restaurant, with Bonnie coloring by her side, when she promised, *But you're going to lose me anyway. I'll turn myself in before I'll let her go to prison for murder. I did it and I'll make it right.*

It all sounded so noble at the time. She held her head high like she was ready to do the right thing and suffer the consequences. Now, those consequences are staring right at her. It was one thing when it was all theoretical, but the reality of never seeing her little girl and boy again floods over her. A tear drops down her cheek that she can't wipe away because her hands are chained behind her. Her lips start shaking, and she sobs for the first time.

Hope has no idea that Grace had anything to do with Jackson's murder. *How do I explain everything? How do I tell her I'm going to prison, and we'll only be able to see each other when you come and visit?*

Grace trusted her dad. *Why did he tell me to tell the truth? I knew the question was bad. I knew the truth would kill me. I could have lied on that one question, and Hannah would still be found not guilty.*

Grace starts to wonder what bright idea her dad has now. *Maybe he can tell them I misspoke? Maybe he can twist my words around so it sounds different than it really was.* The truth is, this all sounds ridiculous. The words came out of her own mouth. It was recorded by the court reporter. All the trickery in the world can't get her out of this.

Now decisions have to be made. *What will I do with my babies?* She considers the idea of Hope and Blake raising them. Hope loves them both so much—especially Bonnie. Grace wouldn't even have to ask. Then Grace realizes this wouldn't be fair. They just got married and they're starting their new life together. Soon they'll have their own kids to raise. No, Dad will be the one to raise Bonnie and Wesley. He's already raised three children, did a great job with Ben, and his grandkids mean the world to him. He'll make sure they have everything they'll ever need.

Sitting here handcuffed, she can't help but wonder how? *How did I think I would get away with it?* The plan seemed foolproof at the time. She was in Thailand, for God's sake. Now it all seems so foolish. So many people must think they can get away with it, but something always trips them up. She was so foolish. She let her anger get the best of her; and now the chickens are coming home to roost.

Grace looks up when the same officer who chained her to this bench, returns and says, "The judge is ready to see you."

He unlocks the handcuffs from the bench, locks her hands behind her back, and escorts her back into the courtroom. This is something Grace could never imagine.

# – CHAPTER 40 –

Everyone in the courtroom hears the side door open, and sees Grace walk back in handcuffed. She looked a lot less shaken when they took her out. Her hair is now a mess, and her face is covered in mascara stained tears. The officer escorts her through the door with everyone watching her every move. Grace starts to tear up. The officer walks her to the middle of the courtroom and stops right in front of the judge. Another officer comes up, and they both stand behind her, like she might flee at any second.

Grace is standing there, all alone, with everyone in the room looking right at her. All you have to do is look at the faces across the courtroom to know Grace is in trouble—big trouble. Two of the female jurors, who've been sitting beside each other from the beginning of the trial, whisper something to each other while shaking their heads at Grace.

"Grace Kennedy," the judge begins.

Grace isn't really sure how this all works. Is she just found guilty and sent to prison, or is there another trial? She looks down and starts to cry.

Speaking through her tears, with a trembling and cracked voice, she barely gets out, "Yes, Your Honor."

More and more people fill the courtroom, as this shocking news gets out.

The judge looks at Grace and says, "Some officers are on the way to take you into custody for the death of Jackson Kennedy."

Ryan stands up from his chair and grabs his briefcase. He walks up to the bench and stops right beside Grace. He puts his arm around his terrified daughter and pulls her close.

The judge drops his pen and says, "Let me guess…now you represent Grace Kennedy?"

"Yes, Your Honor. She's my daughter."

The judge closes his eyes and says, "Of course she is. This is just wonderful."

Right then, the back door opens and four more officers from the Sherriff's Department walk down the aisle and surround both Ryan and Grace.

The judge looks at Grace and says, "Based on your sworn testimony this afternoon, I'm ordering that you be taken into custody. I anticipate you will be charged with Jackson Kennedy's murder." He then gives a quick nod to the officer closest to Grace, who moves in and reaches for her arm.

Ryan raises his hand, which causes the officer to pause just long enough for Ryan to address the court. He catches the attention of everyone in the crowded courtroom. Ryan looks at the judge and says, "Your Honor, before these fine gentlemen here take my client into custody, you might want to pause for a moment."

The judge, with an obvious look of confusion, says, "Why would I pause for a moment?"

"Well, Your Honor, you should be aware that my client has a signed immunity agreement with the District Attorney's office."

The judge drops his glasses, covers his eyes with both hands, and asks, "A what?"

"Yes, Your Honor," Ryan says, like it's business as usual. "She has a signed immunity agreement protecting her from any criminal charges and any prosecution in this case."

The prosecutor, still standing back at his table, comes around and does his best to get his mind around what he just heard. Unsure what to do next, he says, "Your…your honor, I know nothing about any such signed agreement."

Ryan reaches inside his briefcase and pulls out three copies of the document signed by Grace, the District attorney, and himself. He holds the document up in his right hand, and says, "It's nothing special… actually it's pretty standard with a few agreed modifications. I worked out the details with the District Attorney himself."

"Let me see that document," the judge growls.

After handing a copy to everyone, Ryan says, "They asked my client to cooperate—to testify in this case. They told us they were issuing a subpoena. My client could have exercised her Constitutional right and pleaded the fifth. Surely, the prosecutor wouldn't think Ms. Kennedy would testify on behalf of the state, and waive her Constitutional right to remain silent and not incriminate herself, without some agreement to protect her. I did what I do with every client in this situation. A month ago, we signed an immunity agreement protecting Ms. Kennedy from any prosecution."

The judge, so angry at this point he can't see straight, yells, "Counselor, I don't know what the hell you're trying to pull here." He points at Grace and Hannah, and lowers his voice just a bit. "These women have completely different interests. You're telling this court you were representing Hannah Kennedy and Grace Kennedy at the same time?"

"Yes, Your Honor."

"Well, clearly you have a conflict of interest, Counselor."

"You're exactly right," Ryan says, reaching inside his briefcase and pulling out a different document. "Just like you, I was also concerned about any possible conflict of interest. Both Hannah and Grace signed a waiver of any conflict."

He hands a copy of the signed document to the prosecutor and the judge, and points at the last line. "I even had it notarized. It wasn't required, but I wanted to be safe. You might say I wanted to wear both a belt and suspenders, so to speak."

The judge now directs his anger towards the prosecutor. "Is this true, Counselor?"

The prosecutor looks down at the immunity agreement in his hand, scratches his head, ruffling his nicely brushed hair, and says, "I have no idea. I'm seeing this for the first time."

Both Ryan and the judge give the prosecutor a minute to review the document. Caught completely off-guard, the prosecutor says, "We knew nothing about this. It's obvious, however, that the D.A. had no idea she was involved in her husband's death."

"I don't see how that would invalidate this agreement," the judge admonishes.

"But if the District Attorney had known—"

Ryan interrupts, shakes his head, and says, "They didn't know because they never asked…not until today."

The judge looks straight at Ryan like he might explode. He points his long, bony finger right at Ryan's face and screams, "Mr. Brunick, did you put her up to this?"

This would terrify most attorneys, but Ryan simply shakes his head. So cool and calm, he says, "Absolutely not. My client didn't ask to testify today. *They* subpoenaed *her*. *They* called her as a witness. All I did was instruct her to tell the truth, and she did that."

Doing his best to keep the judge's wrath off his client or himself, Ryan says, "Under the agreement, my client must tell the truth. If she lies, even a little white lie, the agreement is revoked and Ms. Kennedy could be prosecuted. I warned her again and again to tell the truth and nothing but the truth…just like you told her to do when she first took the witness stand. Well, it's obvious she did that. Given the prosecutor's specific question, she really had no choice. She was asked a direct question, and she answered honestly"

The prosecutor, looking frazzled, says, "But if we'd known, Your Honor, we wouldn't have asked her why she was shocked."

"Good God, Counselor," the judge yells, shaking his head. "Every lawyer knows not to ask a question if you don't already know the answer."

Ryan turns to the prosecutor and asks, "Then what?"

Unsure what he just heard, the prosecutor repeats, "Then what?"

"What? You'd have an innocent woman go to prison for the rest of her life? I'm sorry, but I don't think that'd be justice at all."

"Justice?" the prosecutor asks. "What about justice for Mrs. Kennedy…and justice for Jackson Kennedy?"

"Ms. Kennedy," Grace interrupts.

The prosecutor gives Grace a look as cold as ice.

Ryan turns to the jurors who've been watching this whole thing in disbelief, and says, "Isn't it better for ten guilty people to go free than for one innocent person to be wrongfully convicted and go to prison?"

The prosecutor slams the paper down and says, "Oh, don't give me that shit."

The judge bangs his gavel and says, "Counselor! I won't tolerate that language in my court."

Ryan throws his hands in the air and says, "I'm just asking."

Grace, standing there with handcuffs digging into her wrists, leans over to her dad, and asks, "Can we take these off?"

Ryan turns his attention back to the judge and says, "Your Honor, my client can't participate fully in this hearing with her hands cuffed behind her back. Given the fact she's free from any prosecution, she'd like to have the handcuffs removed so she can write on her tablet, if that's okay."

The judge points to the bailiff and says, "Take the cuffs off Mrs. Kennedy...I mean, Ms. Kennedy."

Eventually, things calm down. More lawyers come into the courtroom after hearing about this incredible situation.

The judge, in front of a packed courtroom, addresses Ryan. "As much as it pains me, given the fact your client just confessed to murdering her husband, I have no choice but to release her from custody."

He looks at Grace, and says, "I would advise you, if you're smart, to never return to Colorado again."

"Thank you, Judge," Grace says. "I won't."

The bailiff steps forward and unlocks the handcuffs. Showing a little pain on her face, Grace rubs each of her wrists.

Having no choice in the matter, the judge says, "Then I guess you're free to go."

The bailiff steps aside so Ryan and Grace can walk out of the courtroom with every single person staring at them.

# – CHAPTER 41 –

Mentally, physically, and emotionally exhausted, Ryan tells Zimmerman to take all the boxes back to his office and to handle all the reporters.

"The exposure will do you good. Just one thing…Grace is our client, too. Remember that when you're talking to the reporters. For now, enjoy your time in the spotlight."

"Mr. Brunick?" Zimmerman says, causing Ryan to stop for a second. "You are truly amazing. I see why you never lose. Thank you so much for letting me sit with you."

"You're welcome, Mark. You can be amazing too, but you gotta' care about your client. Oh, and work hard."

"I will," Zimmerman says.

A year later, Zimmerman won his first trial. It was just a DWI, but the evidence looked pretty strong. Zimmerman told the jury all about the mother who has two boys who broke a window. Remembering Ryan's other story about the newspaper with some boring story, he turned over the evidence and found his case on the other side. Really, it was pretty easy. You just have to simplify things.

Ryan and Grace walk out of the courthouse and right past the reporters, who are doing their best to put cameras and microphones in their face. They want to get out of Aspen as soon as possible. Hannah is going to meet them at their hotel for a quick celebration.

Back at the Ritz Carlton, Ryan and Grace grab a table at the very back of the bar where they won't be noticed. Ryan sits down, takes off his jacket and tie, and orders a double martini.

"Jesus Christ, Dad!" Grace says, "What did you just do?"

Ryan takes a sip of his martini and says, "That was the backup plan."

"So, you knew? You knew all along?"

He turns his head a little and says, "Did I know for sure? Not really, but over time you get a feel for people. The prosecutor thought this would be an easy win. You see, sometimes a person can be so far behind in a race they actually think they're in first place."

Grace laughs and says, "Where do you get these things?"

"Anyway…they prepared for Zimmerman and thought it would be a cakewalk. They were frustrated. I could tell from their other witnesses that they didn't always think things through. Either way, the advice was still the same. Tell the truth and we'd be all right. If you had lied, they could revoke our agreement and come after you one day. I was thrilled when they asked the wrong questions. It all worked out for the best. Now, you never have to worry about being charged again."

"What agreement?" Grace asks.

"You don't remember signing it?"

"Not really."

"It was that legal document I had you sign. I didn't want to make a big deal out of it, because I wanted it to look genuine. You did good."

"Dad, do you remember when I was a little girl, and I got stuck in that oak tree behind our house?"

"I remember," he says.

"You always told us not to climb past that first branch, but Colt and I climbed up pretty high. I lost my footing and was just hanging there. I was scared to even look down. I kept screaming, 'Daddy! Daddy! Daddy!'" Grace pauses to take a drink. "Colt ran in to get you while I hung there, not sure how long I could last. Next thing, I heard your voice under me saying, 'Let go, Sweetie…just let go.'"

Ryan smiles.

"I didn't know what you were going to do, but I knew you were there, and you were my daddy. I was terrified, but I let go just like you said. You saved me." After this sinks in, she says, "Well, you just did it again. It made no sense to me, but I knew you were my daddy. You've never once let me down."

Ryan gets up and kisses Grace on the forehead.

Right then, Hannah walks into the bar with a smile on her face so big she can barely contain it. Ryan stands up, and Hannah runs into his arms, knocking him back a couple of steps.

Looking at Ryan, she says, "I was so afraid when we started. I was sure I was going to prison. Next thing, you were saying things I never even thought of. I just sat back and watched the show. You are Superman! I owe you my life. Now I just gotta get Savannah back."

"Don't worry about that," Ryan says. "What they did wasn't right. I don't think they want a lawsuit. I'll make a couple calls and have her back by Monday."

Hannah starts crying. Without a thought, she pulls Ryan to her and gives him a quick kiss on his lips, with Grace looking on. She stares into Ryan's eyes, and says, "God Bless you, Mr. Brunick. You have a special place in heaven waiting for you."

They all sit down and Grace says, "We're drinking martinis."

"God, yes," Hannah says.

Ryan goes to the bar and orders three more martinis and their best bottle of red wine. When the martinis are gone, they order appetizers and pour the red wine.

Feeling more than tipsy, Grace says, "I told you. I told you my dad was the best."

"The best?" Hannah says, looking at Ryan and wanting to kiss him again—this time for real. "He is Superman."

The waitress brings the chicken nachos and flatbread bites. While they eat and drink, Hannah and Grace spend almost an hour going over one moment in the trial after another. Ryan sips his wine and nods in agreement every now and then, like it's no big deal.

Finally, taking a break from all the law talk, and loosened up from the alcohol, Grace looks at Hannah and says, "You've got to come back to see my dad's place. It's beautiful. Let's get away from here. We'll take it easy for a while. We can travel around Europe."

Hannah leans back in her chair and gives Ryan the kind of look a woman knows how to give. She looks back at Grace and says, "It sounds wonderful. Let me get Savannah back and I'm in."

Grace takes a sip of her drink and says, "I can't wait to get out of here."

"Me too," Hannah says, reaching out for a toast.

Grace takes down the rest of her wine and says, "Remember the last time we were here?"

"I know," Hannah laughs. "I couldn't drink because I was pregnant with Savannah."

Ryan puts down his drink, leans forward, and looks at both of the girls. Puzzled at what he just heard, he tilts his head a little and says, "Wait a minute. I thought you didn't meet until *after* Savannah was born."

Both girls freeze with their wine glasses still touching their lips. First looking at Ryan, then at each other; they are unsure what to say.

"When she was pregnant?" Ryan continues. "So, you're telling me you girls met *before* Jackson disappeared?"

Hannah and Grace look like children who just got caught with their hands in the cookie jar. Hannah gets up, walks over to Ryan, and puts her soft hand on the side of his face. She moves forward and gently kisses his cheek, leaving her lipstick imprint behind. She reaches out to hold his hand, and for the first time, she calls him by his first name. "You were brilliant, Ryan."

Ryan backs up, and says, "OH MY GOD. YOU BOTH—"

Grace puts down her wine glass and says, "Don't be mad, Daddy."

"Why didn't you tell me?"

Grace leans forward, brushes her hair back with her fingers, and says, "I don't know. We wanted it to look genuine."

Ryan closes his eyes and says, "I don't believe this."

Grace takes her dad's other hand. Trying to explain, she says, "Don't be mad. I knew you couldn't represent Hannah if we were both charged. So, I left for Thailand. It was the perfect alibi. So now you know. Why did Jackson stop his car at the gas station? Hannah was supposed to meet him in Aspen. Then she called and said she was in Austin and wanted to meet at the gas station. He never questioned it. Sean was waiting for him there. It was *Sean's* car who drove through all those tolls."

Hannah's eyes get big and she says, "All that talk about checking the tolls! I was so afraid they'd find Sean's car."

"Son of a bitch!" Ryan says. "This is the most incredible thing I've ever heard." He turns to Hannah and says, "When did you find out?"

Grace looks at her dad and answers first. "It's like I said, I broke into his phone and found everything. I called Hannah and broke the news."

"So, you knew the whole time?" Ryan asks.

Hannah nods her head and says, "Who do you think broke into the vacation home so he'd buy that gun?"

"Oh my God!" Ryan says.

Ryan turns to Hannah and asks. "Okay….it's all over. Tell me the truth. What about the money? The eight million dollars?"

Just to make sure, Hannah asks, "You're still my lawyer, right?"

"Right."

"Attorney-client protection or something like that?"

"Of course."

"Well, let's just say Savannah and I will be just fine."

# – CHAPTER 42 –

Living in Europe is an amazing experience. Hannah came for a month and ended up staying for six months. Ryan watched Bonnie, Wesley, and Savannah while Grace and Hannah traveled like two schoolgirls.

As much as they like Montenegro, Ryan and Grace always talk about returning to the States. The United States will always be their home and whatever time he has left, Ryan wants to spend it with his family all together again.

Three days after turning fifty–nine years old, Ryan made the move. He sold his home in Montenegro, and moved to Carmel, California, to be near Hope, Blake, and their first child.

It took some time, but he found the perfect home located off the beaten path overlooking the ocean. He loved his home in Montenegro so much that he did his best to replicate it here. He changed the back living room wall so it had floor to ceiling glass. Visitors can look out at the incredible pool and the beautiful ocean behind it. He built a large firepit in back where he spends each morning in prayer and meditation and his evenings with a small fire and a glass of red wine.

Ryan has never forgotten about Jesse, so he doesn't take any chances. For the most part, he stays out of the public view. He tore down the existing fence and constructed a new eight-foot electrical security fence around his property that obstructs all outside visibility. He installed a maximum-security gate at the front of his drive made of the strongest steel available. It has encrypted signals to prevent hackers from opening or even tampering with it. He added a state-of-the-art security system throughout the property, with cameras, motion detectors, and ground pressure switches that alert the police the second an intruder is detected. Coming onto the property is virtually impossible. For almost a year, there were rumors going around town that Ryan might be a drug smuggler.

Carmel is the kind of place where everyone knows everyone, so it doesn't take long for Ryan to make friends. He has the kind of personality people want to be around. He found a small church and became a generous supporter, even though he only attends Sunday services by watching from the comfort of his home. He does all his shopping online and has his groceries delivered to a secure lockbox at his gate. His friends mostly come to his house, and when they go out to eat they pick a secluded restaurant with a private room.

Ryan has one exception to his secluded lifestyle. His home overlooks Pebble Beach and watching all those golfers caused Ryan to fall in love with the sport. He joined the country club and took golf lessons for over a year. Now he plays golf with his buddies at least twice a week. Pebble Beach Golf Links is a very exclusive club that doesn't let just anyone in.

A couple of years after moving to Carmel, Ryan starts to worry less and less. By his calculation, Jesse is seventy-one years old. Ryan's investigator once reported back that Jesse was in bad health. This wasn't a big surprise, given how hard Jesse lived.

Ryan has been living in Carmel for two years when his security camera picked up a suspicious visitor at his front gate. A black Suburban stopped out front and stayed there for twelve minutes. Ryan couldn't make out the driver because of the tinted windows, but it looked like the man inside was studying the security system.

Two days later, Ryan is driving down Ocean Drive and sees the same dark windowed Suburban coming from the opposite direction. The driver tries to make a quick U-turn after it passes by, but the heavy traffic allows Ryan to make an inconspicuous exit.

A week later, when Ryan comes in from golfing, he sits with his buddies at the Beach Club Dining Room. Ryan is good friends with the bartender, Sam, so he walks up to the bar to buy the first round of drinks.

"How'd you do today, Mr. Brunick?" Sam asks.

"Ah, I was a little off," Ryan answers, rolling his eyes.

"What can I get you?"

"We're going to have lunch," Ryan answers. "How about four Heinekens for now?"

"Yes, sir," Sam says, pouring four beers from the tap.

After he sets the beers in front of Ryan, Sam says, "By the way, Mr. Brunick, someone came in this weekend asking about you."

At first thought, Ryan figures this must be one of his friends wanting to play golf. "Who was it?" he asks.

"I'd never seen this guy before. He was kinda vague. Said his name was Jacob…or Jerry…or something like that."

Ryan knows no one by those names. "Jesse?" he asks, afraid of the answer.

Sam snaps his finger, points at Ryan, and says, "That's it….Jesse!"

"What did he say he wanted?"

"Said he was an old golfing buddy of yours. Said he was wanting to catch up…maybe play a little golf."

This revelation shakes Ryan, but he does his best to remain calm. "What did you tell him, Sam?"

"Ryan, I've been here seventeen years. I know a golfer when I see one. This guy didn't look like any golfer I've ever seen. I knew from his southern accent that he wasn't from around here. By the way he looked and the way he talked, it seemed like he was up to no good. I said I didn't know any Ryan Brunick. He looked at me with this scowl and said 'Never heard of him, huh? I heard he's a member here.' I shrugged my shoulders and told him that if he is, I've never heard of him. I don't think he bought it. He showed me a photo and said, 'Maybe you know him by Scott Richards.' I looked at the photo and said, 'Nope.'"

Doing his best to fake a smile, Ryan takes three of the beers and says, "Thanks, Sam. You called it right. This guy is up to no good."

Ryan returns to his table, sets down the beers, and says, "Listen, guys, I've got to go. I have a little emergency."

Ryan drives straight home, locks himself in his house, and stays there. Two nights later, his security system detects an intruder and an ear-shattering alarm blares so loud it can be heard for miles. The police arrive in less than fifteen minutes. Ryan, and the first officer on the scene, review the security tapes that show a man dressed in black, with the same size and build as Jesse, trying to break through the back security fence. He ran off when the alarm sounded, jumped into a black Suburban, and sped off.

Within half an hour, there are four police officers in Ryan's living room. Ryan tells them the whole story—well, almost the whole story. He explains how Tom Flint was charged with murdering a man named Zach. Ryan had knowledge of the murder and cooperated with the police—giving them key evidence in the case. When Flint found out it was Ryan who alerted the police, he hired a man named Jesse to find and kill him. The same Suburban was just lurking in front of his gate, Jesse showed up at the Pebble Beach golf club asking for him, and the person now on the security video looks just like Jesse.

The police take everything down and pay Sam a visit. Everything checks out. Sam repeats the whole conversation, and the security camera caught Jesse's face plain as day. They issue a warrant for the arrest of Jesse for attempting to break into Ryan's house.

Ryan hires two security guards to secure his home and has his investigator tracking Jesse. A week later, he calls Ryan to let him know that Jesse is back in Alice, Texas. From that day forward, the investigator puts Jesse under around-the-clock surveillance.

Ryan doesn't leave his home for months. He no longer goes into town, never eats out, and stops golfing with his buddies. Six months after Jesse tried to break into Ryan's home, his investigator informs him that Jesse was arrested for murder. Ryan follows the case closely. A lawyer in Duval County was charged with hiring someone to kill his own wife. When the evidence finally pointed back to him, he admitted everything and turned on Jesse in exchange for a forty-year prison sentence. Jesse is charged with murder for hire and is sitting in jail awaiting his trial after the judge denied him bail. The case is iron-clad. Jesse will never again see the light of day.

For thirty years, Ryan's life has been one big tangle of knots. As hard as he tried, as much as he struggled, he could never free himself. He was like a whale caught in the floating remnants of a long-forgotten fisherman's net. The whale has no idea what he's getting himself into as he swims dangerously close to the peril awaiting him. Now he has no solution to man's horrible trap. He isn't armed with a knife or hands to use it. The more he struggles, the more the net wraps tight around his pectoral fins and tears into his flesh.

Now Ryan is free. It's like a diver has come to his rescue and heroically cut away all his entanglements. Jesse is gone and Ryan is free to go wherever he wants, no longer afraid to walk out of his own front door. He can travel the world, eat at the best restaurants, take a walk on the beach, and golf with his buddies at the best golf courses. He no longer has to look over his shoulder, reliving the past and fearing the future. He's finally free, and who can argue with freedom?

# – CHAPTER 43 –

Two years after winning his freedom, Ryan has a massive stroke that almost takes his life. The right side of his body is paralyzed, and it takes years of physical therapy for him to walk with the aid of a walker and intense speech therapy for him to talk again. He looks helpless on the outside, but his mind is generally sharp—except he's still haunted by Faith, who keeps coming back again and again. Sometimes he's better, but other times he continually obsesses about the past and can't move on. Ryan might be safe from ole' Flint and Jesse, but now he must live alone with his memories and the guilt that robs his mind and torments his soul. The truth that he's the one who created his own demons is too much for his mind to accept, so he does his best to block it all out.

Most nights sleep doesn't come easy—even in the best facility, with the best doctors, the best therapists, the best staff, and the best bed money can buy. There are nights Ryan sits up all night long reading, watching television, or surfing the internet for answers to the many questions that swirl around in his head.

One evening after finishing dinner, Ryan lays down in his bed to get some rest. Unexpectedly, a smiling nurse opens the door, peeks inside, and with a friendly smile, says, "Mr. Brunick, you have visitors."

Ryan strains a little to grab for the washcloth beside his bed. He quickly cleans his face and neck and brushes his hair back to look his best.

When the door opens wide, he extends both his arms to his family and says, "Look who's here!"

"Hey, Dad," Hope says, walking up and kissing her dad.

"Good to see you," Ryan says with a big smile.

Hope's son, Caleb, is now nine and her daughter, Beth, just turned seven. Sometimes they're too busy to visit Grandpa, but not this week. Hope, on the other hand, is never too busy. She comes at least once, and usually twice a week.

Beth comes right up, hugs her grandpa, and says, "Hi, Grandpa."

Ryan gives her a hug with his one good arm.

When Beth pulls away, Caleb takes her place and offers his own big hug. "Hi, Grandpa, how you feeling today?"

The saddest part of the stroke is the fact that the smooth-talking attorney with a quick wit is gone. Speaking slowly, Ryan says, "Good, y'all keeping your grades up?"

"I got all A's on my report card," Caleb says. "I went three-for-three and hit a home run on Saturday."

"That's my boy," Ryan says, patting him on his back. "Sorry I missed it."

"I got all A's too," Beth says with a smile. "Oh, I got the lead role in our school play. Can you come see me?"

"Of course," Ryan answers with a wink. "I'll be the first one there."

After ten or fifteen minutes of friendly chitchat, Beth asks, "Grandpa, can we go down and grab some snacks?"

"Sure," Ryan answers. "Get whatever you want."

The kids love this part of the visit. They run down the hall, past the lounge area, and into the cafeteria that is set up like one of the nicest restaurants in town. It has every kind of coffee, juice, cookies, cakes, and ice cream. It has a private chef that will prepare anything you want. He even gives cooking lessons once a week. This place has a beautiful pool where the kids can swim. It's the best assisted living center in town, and Ryan is one of their favorites.

Hope decided on Stanford Law School and graduated second in her class. She's been a lawyer for seven years now. She owns her own firm: *The Law Office of Brunick and Brunick, PC*. Ryan's name has been on the letterhead, and the Internet has always listed him as a consultant. His name still gives the firm a lot of clout, even though Ryan hasn't been seen in a courtroom since his last trial in Colorado. Still, he often offers Hope valuable advice. Now she's starting to be recognized as an impressive attorney. She always remembers to keep it simple.

Ryan turned over control of all his assets for Hope to handle four months after his stroke. Hope also makes his most important medical decisions after consulting with Ryan and his doctors.

Before stepping in to visit her dad, Hope stopped by the director's office to get her regular update. Some days, Ryan is doing better. Other days, he seems confused about the past. After the kids run out of the room, Hope shuts the door, pulls up a chair, and sits beside her dad. "So, you still having those nightmares, huh?"

Ryan lies back in his bed, covers his face with his good hand, and takes a deep breath. "This was bad. I dreamed your mom went to Thailand. It was horrible. She was caught with drugs in—"

*Okay...not a good day.*

Everyone knows not to bring up the "F word." Once you get Dad started, he can go on and on for hours. Hope learned long ago that all you can do is divert the conversation to a different subject.

"The director says your doctor's going to be in later to change your medicine, so you can sleep. It should also help with the bad dreams."

"Have you talked to her?" Ryan asks.

Sometimes, Ryan can't deal with the reality of Fai—I mean the woman we don't talk about. His mind just shuts out the whole Thailand thing. "Dad," she says taking his hand, "I'm not here about Mom. I'm here to see you."

"You know, she didn't come visit me on Sunday."

Hope gives his hand a light squeeze. With a sympathetic smile, she says, "I know, Dad."

"Is she okay? I don't want anything to happen to her. Is she still with that guy? What's his name? Paul?"

*Divert…divert.*

Hope kisses his hand and says, "Dad, let's talk about you, okay?"

Hope knows the kids and grandkids are always the best distraction.

"Grace said she'll be up to visit you tomorrow, right after she picks up Wesley from school. Bonnie is driving up right after she gets out of class."

Ryan never gets tired of family. "Did we decide where we're having Christmas this year?" he asks.

"I think it'll be at my house this year," Hope says. "Grace will be there. Will you be up to leaving here again?"

"Of…course," Ryan says, like it's a silly question to ask. "Will your mom be there? I need to warn her of something."

*Divert.*

Hope looks at the stack of newspapers beside the bed and asks, "Anything interesting going on?"

Waiving away the newspapers, Ryan says, "Hope, the whole world's going to hell. I wish we could just shut all these computers off and learn to talk to one another again. When I was a kid, we'd ride our bikes to each other's houses. You didn't know who someone voted for, or if they were a Democrat or Republican. All you knew is Mr. and Mrs. Jones are good people. They work hard, keep their yard pretty nice, and have good kids. People just don't know how good they have it today. You know, God's given us everything we need to make us happy—"

"If we don't screw it up," Hope and Ryan both say together.

"That's right," Ryan says. "Don't you ever forget it."

"I won't, Dad."

Ryan is full of these witty little sayings. He's passed so many down to his kids, and now his grandkids. "How's Blake?" Ryan asks.

"He's doing great. He said he's sorry he couldn't make it."

"Holy cow," Ryan says, lifting his hand. "Tell him not to worry. I'm not going anywhere." Ryan takes the bed's remote and lifts the bed until he's sitting upright. After adjusting his pillows, he says, "You know, Hope, you got a good one there. Take care of him."

"I know, Dad. I do, and he takes care of me."

"You know, in some ways, y'all remind me of your mom and me at that age. Gosh, I'd come home from work and she'd be cooking at the stove. She loved to cook and always had dinner ready. You know, she'd always meet me at the door. No matter how—"

Right then, the grandkids come back into the room, each holding an ice cream cone. "They got rocky road," Beth says.

"Rocky road? Rocky road?" Ryan teases. "Well, you should have gotten two scoops."

"I got two scoops," Beth says.

"Then you should have gotten three," Ryan jokes.

Ryan turns to Hope and asks, "How's the Blanchard case going?"

"I don't think it's going to settle," Hope says, shaking her head. "We're the first case set on the jury docket next month."

Ryan grabs his legal pad and his mind starts running. "Make sure you call his supervisor to prove—"

Hope knows the only thing as bad as talking about *you know who* is talking about law stuff. The doctors say he's got to quit, but you can't tell Ryan that. "I know, I know," Hope says, cutting her dad off. "I took his deposition and I've issued the subpoena."

"You know, our strongest claim is Respondeat Superior. They can't get around that no matter how hard they try. The motion for summary judgment cleared the—"

"Dad…Dad," Hope jumps in. "I know. Don't worry about it. It's all going to be fine."

"Hope, just stay focused on what's important. Forget the rest. You know, the dog who chases—"

"I know, Dad," Hope says. Then both grandkids say, "The dog who chases two rabbits catches neither."

"Just keep things simple," Ryan reminds her.

"So a child can understand," Hope smiles.

When the visit is over, Ryan uses the remote control to lean his bed back down a little. *What a nice meeting.* It's all he lives for anymore. Without his family, Ryan would have given up long ago. *Love those grandbabies.*

As much as he wants to lie back down, he's too afraid he'll have another one of his horrible nightmares. *Where do these dreams come from? These kids need to make sure their mother never goes to Thailand.*

Ryan turns on the television and lies back in his bed. *Judge Judy….Jerry Springer….CNN….Fox News….HBO…Netflix. So many channels but nothing to watch.* Maybe his doctor will be in soon with his new medicine. He eventually closes his eyes and dozes off again.

Two hours later, he's zonked out and dreaming again about Faith. The good dreams are always in their younger, happier years, and most bring back memories of Faith's incredible sexuality. She's cleaning dishes in the sink when Ryan comes up from behind and puts his hands on her waist. She looks over her shoulder and gives him a sensual smile. Ryan moves his lips to hers and slides his hand from her waist, under her shirt, and up her stomach, until he's resting his hand on her breasts. As soon as they kiss, Faith turns around, puts her wet hand on his neck, and pulls his face close. She kisses him with such passion, Ryan knows she's thinking the same thing he's thinking.

"Come on, baby," she says, leading him to the bedroom.

Ryan follows her, still amazed by the beautiful figure walking so gracefully in front of him.

Once in the bedroom, Faith slowly releases each of the buttons on his dress shirt, pulls it off his shoulders, and reaches down and kisses him in the center of his chest. He lies back while she kisses down his stomach to his belt. She undoes his belt and unbuttons his slacks, and kisses him some more. She sits back up, unbuttons her own blouse, and shows Ryan her beautiful, small breasts hidden under Ryan's favorite black, lacy bra.

Faith places three fingers on each side of her front bra clasp, twists it open, and frees her breasts. Ryan reaches forward and puts his hands on her rising nipples. Faith starts to moan and then leans forward and covers

Ryan's mouth with her hand, stopping him from talking—or even breathing. At first, this seems like a joke, but as hard as Ryan tries to break free by swinging his head to the side, Faith doesn't let go.

Trying to break loose, he swings his body to the left and then the right. Still unable to breathe, he opens his eyes and feels duct tape over his mouth. Ryan tries to reach up and tear the tape off his mouth, but his hands are zip tied to the side of his bed. He reaches for the emergency buzzer that's always at his side, but now it's gone.

"Is this what you're looking for?" a man asks from the end of the bed, holding the buzzer up in the air. Not wearing his glasses, Ryan can't make out the face. This man looks familiar, but it's been so many years. Ryan starts to panic, as he realizes he's in trouble. It's Jesse! Just when he thought he was safe, Jesse has finally caught up to him and is here to settle the score. Seeing Jesse in front of him blows Ryan's mind. *How the hell did he get out of prison?*

"Jesse!" Ryan tries to scream, but he's silenced by the duct tape.

"Hello, Ryan," Jesse says.

Ryan's unable to speak and can barely breathe. He squints to get a good look at Jesse's face. Jesse walks around and picks up Ryan's glasses sitting on the desk next to his bed. As gentle as a mother, Jesse slides Ryan's glasses across each side of his face and slips them behind Ryan's ears.

Now that Ryan can see clearly again, Jesse's face comes into focus. As soon as he says, "It's been a long time," Ryan realizes who this guy is. Time, being so cruel and unforgiving, has stolen the youthful look of the man Ryan last saw standing at his front door, so many years ago.

It's not Jesse standing over him with the buzzer secure in his hand. It's Jonah—Faith's brother—who came all this way to visit Ryan. Like a gambler on a losing streak, Ryan's been borrowing from the house for way too long. Jonah's here to square up his sister's account.

Just a second ago, Ryan was struggling with all his might to free himself. Now, he exhales loudly through his nostrils and forfeits the fight. He lies back on his bed and closes his eyes.

"That's right," Jonah says, patting Ryan on the shoulder. "Just take it easy. We have a lot of catching up to do."

Jonah walks over to the window and twists the blinds closed. Ryan moves his head to follow him. Jonah turns back around with a smile, and says, "There, I think we might want to discuss things in private."

Jonah walks back to the other side of the bed and slowly pulls up a chair. It sounds like fingernails on a chalkboard as it screeches across the floor. He sits down in the chair, crosses his legs, and looks at Ryan with a crooked smile.

Jonah lifts his shoulders, takes a deep breath, and drops his shoulders as he exhales. His hair is completely gray and has thinned since Ryan last saw him. He's wearing black slacks, a black belt, a white-collared shirt, black socks, and black dress shoes. He looks really professional and impressive—like he's had his own share of success in life.

Sitting upright in his chair, Jonah says, "So….the great Ryan Brunick….how you been doing, buddy?"

Ryan nods his head so slightly it's barely noticeable.

Jonah pats Ryan's leg and says, "You've aged, but haven't we all?"

Ryan lets out a helpless moan.

"What's that?" Jonah says, leaning forward. When Ryan doesn't moan again, Jonah sits back and says, "You know, I once heard we get only so many words in life. I think you've used up all your words."

Ryan doesn't respond.

"It's okay," Jonah says with a scowl. "I came all this way, so why don't I do all the talking? Actually, I don't want to hear a damn thing you have to say."

Ryan could try to scream through the duct tape, but he doesn't.

Jonah pauses a second to think about the situation and says, "This must be pretty hard on you—sitting here so helpless….unable to talk your way out of this."

He reaches down into a satchel sitting beside him on the floor, pulls out two surgical latex gloves, and snaps one on each hand. He pulls out a black leather box that looks like a gift box for a fancy bracelet. He places the box on his lap, unclips the latch, and flips the top open. Secured inside are two needles filled with liquid.

Like a trained nurse, Jonah releases the first needle, raises it to the ceiling, and taps the side three times. He presses on Ryan's arm to find a suitable vein and says, "This here is pancuronium bromide. It's the drug the state uses on prisoners. I'm sure a couple of your clients would have received this drug—except for the work of the great Ryan Brunick. It will help you relax so we can talk."

Jonah is well prepared. The shot won't just relax Ryan. He gives Ryan the exact dosage necessary to paralyze all his voluntary muscles without suffocating him. Soon, the drug sweeps through Ryan's body, and he can't so much as flinch. Completely helpless, all he can do is stare forward and listen as Jonah continues to toy with him. Looking at Ryan's face, you'd never know the excruciating pain he's experiencing all over his body.

Seeing Ryan's face go blank, Jonah can see the drug just took hold. "There…are you comfortable now?" he asks.

Of course, Ryan doesn't answer.

Jonah moves forward, turns Ryan's head towards him, and says, "I want to visit with you for a minute, if that's okay."

Jonah reaches over and picks up one of the photos sitting on Ryan's desk. It's the family photo of Hope, Blake, and their two kids. Jonah turns the photo towards Ryan, and says, "Looky here…this must be Hope. What a beautiful woman." He looks up at the ceiling and says, "It's been so long. She was just a little girl the last time I saw her. Man, has she grown. And this is her husband and two kids? That boy looks a lot like his dad. Congratulations, Ryan."

Next, he picks up the photo of Grace and her two kids. Grace never remarried, so there's no husband beside her in the photo. Jonah turns the photo towards Ryan and says, "And this must be Grace. Oh my, and this is Bonnie….right? And who's this little boy? I never met either one of them." He lowers the photo, looks at Ryan, and asks, "So where's their daddy? Oh yes, he met the same Brunick curse, didn't he? I read about it. Great job, Ryan. It was masterful how you cleaned house on that one."

Jonah studies the photo and his eyes turn red. "You know, Grace is gorgeous. Look at those beautiful blue eyes. . .that same beautiful face of hers. . .and the same beautiful blonde hair." He shakes his head and says, "You know who she looks like? She looks just exactly like" He pauses for a second, wipes his eyes, and says, "Well, let's not get all sentimental here."

Next, he picks up the picture of Colt taken right before he died in that terrible car wreck. He looks back at Ryan and says, "I guess it's true what the Bible says. . .sometimes the son does pay for the sins of the father."

Somehow, someway, a tear rolls down Ryan's cheek. Not a tear for himself, but for everything he did. Jonah looks at the tear falling down Ryan's face and says, "Do you have a picture of my sister around here?" With a big smile, he says, "I bet you don't. Well, lucky for us, I brought one."

He removes a beautifully framed 8X10 photo of Faith when she was sixteen years old. She's in her cheerleader uniform, holding pom-poms at her side. She looks as radiant as ever, with a smile so full of life. He shows Ryan the photo and sets it on the desk right beside Faith's children and grandchildren. "There," he says with a smile. He takes the photo of Ryan and his family, and with a disgusting shake of his head, drops it into his bag.

Protected by his surgical gloves, Jonah arranges all the photos so they're in perfect order. "There," he says with his back turned. "The family is finally back where they belong, even if it's only in photos."

He turns back to Ryan and says, "Ryan, you're a blessed man. You had three beautiful children. My sister would have given you more if you weren't so narcissistic. But you wouldn't have it, would you? It's always been about you."

He looks to the side and says, "You know, I haven't been so blessed. I would have had a hundred children if I could, but my wife and I were never able to have children. Actually, it was all because of me. Can you imagine that?"

Ryan is still alert and listening.

Jonah shakes his head and sighs. "No, I guess it wasn't meant to be. It was all too much for her. Eventually, she packed her bags and moved on. I haven't seen her since."

Ryan can tell by the expression on Jonah's face that he's thinking about his ex. Jonah finally says, "After she left, the only family I had in the whole wide world was my mom, my dad, and Faith. The closest I got to having my own precious children was my beautiful nieces and nephew. And you took them all from me."

All Ryan can do is stare ahead.

"You know, I saw her," Jonah says, like he can still see that horrible vision in his mind. "Yep, I went to visit her in that hell you sent her to. It wasn't good, Ryan. It made me sick just sitting there. Can you imagine having to live there? While you were living in your mansion, eating at all your fancy restaurants, and making memories with Faith's children, my beautiful sister, who could once move mountains with her smile, was just skin and bones. She was so sick…oh my God, she was sick. It was hard to even look at her. But I did, Ryan. I looked close, and I looked hard. You know why? Well, you know how we sometimes forget about things over time? You see, I never wanted to forget the way she looked that day."

Jonah starts to cry. Wiping away his tears, he continues. "My sister had a good heart. All she ever did was take care of you. Who could ask for a better wife? She treated you like a God, and you never appreciated it."

Jonah takes a deep breath and says, "I swore to my little sister that one day…however long it took…I would pay you a visit." Sounding chipper, he slaps both his hands on his knees, and says, "And here we are!"

Ryan watches as Jonah's face turns dark again.

"Ryan, you destroyed our family. I'm sure you've destroyed so many families without thinking twice. To my dad, Faith hung the moon. She could do no wrong." Knowing what Ryan must be thinking, he lifts his hand and says, "I know, I know. She was strong–willed and could have a mischievous spirit, but my dad loved her. He loved you too, Ryan. . .and he trusted you. He put his little girl in your hands and trusted you to take care of her. Faith going to prison just destroyed him. He worried himself to death. You must know you caused his stroke, and my mom followed right behind him. After they died, all I had left was my sister's little babies. I wanted to see them just once…that's all. We didn't have to reminisce or have some long conversation about everything you did. I just wanted to see my sister's babies. And you what? Threatened to have me arrested? Ahh…the great Ryan Brunick."

Since the day he came back from Thailand, Ryan has regretted the horrible thing he did to Faith. His thoughts and dreams have haunted him. Some people might *think* about doing the unthinkable, but they don't do it. Their better sense of themselves won't allow them to do it. But he actually did it. What he'd give to go back and change everything, but this is something you can't ever take back.

If he could talk, he wouldn't argue with Jonah or try to straighten out his view of their marriage. No, he'd tell Jonah that he understands completely and how sorry he is for everything he did. He'd take that second syringe and shoot that poison into his own veins. He'd do all that, but right now he can't move.

"Well, Ryan," Jonah says, shaking his head. "I can't send you to some hellhole for fifty-five years. I wouldn't do that to you if I could. You see, I'm not you. My soul isn't that dark. I don't think anyone's soul is that dark. No, I'm going to be merciful. You know mercy? The mercy you never showed my sister?" He lifts his finger and says, "Now, don't get me wrong. I can't just walk out of here like everything is okay. We've come way too far for that. But you don't have to suffer for years and die a slow, terrible death from poison flowing throughout your body. You don't have to be buried in some mass grave in Thailand where no one can ever find you. I'm sure you'll have a big funeral and a grand headstone. Everyone can come and cry for the great Ryan Brunick."

Ryan knows what's coming, and he's at peace with it.

"I'll tell you what. I'm going to give you a minute to get right with the Lord. Really, I think it's the least I can do. But don't dilly–dally. We don't have much time."

As Jonah pauses, Ryan turns to the Lord and silently prays:

*"Dear Lord, I thank you for giving your life for me. I know all the good I've ever done is nothing but filthy rags in light of my horrible, ugly sin. I beg your forgiveness. Have mercy on my soul."*

*"Lord, watch over my family. Keep an eye on Grace and Hope. Watch over Bonnie, Wesley, Caleb, and Beth. Keep them safe in your hands so they will walk in your ways."*

*"And forgive Jonah. Comfort him… for his heart is broken."*

*"In your hands, I commit my soul. In Jesus' precious name, Amen."*

Jonah stands from his chair and says, "All right…I think that's enough."

He reaches into the box and unsnaps the second syringe. He raises the syringe to the light and also taps it three times. He searches Ryan's arm for the same vein he found the last time. Then he explains to Ryan, "In here is potassium chloride. It induces irreversible cardiac arrest. It might be uncomfortable for a few minutes, but don't worry. Soon it will pass."

Jonah slowly slides the needle into Ryan's arm until it finds its target. Then he says, "Are you ready?" Ryan tries to nod his head but he still can't move. When Jonah hears no answer, he injects the chemicals into Ryan's body. Two minutes later, Ryan lies there motionless—looking up with nothing but a blank stare. Jonah checks for a pulse, but Ryan is gone.

Jonah extends two fingers, touches them to his lips, then touches them to Faith's picture sitting on the desk. He returns to Ryan and says, "I'll see you in hell, Mr. Ryan Brunick."

Jonah removes the tape from Ryan's mouth, careful not to leave a mark. He snaps off the zip-ties with the scissors in his bag. He removes his gloves and puts everything back in the bag and clips it shut. He takes his time putting on the old man mask and sunglasses he wore in here. Pretending to use a cane for support, he walks out of the facility so calm and easy, that no one thinks a thing.

As far as Grace, Hope, or anyone else knows, Ryan had a heart attack and died in his sleep. It doesn't really surprise anyone that Ryan found an old picture of Faith and put it on his desk before he died.

A second later—or maybe ten thousand years later—Ryan sits up from his bed, feeling young again. He lifts his arm, looks at his hand, and opens and closes his fingers a couple of times. His paralysis is gone. He moves his right leg to the floor and stands without any help for the first time since his stroke. He walks—no strolls—forward, without any pain.

A subtle breeze blows against his face, and his nostrils fill with the most wonderful, sweet perfume he's ever smelled. He breathes in until his lungs are so full they might burst. Then a light comes closer and a wonderful, powerful love pours over him. He can see it, feel it, even touch it. It stops him in his tracks. He falls face down on the ground and cries.

Don't miss William Holms' newest release, *The Intruder You Know*.

# SIGN UP FOR MY READER GROUP

Thanks for reading the final book in my Killing of Faith
series. I hope you enjoyed it. Please be so kind to leave a review
on Amazon and tell your friends and family. Support from
readers like you can make or break a book. My next book, The Intruder
You Know, is available. I hope you join me for the ride.

Want more? Click this link and join my reader group. I'll notify you
when my next book is released, provide the background on each book,
sign your book, and give you the lowest price on the internet.

https://readergroup.williamholms.com/

**Notice any errors in the book? Email me and I'll email you the next
book for free!** Feel free to buy my books directly from me and I'll send
you a signed copy. You can buy it for less than the retail price. Want me
to speak at your event or book club, or just want to talk? Email me:

Email me:  author@williamholms.com

# ACKNOWLEDGMENT

Gosh, where do I start. I'm going to miss the Brunicks. I hope you will too. Thanks again to all my great readers. You made *The Killing of Faith* more successful than I ever expected. It's only because of my readers that *The Killing of Faith* became a series. Thanks for joining me on this journey. Keep the reviews and the emails coming in.

I want to thank my advance reader team. You keep getting better with each book. Thanks to Dee Wilson, Deborah Jesensek, Ted Wood, Christie Schneider, Amy Stallings, Jenna Buster, Patricia Montalvo, Shelby Peavler, Pamela Long, Kay Painter, Karen Silver, Sandra Soreano, Ellen Aish, Mary Vanede, Audrey Mayrent, Deborah Donnelly, and Rosanne Meyers.

I want to especially thank Deborah Jesensek who has been the best editor an author could want. Thank you…thank you….thank you.

I want to thank two special people in my life. Thanks to Dean, my best friend and the best brother anyone could ever want. You helped make *The Beginning of Hope* the book it is. Even more, you add so much to my life. I'd be lost without you.

Finally, thank you Curt—my lifelong friend. You're like another brother to me. Your brilliant ideas helped add the final touches to this book. Love you brother.

www.ingramcontent.com/pod-product-compliance
Lightning Source LLC
Chambersburg PA
CBHW051212130726
47988CB00001B/65